"The mystery pleases with its plot and character development." — *RT Book Reviews*

"This is a fun series and the latest is a fantastic whodunit." — Cozy Mystery Book Reviews

Dyeing Wishes

"A light paranormal cozy that will draw readers in with its small-town charm and hidden secrets." — Debbie's Book Bag

"[An] enjoyable mystery . . . filled with a cast of charming characters." — Lesa's Book Critiques

"[This] series is one that I've fast learned to enjoy for its cast of characters, its humor, and its primary setting of a yarn shop. . . . Oh, how MacRae's characters shine!" — Kittling: Books

"Molly MacRae writes with a wry wit." — MyShelf.com

Last Wool and Testament
**Winner of the 2013 Lovey Award
for Best Paranormal/Sci-Fi Novel**
***Suspense Magazine*'s Best of 2012**

"A great start to a new series! By weaving together quirky characters, an interesting small-town setting, and a ghost with a mind of her own, Molly MacRae has created a clever yarn you don't want to end." — Betty Hechtman, national bestselling author of *Knot Guilty*

"A delightful paranormal regional whodunit that . . . accelerates into an enjoyable investigation. Kath is a fascinating lead character." — Genre Go Round Reviews

"A gem." — TwoLips Reviews

"A delightful and warm mystery . . . with a strong, twisting finish."   —Gumshoe

"Suspense and much page flipping! . . . I loved the characters, the mystery; everything about it was pitch-perfect!"
   —Cozy Mystery Book Reviews

"The paranormal elements are light, and the haunted yarn shop premise is fresh and amusing."
   —*RT Book Reviews*

"MacRae has the perfect setting and a wonderful cast for her new series . . . good setting, good characters, good food . . . and fiber and fabric too. *Last Wool and Testament* is a wonderful beginning to a new series."
   —CrimeSpace
                                                          .

PRAISE FOR THE OTHER
MYSTERIES OF MOLLY MACRAE

"MacRae writes with familiarity, wit, and charm."
   —*Alfred Hitchcock Mystery Magazine*

"Murder with a dose of drollery . . . entertaining and suspenseful."   —*The Boston Globe*

"An intriguing debut that holds the reader's interest from start to finish."   —*Kirkus Reviews*

"Witty . . . keeps the reader guessing."
   —*Publishers Weekly*

"Engaging characters, fine local color, and good writing make *Wilder Rumors* a winner."
   —Bill Crider, author of the Sheriff
   Dan Rhodes Mysteries

Also by Molly MacRae

KNOT THE USUAL SUSPECTS

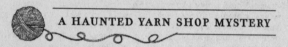

A HAUNTED YARN SHOP MYSTERY

Molly MacRae

AN OBSIDIAN MYSTERY

OBSIDIAN
Published by New American Library,
an imprint of Penguin Random House LLC
375 Hudson Street, New York, New York 10014

This book is an original publication of New American Library.

First Printing, September 2015

Copyright © Molly MacRae, 2015
Penguin Random House supports copyright. Copyright fuels creativity, encourages diverse voices, promotes free speech, and creates a vibrant culture. Thank you for buying an authorized edition of this book and for complying with copyright laws by not reproducing, scanning, or distributing any part of it in any form without permission. You are supporting writers and allowing Penguin Random House to continue to publish books for every reader.

Obsidian and the Obsidian colophon are trademarks of Penguin Random House LLC.

For more information about Penguin Random House, visit penguinrandomhouse.com.

ISBN 978-0-451-47131-4

Printed in the United States of America
10 9 8 7 6 5 4 3 2 1

PUBLISHER'S NOTE
This is a work of fiction. Names, characters, places, and incidents either are the product of the author's imagination or are used fictitiously, and any resemblance to actual persons, living or dead, business establishments, events, or locales is entirely coincidental.

The recipes contained in this book are to be followed exactly as written. The publisher is not responsible for your specific health or allergy needs that may require medical supervision. The publisher is not responsible for any adverse reactions to the recipes contained in this book.

Penguin
Random
House

ACKNOWLEDGMENTS

Writing the Haunted Yarn Shop Mysteries is a joy—for the opportunity to write another one, I thank Cynthia Manson, my agent, and Sandy Harding, my editor at NAL/Obsidian. For encouragement along the way, I thank critique partners Betsy Hearn, Janice Harrington, Sarah Wisseman, David Ingram, Steven Kuehn—the value of your help and friendship is immeasurable. Thanks to Nick Freer for letting me try my hand with his kumihimo loom. Thanks also to Michael Newton for letting me put a copy of his book, *The Naughty Little Book of Gaelic*, in Hugh McPhee's sporran. Thanks to the members of An Comunn Gàidhealach Ameireaganach (ACGA—the American Scottish Gaelic Society) who let me join them at Lees-McRae College in Banner Elk, North Carolina, for their Gaelic-immersion week and use the time as a writing retreat, and to Sherry Kreamer for waking us each morning with her pipes. Thanks to Johnson City, Tennessee, for not complaining that I took the name Blue Plum. You had the name first, but you discarded it when you thought you'd found a better one. Kate Winkler—you're a gem. Thank you for providing the patterns in my books and for your continued enthusiasm for the series. Special thanks to my generous colleagues at the Champaign Public Library—Debbie Keith, Aaron Carlin, and Thea Green lent me their names; Mike and Val Rogalla lent me Al and Bruce; and Larry Damski let me have Bill the Border Collie. Mike, Ross, Gordon, Milka, and Michael—I love to write, but you are my true loves.

CAST OF CHARACTERS

At the Weaver's Cat

Kath Rutledge: Textile preservation specialist formerly of Springfield, Illinois, now owner of the Weaver's Cat, a fiber-and-fabric shop in Blue Plum, Tennessee

Ardis Buchanan: Longtime manager of the Weaver's Cat

Geneva: The ghost who lives at the Weaver's Cat, Ardis Buchanan's great-great-aunt

Debbie Keith: Part-time staff at the Weaver's Cat, full-time sheep farmer

Abby Netherton: Teenager working part-time at the Weaver's Cat

Argyle: The shop's cat

Members of TGIF (Thank Goodness It's Fiber) and the Yarn Bomb Squad

Joe Dunbar (Tennyson Yeats Dunbar): Kath's significant other, fly fisherman, watercolorist, sometimes called "Ten"

Ernestine O'Dell: Septuagenarian, retired secretary

Melody (Mel) Gresham: Café owner, calls Kath "Red"

Thea Green: Town librarian who came up with the idea to yarn-bomb Blue Plum

John Berry: Octogenarian, retired naval officer

Zach Aikens: Teenager

Rachel Meeks: Banker

xii   CAST OF CHARACTERS

Tammie Fain: Energetic grandmother
Wanda Vance: Retired nurse

Supporting Cast

Shirley and Mercy Spivey: Twins, Kath's cousins (several times removed)
Hugh McPhee: Bagpipe player, former Blue Plum citizen
Gladys Weems: The mayor's mother
Olive Weems: Organizer of the arts and crafts fair Handmade Blue Plum, the mayor's wife
Palmer (Pokey) Weems: Mayor of Blue Plum
Al Rogalla: Accountant, volunteer fireman
Ellen: A knitter in town for Handmade Blue Plum
Janet: A knitter in town for Handmade Blue Plum
Aaron Carlin: Odd-jobs man, significant other of Angie Spivey
Hank Buchanan: Ardis' daddy
Ambrose Berry: John's older brother
Angie Spivey: Mercy Spivey's daughter

Sheriff's Department

Cole (Clod) Dunbar (Coleridge Blake Dunbar): Deputy, Joe's brother
Darla Dye: Deputy
Shorty Munroe: Deputy
Leonard Haynes (Lonnie): Sheriff

Chapter 1

Waiting for twilight would have been a good idea. Waiting for full dark even better. A sunny Tuesday morning was hardly the best time for scuttling up the courthouse steps and sliding behind one of the massive columns—not if I wanted to call myself "sneaky."

I hesitated at the bottom of the steps. My friends and former colleagues back in Springfield, Illinois, might not think so, but from where I stood Blue Plum, Tennessee, bustled. Crowds didn't jostle me, but in the way of small towns, as long as *anyone* was around, there was a chance that someone would see something and mention it to two or three others. The problem was partly my own fault. If I'd completed this measuring assignment for TGIF sooner, I wouldn't have to worry about being surreptitious in broad daylight now. Then again, if we'd included the courthouse in our original plan, I would have had weeks, not days, to get it done. The occasional criminal investigation aside, TGIF (Thank Goodness It's Fiber—the needle arts group that met at the Weaver's Cat) was not an organization ordinarily dedicated to furtive operations, though, so I didn't want to let the others down now, as we prepared for our first-ever clandestine fiber installation event.

The way to sneak successfully, I decided, was to act normal. Eyes open, not casting shifty glances left and right. Shoulders square, not hunched as though ready to creep. Air of confidence. Relaxed smile.

A familiar-looking woman came down the stairs toward me. Her face didn't jog a name from my memory, but I liked the popcorn stitch cardigan she wore and I smiled as she passed.

"It's Kathy, isn't it?" she asked, turning back to me.

"Close," I said. "Just Kath."

"I hope you know how lucky you are."

"Pardon?"

"Lucky to have the Weaver's Cat. Your grandmother made the right decision in leaving the shop to you."

"Oh. Thank you."

"I keep meaning to stop in. Later this week, though. Not today—must rush."

"Great—" Before I could say anything more, her rush carried her away.

I walked up the dozen worn limestone steps, looking for all the world like anyone else on her way to renew car tags, attend a trial, or probate a will. But at the top, rather than follow an older couple across the portico and through the doors, I stopped, turned around, and pretended to enjoy my elevated view of Main Street.

I didn't really have to pretend. The streetscape, a mix of mostly Federal and Victorian architecture, looked and felt exactly right to me. Pink and purple petunias spilled from half-barrel planters along the brick sidewalks. Window boxes with red geraniums and sweet potato vines brightened storefronts. Looking right, I saw the bank and half a dozen office buildings and shops and, down at the end of the next block, the sign for the public library. To the left, along past Mel's café, my own shop, the Weaver's Cat, basked in the morning sun. This view, this town, had been part of my life through all my childhood summers when I'd come to visit my grandmother in her hometown. Now, thanks to her generosity in leaving me her house and the Weaver's Cat, Blue Plum was my hometown, too.

I watched Rachel Meeks, the banker, deadhead a couple of geraniums in the planters at the bank's door. Somewhere in her mid- to late fifties, Rachel's business suit mirrored her straightforward business sense. Apparently so did her sense of gardening decorum. She carried the withered flowers inside with her. I strolled to the end of the portico, still looking out over the street and assuming I looked casual, then sidled around behind the last column where I'd be in its shadow and couldn't be seen from the steps or the door. There I took a coil of string from a pocket in my shoulder bag.

A second pair of hands to hold one end of the string would have helped. Unfortunately my favorite second pair of hands had other business that morning. Joe—the Renaissance odd-job-man-about-town who'd worked his way into my heart—had gone over the mountains early to deliver half a dozen fly rods he'd built for an outfitter in Asheville. That was just as well; two of us fiddling around a column would draw more attention. I took a roll of painter's tape from my bag, tore off an inch-long piece, and pressed it over the end of the string, sticking it to the column at about waist height.

The plan was to circle the column with the string and mark the string where it met itself again, then remove the tape, recoil the string, return string and tape to my bag, and retreat to the Weaver's Cat. I'd barely started around the column, though, when a familiar voice made me pull back out of sight.

"Ms. Weems, ma'am—*oof*—now, that was uncalled for."

"You're a quack, and I'll tell anyone who asks."

"Let's step on inside, then, ma'am, and you can tell the sheriff."

I inched around the column in time to see Joe's uniformed and starched brother, Deputy Cole Dunbar, ushering a tiny, elderly woman through the courthouse doors. The woman, Mayor Palmer "Pokey" Weems' mother, wore tennis shoes, and it was a good thing. As she passed Joe's brother, she hauled off and kicked his shin. He winced, but there was no second "oof." That led me to believe the first "oof" had been a reaction to a different kind of assault—maybe a swift connection between Ms. Weems' pocketbook and his midsection.

Snickering at someone else's pain isn't nice, even if that person is a clod. And even though Cole Dunbar would always be "Clod" to me, I was fairly sure I *hadn't* snickered. But before the door closed on him, something made Clod turn toward me and my column. I immediately knelt and retied my shoe, pretending not to notice him noticing me.

"I'm not sure he fell for that," a voice from farther around the column said.

At one time in my life an unknown and unexpected voice addressing me out of the blue might have startled me. Not anymore. Now I practically yawned to show how blasé I was about such surprises. I also flicked an inconsequential speck of dust from the toe of my shoe to show I wasn't worried about whether or not Clod fell for my pretense. Then I stood up to see who'd spoken. That I *could* see a living, breathing human standing there was a plus, even if I hadn't ever seen him before and had no idea who he was. Judging by the light gray overtaking the dark gray in his beard, I guessed he was in his fifties—older than Clod by at least ten years and Joe by more than a dozen.

"That was one of the Dunbar brothers, wasn't it?" he asked. "Weren't they named after composers?" The camera around the stranger's neck made him look like a tourist. The soft twang in his question sounded local.

"Poets. That was Coleridge," I said.

"And the other one's name . . ." He tried to tease it from his memory by tipping his head and waving his hand by his ear.

"Tennyson," I said.

"That's it."

"Coleridge Blake Dunbar and Tennyson Yeats Dunbar," I said, "except the deputy there goes by Cole and his brother is Joe."

"Smart move." The stranger nodded. "Better than Cold Fridge and Tennis Shoe, both of which I remember hearing when the boys would have been at a tender age. Huh. I haven't thought about them in years. But even back then I wondered how they'd turn out, weighed down with those names." His tone was mild rather than judgmental. It had a reminiscent, storytelling sound to it.

"You're from Blue Plum?"

"Not for a few years, anyway," he said.

Not for a few decades, if he hadn't known Clod was a sheriff's deputy and that Joe was, well, Joe.

"Can I give you a hand with your string there?" he asked.

"Oh." I'd let go of the string when I pretended to tie my shoe. The end was still stuck to the column with the painter's tape.

"Measuring it for a school project, right? You hold it there and I'll—" He picked up the dangling end and walked around the column to meet me. "One of my proudest moments in the fourth grade was when I made my cardboard model of the courthouse. Of course, a flexible metal tape measure would be the best way to do this, but your string works, too."

I took a felt-tip pen out of my shoulder bag and marked the string. He pulled the tape off the column, coiled the string, and handed it to me. "Thanks," I said, tucking the string and pen back in my bag. "It was nice of you to help." I turned to go.

And I saw Clod. He'd come back out of the courthouse and stood beside the door in his police-issue posture, arms crossed, watching me and whoever the guy was who'd just helped me with my string-and-column project.

"Hey, Cole," I called, with a wave as wide and insincere as my smile. "Here's an old friend of yours." I pointed over my shoulder, then turned back to my new friend to reintroduce him to his old acquaintance. But no one was there.

Chapter 2

Clod started to say something—possibly *Good morning, Ms. Rutledge. Why are you lurking?*—but the radio at his shoulder burped static. He listened and responded with a curt, clear "Ten-four" that I imagined spitting out the other end in another eruption of static, intelligible only to the starched and initiated. Without a wave or a nod, he put on his sunglasses and went down the steps and around the corner to where he parked behind the courthouse. I looked around again for the helpful stranger, didn't see him, and headed for the Weaver's Cat.

When I'd decided to stay in Blue Plum (due to one thing or another—one thing being the loss of my job as a textile conservator at the Illinois State Museum and the other being the lucky inheritance of Granny's house and business), Ardis Buchanan told me her secret for getting anywhere fast in our small town. No matter how short the distance, she got in her car and drove. *If I walk,* she'd said, *I'll run into someone I know, and you and I both know that I am incapable of walking past the opportunity for a good chin-wag.* Ardis, longtime manager of the Weaver's Cat, wise in the ways and means of Blue Plum, was always worth listening to. I'd adapted her solution for bypassing unavoidable chin-wags, taking it in a more ecological and heart-healthy direction. I walked, but I took the less traveled driveways that threaded between some of the businesses on Main Street and the service alleys running behind them.

The electronic chime on the back door of the Weaver's Cat was another reason I liked taking the alley way to work. The chime—courtesy of my creative friend Joe, né Tennyson, brother of the lamentable Clod—said "Baaaa" every time the door opened. I loved it. Argyle, the cat in residence, liked the chime, too, and he came to greet me in the kitchen, his tail up like a signal flag that read *feed me*.

"Hasn't Ardis already given you breakfast this morning, sweet pea?" I asked.

Argyle twined his yellow-striped body between my ankles. I stepped over him, he followed and twined, I stepped, he twined. Together, we moved toward the cupboard that held the dry cat food, doing what I'd come to think of as the "Paw de Deux." I tipped a few kibbles in his dish, and he thanked me with one last circuit of my ankles.

"She never gives him enough," a voice grumped from somewhere near the ceiling. I looked up and saw Geneva, the ghost in residence, do a fade-in on top of the refrigerator. "In my experience, young gentlemen require and enjoy unbelievable amounts of what's good for them."

I sidestepped Argyle's thank-you maneuver and looked down the hall toward the front of the shop. Talking to Geneva had gotten somewhat easier in the past couple of months. When she and I had first met, I was the only one who saw or heard her, and communicating openly—without looking or sounding crazy—had presented problems. But now that I'd found a way for Ardis to see and hear her, I only needed to be careful around everyone else in the world. I saw no one in the hall and went back to the refrigerator. Geneva sat with her knees drawn up so that she looked like a wispy gray lump.

"He's not a young cat, Geneva. The vet says he might be as old as fifteen."

"When you are one hundred and fifty-nine years old, then you come back and tell me if you still think fifteen isn't young."

"But for a cat, especially one who had a rough early life, fifteen *is* old. The shop is Argyle's retirement home, and we need to take good care of him."

She pulled her knees closer and rested her chin on them, a pose that said "hmph" as clearly as words.

"Anything going on this morning?" I asked, watching her body language for further clues about her attitude in general and the current state of affairs between her and Ardis in particular. Watching her "mist" would be more accurate. She rarely appeared more substantial than a film of rainwater on a dark window, or more solid than an Orenburg lace shawl—garments made of lace so fine they can be gathered and passed through the hole in a wedding ring. "How's Ardis this morning?"

"Hmph."

"Give her time, Geneva."

She said nothing and shifted like an annoyed hen ruffling its feathers.

"Would you like me to talk to her?"

"*I* certainly do not want to talk to her," she said. "Her happy prattle is like the yapping of a small dog. I find it enervating."

Oh, brother. Now that Ardis did know about her, communicating with Geneva might be somewhat easier, but dealing with her doleful whims was somewhat less so.

"'Enervating' is a very good word, which you can substitute for 'exhausting,'" Geneva said. "So is 'depleting.'" With her chin on her knees, she wasn't easy to understand; I thought she'd said *defeating*. I was beginning to feel defeated myself. "'Wearying' is another one," she said. "And 'paralyzing.'"

"Okay. Thanks. I've got it." I spoke louder and sharper than I meant to.

"You've got what, hon?" Ardis called as she came down the hall.

"Also 'dispiriting,'" said Geneva, and she disappeared as Ardis came through the door.

Ardis blinked. "Was that Great-great-aunt Geneva?"

"Hmm, I don't see her. Maybe she's up in the study." I was glad I could sound genuinely unsure.

"But Argyle is down *here*."

"Cats and ghosts are a lot alike, Ardis. As soon as you think you see a pattern to their behavior, and you think you can count on it, they figure out that you know, and then off they go and start doing something else completely different. Argyle's just here having a second breakfast and adding another layer of fur to my ankles. Geneva's probably off having her morning alone time."

"The morning alone time—is that a pattern you've noticed?" Ardis asked.

"Not so much a pattern as . . ."

"As what? I keep feeling as though I should be taking notes." She patted her pockets for the pencil she'd stuck behind her ear.

"Alone time isn't so much a pattern as something she seems to need a lot of."

"Ah." Ardis nodded, looking solemn. "It's what she's used to, isn't it. She hasn't known much else for the last hundred and twenty or thirty years and it might be hard to adjust."

"Alone time punctuated by a regrettable decade or two of nonstop television."

"But that wasn't in any way her fault," Ardis said, "and her addiction is understandable. And under control, too, wouldn't you say?"

I held my hand out and tipped it back and forth.

"Well. I'll let her have her privacy." She stooped to rub Argyle between his ears, making it look as though that required all her concentration. Then, sounding wistful, she asked, "Have *you* seen her today?"

"For a minute or two. She seemed tired."

"Is letting her have alone time enough, then? Is there anything else I can do for her? I mean, after all these years, to find each other, it's nothing short of miraculous. Odd, too, what with me, the great-great-niece, pushing seventy and her, the great-great-aunt, stuck in her early twenties. But the whole situation is miraculous. You see that, don't you?" She didn't wait for an answer. "I've been making a list of questions to ask her. After she gets better used to me, of course. That's the best plan, don't you think?" She was entering into the small-dog phase Geneva objected to.

"Give her time, Ardis. And space."

"It's all pent up, though. The questions and ... everything." Her eyebrows inched up her forehead, as though illustrating the increasing level of things pent up. "And it's been weeks since she and I met each other on that wonderful, amazing day. More than a month. Closer to two. And I still don't always see her, if you know what I mean. I can't always bring her into focus, which is so frustrating."

Ardis fiddled with the braided bracelet on her wrist. I'd made it for her, using cotton warping thread I'd dyed with one of Granny's recipes. The bracelet wasn't anything fancy or stylish, although it was a lovely grayish green and I'd done my best not to make it look like a summer camp arts and crafts project. But the bracelet did have an interesting quality. Thanks to following the recipe my grandmother had called "Juniper for Long Lasting and Friendship"—which came from dye journals she'd kept secret and then left to me—the bracelet somehow let Ardis see and hear Geneva. Whether it would let *anyone* who wore it see her, or if the bracelet only enhanced a connection between Ardis and Geneva, I didn't know. That it worked at all was astounding and weird and messed with my science-oriented mind. But, for better or worse (and lately for grumpy and disheartened), it brought my two odd friends together.

"I've never asked you how the bracelet is involved—"

I held a hand up and she stopped.

"I understand," she said. "Don't ask, don't tell. I just wondered if something is, I don't know, wearing off?"

That was a possibility, I guessed, but because I didn't really understand it, either ... "Do you hear her or see her any less clearly than when you first wore the bracelet?"

"No, and that's why I keep hoping that if I can talk to her, engage with her more, then the focusing problem might improve. Was that your experience with her?" She stopped and looked at me and gave a frustrated cluck. "It wasn't, was it. Do you wear something?"

I shook my head.

"You must have a natural talent for this, then. For ghosts. You and Ivy."

My "talent" for ghosts was something else I'd inherited from Granny—Ivy McClellan—along with the shop, her house, the secret dye journals, and another "talent." The other "talent"—more a "glitch" to my mind—let me feel a person's emotions if I touched a piece of clothing. It didn't always happen, I didn't understand it, and the jolts I received when it did happen made me think twice about casually patting strangers on the back. The dye journals and "talents" had come as an unexpected bonus after Granny died. Or, as Geneva might say, "unexpected" and "bonus" were words that, when combined, made a good substitute for "wow, I did not see that coming."

"What should I do?" Ardis asked. "You know Geneva so much better."

"Please believe me when I say I still have a lot to learn, Ardis. Beyond time and space, I don't really know. But time and space can't hurt."

"I know. You're right." She folded her hands, holding them tightly in front of her, keeping pent-up things in check. "I'm trying."

"She's dealing with so many different emotions and her situation has changed so drastically in the last seven or eight months."

"I know. And more so recently. She's like some of the

kiddos I had in my classes. The ones from 'complicated home situations.' That's how we described those situations when we wanted to be polite. There was so much you wanted to do for the little buttons and so much that no end of doing would ever fix."

"That's a good analogy, Ardis. Geneva's pretty resilient, though."

"Most of the kiddos were, too."

Ardis wouldn't have liked the comparison, but she and Clod adopted similar poses when they had serious matters to think over—pursed lips, drawn brows, gaze fixed on the floor. They were also both six feet tall—a height not unusual for a man, but imposing in a seventy-year-old woman with the steely nerve of a former elementary school teacher. Especially such a woman who also relished standing toe-to-toe or nose-to-nose with stubborn authority. And Clod was born to be upright and mulish.

"Maybe if I run upstairs and let her know I'm here for her," Ardis said. She looked up the back stairs, in a way that could only be described as longingly. The study was in the attic, two flights up, and Geneva and Argyle spent at least part of each day hanging out up there. "So she knows she can come to me anytime." She put a hand on the banister and a foot on the bottom step, her instinct to mother giving a strong tug.

"That's a nice thought—" I was going to add a "but" to that statement when the string of camel bells jingled at the front door, doing it for me.

"I'll go," Ardis said, her business instinct and dedication to customer service winning out.

"Thanks, Ardis. I'll put my purse away and be with you in two shakes."

"But before I forget, and at the risk of being a nag, did you get the last measurements?"

I clicked my heels and snapped a salute. "Yes, ma'am. We are all set to bomb the Blue Plum Courthouse."

Chapter 3

"Excellent." Ardis rubbed her hands. "We shall continue to keep mum while the knitting public can overhear us, but, may I just say, I can hardly wait for Thursday night?"

"It's going to be a blast."

"Utter," Ardis said, "and absolute."

She trotted down the hall to the front room and Argyle joined me for the trek up the back stairs. Despite what I'd told Ardis about the ever-changing habits of cats, Argyle's nap schedule didn't have much room for variation. Nap time called frequently and often, and the window seat in the attic dormer was a favorite place. He leapt onto the cushion now and curled into a skein of snoring yellow fur. I took the coil of marked string out of my shoulder bag and tucked it in a pocket. The bag went in the bottom drawer of the oak teacher's desk.

The study had been Granny's snug and private space. Now it was mine. Except that I shared it with Argyle and Geneva, and that made the snug space . . . snugger. Granddaddy, as creative in woodworking as Granny had been with fibers and fabrics, finished the wide-plank floor, fitted bookcases and cupboards under the eaves, and built the window seat in the dormer. He'd also hidden a tall, narrow cupboard behind one wall. He'd painted the inside of the cupboard Granny's favorite deep indigo blue and printed MY DEAREST, DARLING IVY along the edge of the shelf he'd put in the cupboard. Granny had kept her private dye journals on that shelf. Geneva claimed the cupboard as her own "room."

"Geneva?" I called.

"Boo."

I turned around. She was floating behind me.

"You do not jump as much as you used to when I sneak up on you."

"Have you been up here since you disappeared in the kitchen?"

"I sat on the stairs while you talked to Ardent. That is what her name means. Did you know that? And that is what she is, too. Putting up with Ardent is arduous."

"I asked *her* to give you time and space," I said. "Do you think *you* can be more patient with her? This is a new situation for both of you. And you're right; she is ardent. But she's tickled pink that you're here and that you're her great-great-aunt."

"Her great-great-aunt who has never liked the color pink."

"Come on, Geneva. It really would help me out if you two could meet each other halfway."

"On the stairs? I do not think her creaky old bones will be comfortable sitting on the stairs. I did not get where I am today by having creaky old bones."

I was feeling enervated and didn't say anything.

"That was haunted humor, in case you did not notice."

"I'll come back when you're ready to take this seriously," Geneva said.

"But you cannot tell me you did not cringe when she started prattling."

"She's excited. You get the same way when you're excited. You two are a lot alike. I'm kind of surprised I didn't notice that sooner. Come on, Geneva. You heard her say she's willing to give you time and space. There needs to be some give-and-take here. That's how friends and family work things out and how they help each other out."

"Shall I tell you what will help me out?"

I pinched the bridge of my nose between my thumb and forefinger before answering. It didn't help me out much. "Sure. What?"

"Go back downstairs and let me have my very valuable alone time."

The shop stayed busy all morning. That kept us from discussing our plans for Thursday night, but it was good for the till. It was also good for ignoring the difficulties Ardis and Geneva were experiencing. I loved them both, but I didn't love my new role as counselor and mediator for the suddenly and hauntingly related. It was so much easier helping the shop's customers develop relationships with the comforting textures and colors of fibers and fabrics. Thank goodness Ardis *was* willing to be patient with Geneva, though, and that we shared the fiber and fabric passion.

"I get a particular joy from watching neophytes cradling their first tools and materials," she said after two young women left with bulging bags. "I feel as though I should follow them to the door and hold it open, blessing them as they go."

"Telling them to fly free and come back to us when they've learned to soar?"

"Exactly," Ardis said. "In reality, they'll be back to-morrow for help with a problem, but getting them back on track will bring its own kind of joy. Didn't I tell you we'd be run off our feet this week?"

"You did."

"Like sap rising in the New England sugar bush," she said, "the creative juices in Blue Plum awaken, they stir, and now they're in full spate."

"You're full of good analogies this morning, Ardis, except this is October and I think maple sap might rise in February."

She waved the quibble away. "It's a natural phenom-enon like any other, and you can count on it happening every year when the kiddos go back to school. It's that whiff of school paste in the air."

"It's probably all glue sticks these days."

Another dismissive wave. "Crafty-minded folks aren't so particular. They're in tune. They catch whatever whiff it is, and they see visions of handmade gifts dancing in their heads—hats, scarves, ornaments."

"Table runners, afghans, stockings, and tree skirts?"

"Yes, oh yes." Ardis put a hand on my shoulder. "And sweaters. Close your eyes, Kath. Can't you picture those glorious projects?"

I closed my eyes, though I didn't need to; we had sam-ples of sweaters and hats and all the rest displayed ev-erywhere in the shop.

"And although we know an awful lot of those embroidered, quilted, crocheted, and knitted visions are unrealistic," Ardis said, "there's nothing wrong with embellished dreams and hopes. We all have them. *I* have them. And I need them. They give me respite—from reality, from the world, from Daddy's increasing infirmity. They give me strength."

"That's really nice, Ardis."

"I can't lay claim to the analogy or the philosophy. They were Ivy's. Your grandmother knew human nature as well as she knew knitting or any other needle art. I'm sure creativity bubbles up and burgeons all over the country in the fall, but you watch, the local flow will turn into a flood—beautiful and abundant. This was Ivy's favorite time of year, and especially the weeks before and after Handmade Blue Plum."

"I haven't been here in the fall for years. I should've come to visit her more often."

"She didn't expect you to run down here every few months. She couldn't have been more proud of you, or more proud of your career."

I closed my eyes again, this time picturing Granny—gray braid and blue jeans, blue eyes with crow's-feet to prove her good humor, and a tilt to her head to show she saw and heard more than some. "I'll take a walk around, Ardis. See if anyone needs help." I moved away before she could reach over and squeeze my shoulder, and a few tears from my own blue eyes. As I started up the front stairs to check on shoppers on the second floor, I heard the smile in her voice as she greeted the next customer at the counter.

"Good morning. You've made an excellent choice with that turquoise bouclé. Soft and cozy, yet carrying with it underlying hints of daring and whimsy. I think you'll be very happy."

I paused on the stairs to listen for an answer and wasn't disappointed.

"I picked it up," an almost breathless voice said, "and I couldn't put it back down. A scarf, don't you think? Or no! A cropped vest!"

I went on up the stairs, missing the rest of their discussion. Ardis was right about the upwelling of creativity in and around Blue Plum in the past month or so. And Handmade Blue Plum, the arts and crafts fair held the second weekend in October each year, was perfectly timed—either to feed the flow of creative energy, or to take advantage of it. The fair, opening Friday at noon in the school gym, was also perfectly timed to take advantage of the three-week fall break in Blue Plum's year-round school calendar. Having the fair at the school was a win-win. The crafters were under a roof with classrooms for demonstrations and workshops, and the school received ten percent of the crafters' booth registration fees.

The Weaver's Cat couldn't be an official part of the fair, because commercially produced goods and materials were prohibited, but some of the more prolific crocheters, crafters, knitters, knotters, weavers, and whatnot who belonged to TGIF would be selling their handmade wares. In the meantime, we stayed busy in the shop ringing up all manner of needles, hooks, hoops, patterns, and the manipulable fibers and fabrics that dreams and finished projects were made of. We were busy enough that Debbie Keith, who worked part-time for us and full-time raising sheep on her farm outside town, was coming in for a couple of extra afternoons during the week, and we'd hired a fiber-smitten high school student for week-end hours. The student, Abby Netherton, dressed goth and worked a drop spindle like a pro.

Ardis was also right that fall might have been Granny's favorite time of year, although I seemed to remember Granny saying that about every season at one point or another. She would definitely have loved the *un*official part TGIF and her beloved Weaver's Cat intended to play in Handmade Blue Plum. The project—the clandestine fiber installation project I'd been measuring for, concocted and devised by a select splinter group of TGIF—would have blown her away.

A whiff of conversation and the scent of coffee led me to one of the front rooms on the second floor. We encouraged drop-in needlework, and a couple of women sat knitting in the comfy chairs near the windows that looked down on Main Street, one working on a blue baby sock, the other something voluminous and raspberry. Their project bags, a thermos, and two steaming mugs sat on the low table between them. The baby sock woman raised a mug when she saw me.

"It's okay that we brought our own brew, isn't it?" She held the mug under her nose and steamed her glasses before taking a sip.

"We're in town a few days early for the craft show," the raspberry woman said. "I'm Ellen and she's Janet. We came last year and found this shop and decided it was a perfect spot. We promised ourselves the perfect morning in these chairs."

"It's what they're here for," I said, "and we're glad to have you, coffee and all. I'm Kath. Ardis is downstairs. Let us know if there's anything we can find for you."

"There was an older woman here last year," Janet said. She'd put her mug back on the table and picked up her needles. "She talked me into the extravagance of handspun, hand-dyed wool."

Her friend looked over the tops of her glasses at her. "It didn't take much talking."

"Well, no, it didn't. But I think she had me sized up. Somehow she knew I wouldn't be able to resist it—it was a gorgeous indigo and knitted up into a shawl that I'll treasure forever. And I've been wondering what she can show me this year that I won't be able to live without."

It didn't happen often anymore, that someone came in the shop who didn't know Granny had died in the spring. Still, I should have had a response at hand—something less distressing to customers, anyway, than silence and what must have been the stricken look on my face. It was the woman's mention of the indigo wool that threw me. That would have been wool Granny had spun and dyed. Indigo was her favorite and her specialty.

The women stopped knitting.

"I'm so sorry," I said. "She had the amazing knack for remembering everyone who bought her wool, and she would have loved seeing you again."

"You were related?" Janet asked.

"My grandmother."

She nodded. "You favor her. She must have had your dark red hair when she was younger. We're sorry for your loss. And the store's."

"Thank you." I backed out of the room, hoping I hadn't made their perfect morning too awkward, leaving them to their socks and the raspberry cloud.

The other two upstairs rooms were quiet, and I took

a few quiet minutes to straighten them. Tidying the shop had been my "job" during my childhood visits to Granny. I'd liked doing it, liked pleasing Granny by putting things in order. I liked tidying now, too, because I found *her* in each room. In every skein I returned to its bin and every pattern or notion that went back where it belonged, I found her love for everything to do with fibers.

During the next lull in business, when we were both behind the sales counter, Ardis slid closer to me, casting glances left and right. "Yours is the last piece of intel we need," she said. "So, how does it look? Are all systems go? What do you think?"

"That you're mixing spies and astronauts in your jargon."

"Pshaw. Mission accomplished? Can we move forward?"

Ardent Ardis—Geneva had her pegged perfectly. Ardis was fired up and raring to bomb the courthouse and the entire town—with knitting and crochet work. With tatting, macramé, braiding, weaving, and coiling, too, for that matter.

Ardis hadn't come up with the idea that we should yarn-bomb the town on the eve of Handmade Blue Plum. But as soon as she'd heard the suggestion, she was behind the project one hundred percent. She was primed and ready to be pointed in the right direction as soon as darkness fell Thursday night. She was gung ho to leave her mark on Blue Plum with yarn graffiti.

I copied her left-right glances. No customers were in sight. I pulled the coil of string from my pocket, put it on the counter, and held out my hand. "Measuring tape," I whispered.

Ardis slapped a measuring tape in my hand and whispered back, "Measuring tape, Dr. Rutledge. This is very exciting."

I uncoiled the string and measured from the end to the point I'd marked with the felt tip. "Twelve feet, Dr. Buchanan, plus seven and one half inches. Congratulations, you have four strapping courthouse columns."

"Quadruplets," Ardis said. "And I thank my stars they aren't real babies. But who would have thought the columns were so big around?" She entered the number in a notebook, under a long list of other measurements. "It's kind of fun sneaking around like that, isn't it? I had no idea I'd get such a kick out of it. When did you go?"

"Um . . ."

She looked up from the notebook. "You didn't have any trouble, did you?"

"Not exactly."

She put the pencil down. "Exactly *how* not exactly?"

"It's possible I might have been seen."

"Possible? Might?"

"Was. Sorry, Ardis. I was seen."

She studied that problem, and the countertop, drumming her fingers on compressed lips. "Okay," she said, dropping her hands to her hips. "Being seen is the risk we'll be taking Thursday night anyway, so it's good to see how we'll handle that kind of pressure. Besides, in the dark, in the shadows, and as small as you are, you probably weren't recognized, so it might not be so bad."

"Um . . ."

Ardis stepped closer, looming much the way her great-great-aunt occasionally did. Really, their similarities were much more uncanny—although completely natural—than the superficial similarities between Ardis and Clod. I moved down the counter and smiled, going for the same confidence and nonchalance I'd used while accomplishing my column-measuring mission.

"You," Ardis said, moving down the counter after me, "look guilty. Because you didn't go after dark, did you. That's not a question, so don't bother to answer."

I didn't bother and I moved farther down the counter.

Ardis was ardently relentless. "*Mel*, who is busier than any two of us combined, finished *her* assignment last week."

"This was a last-minute assignment. A rush job."

"Which you've known about for three days. You should have been able to find time *not* in the middle of the day to complete this paltry part of the preplanning for this project."

"All those *p* words are making you spit, Ardis."

"You slacked, Kath Rutledge. *And* you went out in daylight? Who saw you?"

Thank goodness she couldn't billow and swirl the way Geneva did. Humor and a confident smile weren't soothing her, so I tried for calm and matter-of-fact. "It's okay, Ardis. Everything's fine. I got the measurement with no harm done. Two people saw me and neither one will be a problem. One was basically a tourist who thought I was working on a school project for my kids. And the other was Cole Dunbar."

"You don't have kids."

"See? So no problem."

"And I didn't catch the second person's name," Ardis said.

She wouldn't have. I'd mumbled it, having failed at feeling matter-of-fact at the last minute.

I moved around to other side of the counter, so that it was between us, and tried another smile. Ardis closed the space—a mere counter being no barrier for a woman of towering height and piercing eye. My smile faltered.

The camel bells jingled as the front door opened. I hoped Ardis' customer service ethic would kick in and give me a reprieve. It didn't.

She leaned closer and said, with what would have been a threatening hiss if there'd been sibilants involved, "Cole Dunbar."

At that point I stood up as tall as my five foot three let me, and I owned my mistakes. For the most part. "Ardis, I'm sorry I didn't get it done sooner, and I'm sorry I didn't do it after dark. But it doesn't matter if Cole saw me. He was busy being a deputy and getting a kick in the shin from the mayor's mother. He had no idea I was up to anything, much less anything secret, sneaky, or clandestine."

"Until now," the deputy himself said behind me.

Chapter 4

I didn't turn around and look at Clod Dunbar. Acknowledging him wasn't going to add anything positive to the situation. Ardis didn't add anything positive, either, when she crossed her arms at me and said, "Mm-hmm." But choosing Clod's side over mine was against her better nature.

"Good morning, Coleridge," she said. "Hat off. Someone will be with you shortly." He made a huffing noise behind me—a noise that ceased when Ardis gave him a sharp look, lowering her glasses to half-mast so he experienced the full power of that look. "Kath, hon," she said, still holding Clod with her eyes, "come on back here and take a look at these figures for me. See if things are adding up to anything of *significance*." She held up the notebook with her list of measurements, emphasizing the word "significance" in Clod's direction.

"Of course, Ardis. Happy to." I scooted around to the business side of the counter and took the notebook from her. For Clod's sake, I whistled and said, "Wow."

"That's what I thought, too," Ardis said. She glanced

over when I picked up the pencil and made a note. When she broke eye contact with him, Clod harrumphed and reasserted himself.

"Until now," he said, "no, I did not know you were up to anything. But I'll hazard an informed guess. *You* think you're up to something. Something secret and sneaking. And I imagine you think you're good at that kind of thing. But our fair city isn't engulfed in any major crime waves, so I'd say it's unlikely that you're really up to anything. Anything illegal. Or anything that will hinder the performance of my duties. Sad to say, but there hasn't been much opportunity in the last month or so for you to dabble in detective work."

Unpleasant noises threatened to erupt from his nose. Something in his long-winded and priggish speech must have struck him as funny. Either that or he had indigestion.

"Ms. Rutledge and Ms. Buchanan," he said, after recomposing himself, "here's something that might interest you—a bona fide case for you to work on that's worthy of your deductive skills." He didn't say anything more, being the kind of irritating person who stands and looks pleased, waiting for other people to ask him what he's talking about.

And I'm the kind of person who can't stand that kind of suspense and always has to ask. "Is that why you came in, Deputy Dunbar? To ask for our help with a mystery that's baffling you?" Unfortunately I'm also the kind of person who's been failing with her latest sarcasm abatement program. "You know us. We're always happy to lend a hand. Hang on a tick." I turned to a blank page in Ardis' notebook and licked the end of the pencil. "Shoot—not literally, of course. But what have you got for us?"

"I meant it as a joke."

"I know. But my keen powers of observation told me that you really did think of something, just then. So even if it is a joke, why don't you tell us? How can it hurt? And if our baffled bumbling gives you a few more laughs, then it'll even be good for you. It'll help loosen up your auras or chakras or something."

"Do you know about auras and chakras, Kath?" Ardis asked with some surprise.

"No."

She turned back to Clod. "She's right, though, Coleridge. Life is better with a few laughs, so lay it on us."

On a personal level, Clod might be a clod, but as a policeman he was no slouch. He proved that by narrowing his eyes—in suspicion, no doubt—a good trait for someone in law enforcement.

"I do like a good laugh as much as anyone," he said after a pause. "So I'll give you a clue. Remember what I said about dabbling in detective work? That's it. That's your clue. So go ahead and knock yourselves out. But now that we've all had our fun, may I get down to the business I came in for?"

Ardis slid over next to me so that we stood shoulder to shoulder—solidarity.

"Ms. Rutledge, outside the courthouse earlier this morning," he said, "was that Hugh McPhee you were talking to?"

"Beats me. We didn't exchange names."

"*Never,*" Ardis said at the same time. "I haven't seen Hugh in years. Are you sure, Cole?"

Clod's left eye narrowed farther as he thought that over, but the narrowed focus didn't appear to deliver the information he needed. Neither did turning his gaze to the ceiling in the corner of the room, despite a flicker in his eyes that suggested sorting and comparing mental images. Images from where, though? Old memories? Photo albums? Mug shots? Clod's inventory didn't take long.

"I can't make a positive ID," he said, "but I *will* find out. And I'll find out before Rogalla does."

"Who?"

He didn't answer. He put his Smokey the Bear hat back on, returning it to its upright and officious position, and marched out the door.

"See?" I said to Ardis after he'd left. "He didn't care what *I* was doing at the courthouse. He didn't even realize I was doing anything. He's more worried about McPhee and someone whose name sounds like a gargle. It was the Case of Clo—" I almost slipped and called him Clod, something I tried not to do out loud, *Clod* being a private pejorative. "The Case of the Clueless Deputy, and we have nothing to worry about."

She didn't say anything, just stared out the front door.

"Ardis?"

"I'll be back," she said, but not to anyone in particular, and she, too, left.

Chapter 5

"Losing friends left and right, I see." Geneva drifted into view and curled around the blades of the overhead fan. I didn't turn the fan on, not wanting to lose another friend, tempting though that might be from time to time. "Whatever possessed *Ardent* to dash out the door like that? She is so rarely ardent about moving anywhere fast."

"It's *Ardis*," I said reflexively, then, "Beats me."

But I wouldn't have been much of a dabbling detective if I didn't realize Ardis had reacted to the name Hugh McPhee. Reacted and left. I went out on the front porch and looked up and down Main Street. Geneva was right, though. Ardis had moved fast. She wasn't in sight walking, and if she'd hopped in her car she was long gone. Curious and interesting.

Before going back inside, I took a minute to look at our front-window displays. I used to do that every morning, before I'd fallen for the electronic charms of the "baa" at the back door. I enjoyed trying to see the business the way a new customer would, and I realized I should get back into the habit.

Our building, simply because of its age and style, attracted people. We were in one of three attached houses—part of the two-story, mid-eighteenth-century row house that my grandparents had called home from the time they married. People couldn't help responding to the warmth and charm of the building's rosy handmade bricks and the millwork "gingerbread" added in the 1890s. The front steps and graceful handrail invited customers and old-building aficionados up on the shady porch that stretched the length of the building. Our window displays did the rest. Debbie knew how to create displays that lured the eyes and then the feet through our front door. That was how Ardis liked to put it, anyway. Although, if she said it in Geneva's hearing, Geneva sniffed and made remarks about the horrible sight of stray body parts mingling with our more "full-bodied" customers.

At the moment, Geneva mingled in the window with Debbie's display of Japanese kumihimo weaving materials. Geneva made an interesting watery gray backdrop for the jewel-colored threads and cords. She treated the window as her personal large-screen TV. If she wanted to, she could float through the window and perch on one of the porch rockers or the railing for a better view. But after she'd moved into the shop—with its colors and textures and fibers and fabrics—she said she felt settled and content, and she tended to stay inside looking out. Settled and content were relative terms, though. And by the way she motioned me in with her hand now, she wouldn't be content until I was back inside looking out, too.

"She is flighty and a bad example," Geneva said as soon as I was through the door.

I looked around for customers before answering. All clear, but I took my phone from my pocket, just in case. "If you're talking about Ardis," I said into the phone, "then you know that isn't true. She's solid and reliable."

"Is that a dig about those of us who are no longer solid?"

"No! No, and I'm sorry if it sounded like one. But a few minutes ago you said Ardis wasn't ardent about moving fast, and now you're saying she's flighty. You can't have it both ways, Geneva."

"Hmph."

"What happened to your alone time?"

She yawned and stretched. "I am feeling quite refreshed. Also, I heard the voice of the long arm of the flatfoot and came to see why he was disturbing our peace. What was his silly clue about?"

"Beats me." I went back behind the sales counter and sat on the stool.

"That saying reflects a defeatist attitude. You should stop using it and adopt something more positive."

"Such as?"

"I will think and let you know. In the meantime, repeat the driveling clue for me."

"Come on over here. I'll write it down."

She floated as far as the ceiling fan and wound herself around it. I wrote *dabbling in detective work* on the blank page in Ardis' notebook.

"You thought of something when you wrote that down," Geneva said. "I can tell by the way your mouth is hanging slightly and unbecomingly open and by the way you're staring at, but obviously not seeing, that corner of the ceiling you haven't thought to dust for cobwebs in at least two months." She uncurled from the fan and drifted down to sit on the counter where she could see what I'd written. Except she didn't just sit. She bounced. "What is it? What did you think of? Is it something useful? Will it solve the mystery? Have there been diabolical doings? What did you think of? What?"

I looked at her. She stopped bouncing.

"You've forgotten what you thought of," she said, starting to droop. "I can tell that, too."

"Your bouncing might have driven it right out of my head."

She took offense at my remark, I could tell that easily enough. But the jingle of the camel bells at the front door, and the two people walking through it, distracted her from drooping further. I put my phone back in my pocket. Ardis was back, with dimples in her cheeks that only showed up on the most joyous of occasions, and with her was the man I'd last seen with my coil of string at the courthouse.

"Hugh," Ardis said, "this is Kath Rutledge. Kath, I'd like you to meet one of my all-time-favorite students, Hugh McPhee."

"Nice to meet you," I said. "And nice to see you again."

"Hugh remembers coming into the Weaver's Cat with his mother," Ardis said, "away back at the beginning, when Ivy and Lloyd still lived here, and you'd find Lloyd reading his newspaper in the comfy chair next to the knitting needle display. And, Hugh, I remember when your mother knitted an Abraham Lincoln beard for you and you wore it to recite the Gettysburg Address at the Blue Plum Elementary Spring Fling. Unless I'm not remembering that right; a knitted beard sounds outlandish in retrospect, and your mother was more of a straightforward pullover-and-baby-blanket needlewoman."

"You're right on both counts, Ms. Buchanan. I did wear hand-knitted whiskers. And no, my mother didn't make them. If she had, the beard wouldn't have been so full of dropped stitches and unintentional yarn overs. And it would have been cabled. But she taught all her children to garden, cook, sew, and knit. I made the beard myself."

Geneva had returned to the blades of the ceiling fan when Ardis and Hugh McPhee came in. He stood under the fan, and as he told the beard story, she leaned down to stare at him, her hollow eyes wide. The ceiling and the fan were high, and Ardis hadn't noticed her yet.

"Hugh's only in town for a few days," Ardis said, "but, Kath, I thought we might let him be an honorary member of TGIF."

"Sure."

"What's TGIF?" Hugh asked.

"What are your plans for the day?" Ardis asked.

"Nothing pressing."

"Good. Then we'll have an early lunch, my treat, and I'll tell you about TGIF on the way." She put her arm through Hugh's. "Shall I bring you something, Kath? I'll take him to Mel's."

"Sure, how about—"

"You'll love Mel's," Ardis said, turning back to Hugh. "Everybody loves Mel's. Mel herself is another story. Come on, we'll take the alleyway—the scenic route." Patting his arm, she led him out of the room and down the hall toward the kitchen. The back door said, "Baa," when they left.

"She will probably be kind to your hips and bring you a salad," Geneva said from the ceiling fan, "if she remembers to bring you anything at all." She floated down and perched on the shoulder of the mannequin that stood near the counter. She almost blended in with the gray cowl the mannequin wore. That made for a surreal moment when she waved a hand at me, two fingers raised, and it looked for a second as though the cowl had unraveled and flapped in a breeze.

"I have two things," Geneva said, "two important points to discuss."

I held up one finger, pulled out my phone again, and put it to my ear.

"First," she said, "you might not have been able to see from down at this level where you dwell, but that man had a bald spot on top of his head. Second, you were right, and I have reassessed my opinion."

"Your opinion of what?"

"Not of what, of whom. My opinion of my relative. She is not flighty. She is giddy."

"Giddy, huh?" Ardis did have her excitable moments, but attaching "giddy" to her six-foot frame and sensible shoes didn't work much better for me than "flighty."

"She's certainly happy to see him."

"Bald spot and all."

"Since when have you got a thing about bald spots? Anyway, from the way she acted, it's easy to believe he *is* one her all-time-favorite students."

"You are not seeing the bald—I mean the *big* picture," Geneva said. "I mean giddy in *love*. In love with a *younger man*!" Having an excitable moment herself, she nearly fell off the mannequin. She righted herself, clasped her hands in her lap, and pressed her lips together primly. "I would say," she continued, sounding now as though she'd sucked a lemon, "that I am scandalized over the behavior of my great-great-niece, but I think you know that I am not one to make a scene. *Arduous* is old enough to be in charge of her own heart and more than old enough to know better. Also, worrying about her as if she were of a natural and decent age for a great-great-niece, instead of one with wrinkles and former students practically at retirement age, makes my head swirl as though you turned the fan on while I was sitting on it." She shuddered and drew her shoulders up.

"That's not true, you know."

"You do not believe me?" she asked.

"That she's in love with him? No, I don't."

"Maybe the bald spot puts her off, too." She sighed. "Just as well. I do not have time to worry about her flibbertigibbet self."

"Busy schedule?"

"Busy noticing. That is what crackerjack detectives, like you and me, do. Those who only dabble in detective work default on the title 'crackerjack.'"

"They're dilettantes?"

"Dead on," she said. "That was more haunted humor."

"Good one. So, what did you notice?"

"*She* never stopped smiling. *He* never started."

"That's—" I had a knee-jerk reaction to say that wasn't

true, but she was right. Hugh McPhee hadn't smiled at the courthouse, either. He hadn't even smiled when he told us about knitting the beard. "Huh."

"Stick with me," she said, "and call me Eagle Eye."

She was so pleased with herself I didn't want to dampen her moment by listing the half dozen reasons that immediately sprang to mind for why someone might not smile—unhappy memories, illness, accident, not being a natural smiler. Worry about a bald spot. "Did you notice anything else?"

She clapped her hands. "Of course, but now it is your turn."

"He had a camera."

"Pffft. Boring."

"His voice—" Speaking of voices, I heard Ellen and Janet, the two knitters I'd spoken to earlier. They were on the landing at the top of the stairs. Their coos and aws gave them away. Debbie had hung a row of sweet baby sweaters from the railing up there, and they were probably fondling them.

"She who hesitates loses her turn," Geneva said. "So it is my turn. Let me see . . ."

That sounded suspiciously like a hesitation to me. I didn't call her on it, though. Ellen and Janet were coming down the stairs, and the camel bells at the front door jingled, bringing the lull in business to an end and me on my lonesome to deal with it.

The mayor's mother came in, stopping inside the door and looking around as though she'd never been in the shop before. In fact, I'd never seen her come in. Not that I saw or knew every customer who did come in, but in terms of fiber and fabric, the mayor's mother was an unknown quantity to me. She was an unknown quantity to me in terms of *most* things, including her name. I liked her for the decisive connection her foot had made with Clod's shin, though, and I smiled and waved to her.

"I have to have go now," I said to Geneva through my unconnected phone—my "dead phone" as Geneva liked to call it, always reminding me, when she did, that "dead phone" was more of her haunted humor. She didn't seem to understand that if she explained or identified her jokes, they weren't as funny.

"But it is still my turn," she said.

"I'll talk to you later, okay?" I said.

The mayor's mother—Mrs. Weems, I assumed—smiled and waved back at me. In addition to her fast-moving tennis shoes, she wore a pair of mocha-colored capris, a French vanilla Henley, and a puffy taffeta vest in a blue close to—or exactly—the color of blue plums. Her pocketbook, the one that might or might not have met Clod's midsection at the courthouse, hung on her arm. She stopped at the display table near the door and stood fingering the skeins of cotton chenille Debbie had put there to waylay the unwary.

She didn't appear to be any the worse for whatever reason Clod had escorted her into the courthouse. She was five foot two at most and might weigh one hundred pounds with the pocketbook, but she was obviously her own woman. Her hand seemed stuck on a skein of mango-colored chenille that would make a beautiful soft baby blanket or yummy scarf.

Equating colors with foods and describing yarns as

"yummy" were early warning signs. Stomach growling would be next, and I hoped Ardis would come back with my lunch before that happened.

Geneva moved in front of me. "Is this later enough?" she asked.

"Sorry. It'll have to be later-later," I said, slipping the phone into my pocket.

"Well, if that is the way you are going to be about it," she said, "I will not tell you anything else."

Ellen and Janet came in then. "We're going to stretch our legs," Ellen said, "and grab a bite to eat. We don't want you to think we're abandoning our perfect spot, though."

"For instance," Geneva continued, with a sniff, "I will not tell you anything more about the bald spot."

"Sounds good," I said, answering her and the knitters.

"And may we leave our project bags with you?" Janet asked. "Rather than lug them around?"

"Not about the bald spot or about the dreadful case of the willies I am now suffering," Geneva said with her nose in the air, "because of the scar."

"Really? Where?" Drat. She'd got me.

"Um," Janet said, naturally thinking I'd said that to her, "we thought you might not mind keeping them behind the counter. But if that's a problem—"

"Here." Geneva put the tip of her index finger in the center of the top of her head. "Shaped like a crescent moon. I think crescent moons are mysterious and romantic, don't you? Unless the scar is shaped more like the bottom of a broken beer bottle, and that is not mysterious or romantic. It just screams 'bar fight.'"

"We'll take our bags with us," Ellen said. She and Janet exchanged glances and backed toward the door. In backing, they bumped into the mayor's mother, who'd worked her way around the display table and had her back to *them*. It was unfortunate.

All three jumped and Geneva screamed, "Bar fight!"

Chapter 6

That scene probably didn't appear more than mildly chaotic to the other three women in the room. On the other hand, the ghost in the room did her best to encourage pandemonium.

Geneva circled the women feinting punches and ducking in case they threw one at her. Ellen picked up the skeins of chenille the mayor's mother had been holding and then tossed in the air when they collided. The mayor's mother steadied herself by latching onto Janet's arm. Janet and Ellen tried laughing and they all apologized to each other. The women had no idea Geneva swirled around them, even though she continued yelling, "Bar fight!"

Into that scene, the back door said, "Baa," and Ardis returned—with no bag or box lunch in sight.

"Did I hear someone yelling bar ..." Ardis stopped when she caught the flicker of Geneva's movement.

Geneva stopped, too. Then she swirled one more time around the women, silent and pouting, and disappeared.

Ardis squinted after her and sighed. But she pulled

herself together, resuming the mantle of good customer service. "Now, who can I help?"

"We have some early arrivals for Handmade," I said, waving Ellen and Janet back to the counter, "and we're going to keep their project bags for them while they go eat lunch." They handed me their bags readily enough, but I apologized to them for the confusion anyway. "Thinking of too many things at once," I said. "But of course we'll keep your bags for you. And if you need a suggestion for lunch, try Mel's down on the next corner. Best food in town. Save room for a slice of her tunnel of fudge cake, though. It's ooooh and mmmmmm all in one." If I wasn't careful I'd embarrass myself.

"We remember Mel's," Ellen said, "and we're already drooling."

"And we're so sorry for bumping into you," Janet said to the mayor's mother. "Are you sure you're all right?"

"I'm fine," Mrs. Weems said. "It takes more than a bump in the rump to knock me over. Besides, it's always a pleasure to *bump into* folks who can't stay away from Blue Plum. You-all enjoy your stay. What's the slogan they're using for the craft show this year?"

"Plum good," Ardis said.

"There you go. You-all have a *plum good* time. Bye, now." Tiny as she was, with her hands now on her hips, Mrs. Weems gave the impression of being in charge of things. The puffy vest gave her some heft, and I could picture her as a crossing guard at the elementary school. Or a wizened superhero—instead of the Green Lantern, the Blue Prune.

Ellen reached her hand out, as though she meant to

pat Mrs. Weems on the shoulder in passing. But something in that superhero stance, or the snap in the Blue Prune's eyes, made Ellen pull her hand back. She and Janet scooted for the door and as the camel bells jingled behind them, Ardis stepped into the slightly awkward breach of etiquette.

"What a nice surprise seeing you here, Gladys. Are you keeping all right?"

"Afternoon, Ardis. I could hardly be feeling better. How's that devilish daddy of yours?"

Ardis' eyebrows shot up, but she wrestled them back down and answered with her usual honeysuckle manners, "Daddy's fine. I'll tell him you asked. Now, what can we do for you? Don't tell me the needlework bug has finally bitten you?"

The mayor's mother—Gladys—laughed. "Wouldn't that be a stitch? And a dropped one more than likely. No, you know me better than that, Ardis Buchanan. What I came for is to ask this young woman a question." She pointed an arthritic finger at me.

"It's nice to meet you, Mrs. Weems," I said. "I'm Kath. Ivy's granddaughter."

"I know who you are," Gladys said, "and I'm pleased to meet you, but what I want to know is this—was that Hugh McPhee you were talking to at the courthouse this morning?"

"Yes, ma'am."

Her question was an eerie echo of Clod's. Her reaction wasn't like his, though. Gladys Weems slapped her thigh. Then she put that hand to her cheek, and shook her head, and sank both hands in the pockets of her vest.

At that point she stopped shaking her head and started nodding. "I thought so," she said. "Yes, indeed, I thought so." Her eyes were the slits of a satisfied cat.

"Tell me about Hugh McPhee," I said.

I'd held the door for Gladys Weems, and then told Ardis about my image of her as the caped and crusading Blue Prune. Ardis had collapsed on the stool behind the counter and was taking a calming sip of the iced tea she'd brought back from Mel's. For herself.

"He was one of your favorites, and you're happy to see him, but he seems to be stirring some other interesting reactions around town. Including forgetfulness. And a certain lack of lunch for coworkers."

"You only think I forgot your lunch because I didn't bring you any," Ardis said.

"Could be."

She held a finger up, holding off further grousing. As I was thinking about biting that finger, the back door said, "Baa," and familiar footsteps came our way. Ardis looked smug. "What was that you were saying, O ye of little faith?"

"Um, hello, Joe, and hello, lunch?"

"Hey, Kath. Hey again, Ardis." Joe put a bag from Mel's on the counter in front of me and leaned in for a quick kiss. "I'd have been here sooner, but Mel needed a few more people to test the new lentil salad."

"Did you like it?" I asked.

"We can compare notes after you've tried your share."

I looked at the bag. Visions of the countless well-intentioned lentil salads I'd experienced at potlucks and neighborhood get-togethers trudged through my head. I poked the bag with a finger; the bag felt heavier than any decent sample portion of lentil salad should.

"Lentil salad can be a hard sell," Joe said. "That's why Mel's trying to build a better one. And why she sent along an incentive — tunnel of fudge is in there, too."

"Oooh."

"The last piece. You're lucky."

I picked the bag up and cradled it. Poor Ellen and Janet would have to settle for something else if they wanted dessert.

"Run on back to the kitchen," Ardis said. "I'll hold down the fort."

Mel Gresham, owner-operator of Mel's on Main, took her recipe experiments seriously, so I gave my full attention to the lentil salad and the questions on the recipe rating card she'd sent along. Or as much attention as I could with Joe, Geneva, and Argyle sitting across from me. Argyle sat upright on Joe's lap. He and Joe watched me — Joe because he took Mel's experiments as seriously as she did, and Argyle because he thought he might like to stick his paw out and grab my pencil. Geneva huddled in the chair next to them. I wasn't sure why; she didn't usually hang around when Joe and I were alone together in the store. *Because of the canoodling,* she'd told me early on in our relationship. *I have an aversion to it and am easily shocked.* A shocking canoodle, to Geneva, was anything less chaste than Joe shaking my hand while standing several feet away. She sat now with her head turned so she couldn't see Joe.

"There's something I'm tasting here . . ."

"Fresh mint," Joe said.

"Nice."

"Make a note of that on the card." He wiggled a finger at the rating card. "Then read what you've got so far."

"Keep your shirt on."

Geneva said, "Eep," and put a hand up to further blinker her view of Joe.

I scooped up the last bite and mulled the last question on the card. After savoring, swallowing, mulling, and marking, I picked up the card and read. " 'Lentil Salad, Version 3.0, question one: Would you eat this dish again?' Yes. 'Question two: Would you order this dish when faced with other options?' Yes. 'Question three: What did you like about this dish?' Mint." I stopped and looked at Joe. He blew me a kiss. "I like *that*, too," I said.

Geneva, who'd been peeking between her fingers, said, "Eep," again.

"I also like the lime vinaigrette and the addition of sliced radish, roasted potatoes, and generous chunks of avocado that contribute to the mixture of interesting flavors and textures. The crumbled cheese was perfect. How am I doing?"

"Nicely thought out."

"Thank you. Next question. 'Was there anything you disliked about the dish?' No, although it could use a tad more salt and pepper. And the last question: 'What is your overall rating?' " I turned the card around so Joe could see the answer—OMG followed by four exclamation points and the *O* as a smiley face. Mel would hate the text abbreviation and smiley, but she would love the sentiment. And I meant every fan girl exaggeration of it.

"I'll take the card back to her later," Joe said.

"And I'll take my reward now." I handed him the card and unwrapped the slice of cake.

Geneva was suddenly sitting next to me—eyes closed, hands clasped under her chin, leaning toward the cake as though drawn there by her nose. I looked from her to the cake. Then I cut into it with my fork and held a mouthful of it closer to Geneva. I swished the fork once, twice under Geneva's nose. She inhaled deeply . . .

"Something wrong?" Joe asked.

I ate the bite, shaking my head at the same time. The cake was perfect—and it was studded with chunks of crystallized ginger. Although Geneva had an aversion to canoodling, she had a tremendous fondness for ginger.

"Is Mel trying a new version of tunnel of fudge?" I asked.

"This is her fall recipe," Joe said. "Closer to Christmas she'll add bits of peppermint candy. Good, isn't it?"

If he'd been able to see Geneva, he wouldn't have asked. She was floating above the table, on her back, arms crossed, humming. To be consistent, not to say eccentric, I swished each bite before eating it to give her maximum olfactory joy.

"So, what do *you* know about Hugh McPhee?" I asked after swallowing the last bite of that chocolate bliss.

Joe started to shrug, but Argyle interrupted him with a growl low in his throat. Then, from the look on Joe's face, Argyle dug his claws into Joe's thighs. But that was only for traction, because in the next instant, Argyle launched himself off Joe's lap and tore up the back stairs.

"What the—" Joe bit down on the rest of that agonized statement.

"The fiends of hell!" Geneva cried, coming out of her ginger stupor. She clapped her hands to her ears and squeezed her eyes shut.

"Hey, it's okay," I said, trying to calm her, wondering what she and Argyle heard that neither Joe nor I could. What she still could. She wasn't panicking like Argyle, thank goodness, but she looked as though she was in pain. "It's okay," I said again.

"Easy for you to say; I'm in pain here," Joe said. "I'm pierced in twenty places at least."

I stood up, trying to get Geneva's attention without looking like a loon by waving my arms.

"Lordy, Lordy," she moaned. "I am pierced as well. My eardrums, at least, and possibly my very soul."

Then Ardis called from the front room, "Kath, Joe, can you hear it?"

"Pretty sure the cat did," Joe answered with more volume and less of his pleasant drawl than usual. "What are we supposed to hear?"

"The pitiful wails of some poor strangled beast," Geneva moaned.

"It's called skirling, isn't it?" Ardis called. "Someone's playing bagpipes out on Main Street. Over near the courthouse, it sounds like. Don't you love it? There's something about that wild music that makes your blood rush, doesn't it?"

"You got that right," Joe muttered.

"Oh, but it's stopped," Ardis said. "Just as it really got going, too. Cut off midskirl. What a shame."

Geneva took her hands from her ears. "The shame comes in calling that howling shriek 'music.' Mark my words," she said, wrapping her arms around herself and shivering, "no good can come from frightening a peaceable cat or torturing a ghost who would never dream of shattering another creature's eardrums."

I expected to hear a self-righteous sniff at the end of that ironic but obviously heartfelt statement. It didn't come.

It was a warm day, but Geneva shivered again. She took a last, sad look at the cake crumbs on my plate, and floated away and up the back stairs.

The warm day turned into a stuffy night as our temperatures zigzagged their way toward first frost. Tonight was warm enough to sleep with the bedroom window open three or four inches. Sometime between midnight and one, a skirl of sound came in on a breeze and woke me. Bagpipes. How odd. But Ardis was right; something about that wild sound stirred my blood and I sat up in bed.

It was a strange time for a pipe concert, though. Downtown, too, judging by the orientation of my window, and the direction of the breeze. Downtown and disturbing the sleep of the countless Blue Plumians within earshot, including the inmates in the jail behind the courthouse and the deputies guarding them and the ducks quacking in the creek . . . I might have dozed sitting up.

The tune changed, slowed, didn't grow softer. I'd heard it before, possibly in a movie. Melancholy . . . haunting . . . Geneva and Argyle! I pictured them cowering in the attic at the Weaver's Cat.

I threw back the covers, but before I'd put a foot on the floor, the pipes quit—one short wheeze of a sour note, and then silence.

Chapter 7

Geneva and Argyle were waiting for me in the kitchen at the Weaver's Cat the next morning. Argyle held no grudges over sleep interrupted by bagpipes. He accepted a rub between the ears and a helping of fish-flavored crunchy things with his usual good grace and shedding fur. Geneva looked grumpy and seemed to expect an apology.

"It wasn't me playing the pipes after midnight, Geneva, but I'm sorry they bothered you. Do you really hate them that much?"

"I hid under your desk with Argyle and we yowled to drown them out. I believe several dogs in the neighborhood joined us. The yowling was cathartic, but that does not mean I would like the fiend to repeat his performance again tonight."

"Have you ever heard bagpipes in real life?"

"As opposed to in real death? You are particularly insensitive this morning."

"That *was* insensitive, and I'm sorry. I just wondered if anyone around here played them in your time."

"Such a villain would have been ridden out of town on a rail."

Ardis was waiting for me in the front room, looking about as sleep-deprived and grumpy as her great-great-aunt.

"I'm trying to put a good face on it," she said, "because I dearly love the pipes. But you and I both know that I also dearly love my sleep, and this morning when I looked in the mirror I had a hard time convincing myself that I wasn't hungover. It's my eyes, Kath. Look at my eyes." She leaned toward me and almost fell off the tall stool.

I immediately went to Mel's and bought a large coffee for her.

Clod Dunbar was waiting for me when I got back from Mel's. He and Ardis weren't exchanging small talk when I came in. Small talk wasn't Clod's strong suit, and Ardis hadn't had enough sleep to bait him into engaging in it. I gave Ardis the cup of coffee and stood beside her. She took a sip, gauging the brew's temperature, then took a long swallow.

"Ah, Coleridge," she said. "Now that caffeine has propped open my eyelids, good morning." She breathed in the coffee's aroma and took another swallow. "To what do we owe the pleasure of your presence two days in a row? Are you here to tell us that the mad piper will pipe no more? That would be a kind thing for you to say and music to my ears. Especially as you tracked mud in through our front door."

Clod didn't look over his shoulder or check the soles

of his shoes. Instead he cleared his throat. His harrumph was out of uniform, though. *He* wore his khaki and brown, and held his Smokey the Bear hat at attention in the crook of his arm, but the harrumph was . . .

"Something's happened," I said quietly, trying to read it on his face. "What?"

His voice was out of uniform, too. He spoke to Ardis. "It's Hugh, Ms. Buchanan. I'm sorry. He's dead."

I took the cup of coffee from Ardis before she crumpled.

"I need to get back there," Clod said, talking to me now, "but I didn't think she should hear about it from some—"

"Where?" I asked.

"I'm not authorized to—"

"Back where?" Ardis asked. "Where did it happen?"

"Ms. Buchanan, ma'am," Clod said, "we don't need to go into that now."

I couldn't see his feet, but I got the impression he shuffled them. If he did, it was another chink in his professional starch and Ardis noticed, too. The chink must have given her strength. She stood up.

"*What* happened to Hugh, Coleridge? Tell me how and when and where."

Expressionless, Clod looked from her to me and back to her. "Unofficial. Off the record. We are investigating. Do not repeat this." He looked at each of us again. We nodded. "He was found a short while ago. His body was obscured by the reeds alongside the creek behind the courthouse."

"And the rest?" Ardis asked.

"Probably sometime last night, and not an accident.

Those are best guesses only. Again, unofficial and please do not repeat any of this."

"Why are you suddenly trusting us with unofficial information?" I asked.

He answered my question, but looked only at Ardis. "Because we might need your help, Ms. Buchanan. We found something in his, his . . . we found your name on a piece of paper in a book in some kind of purse around his waist. Not a purse. I know that's not what it's called. But it's part of the getup he was wearing."

"Getup?" Ardis mouthed the question.

I asked it out loud. "What getup? What are you talking about?"

"A kilt," Clod said, "and . . ." He stopped, maybe at a loss for the right words to describe the rest of Hugh's "getup." Or he might have faltered because he saw the look on Ardis' face.

"A kilt and *what*?" she asked.

"A kilt and *nothing*," Geneva whispered in my ear. She suddenly hovered at my other shoulder, making me a sandwich between a ghost and her great-great-niece. "I have heard about those 'getups' and what they leave out."

I put my hand up to hide my mouth and pretended to rub my nose. "Hush," I said quietly in Geneva's direction.

"I would like to know what a self-respecting great-great-niece of mine was doing consorting with the likes of a risqué man like *that*. I am scandalized." She made a rude noise in my ear and disappeared.

"*Regalia*," Clod said too loudly, as though he'd suddenly remembered the correct answer to a stumper and he'd expected a buzzer to sound, or a fourth-grade teacher's ruler to smack a desk. "Regalia," he repeated. "Socks, tassels, that, that hairy . . ." Vocabulary failed him again, and his hands took over trying to describe what he'd called a purse earlier, and where it hung below Hugh's waist. He turned red and crossed his arms when Ardis looked at him over her glasses, eyebrows raised.

"Perhaps you're talking about a spermin," Ardis said.

"Sporran," I said.

"*Anyway,*" Clod said, "it looks like McPhee was the ass—the um, the individual reportedly playing bagpipes in the middle of the night."

"Reportedly? You didn't hear them?" Clod lived around the corner from me—half a block closer to downtown.

"They were reported because they were heard," Ardis said. "I heard them. I reported them. Do not use legalese or dismissive language with me."

"I'm sorry, Ms. Buchanan. And I am truly sorry about Hugh. I know you thought highly of him. Now, because we found your name in his . . . with him . . . someone will be contacting you later today to make a statement. In the meantime—"

"A statement about what?" Ardis asked.

"Whatever it is that you know about—"

"But I don't know anything about Hugh," she said. "Not really. Until yesterday, I hadn't seen him or heard anything about him in years. I took him to lunch, we chatted, and that's the sad sum total of what I know about Hugh."

"You can explain that when you speak with the officer. In the meantime, what I want to know is—"

"Finding her name in his *sporran* doesn't prove that she knows anything," I said.

"I know that." He might have briefly ground his teeth. "Thank you, Ms. Rutledge," he said, teeth still gritted. "Ms. Buchanan, please, answer this one question—what did Hugh tell you about being in town for Half-baked Blue Plum?"

Silence followed his question. A silence louder than the clodhopping boots of ten thousand deputies. A silence into which Clod put his metaphorical foot one clomp further.

"What?" he asked, looking genuinely perplexed. "Half-baked—that's what everyone calls it, isn't it?"

"No, Coleridge, it isn't." Ardis used the tone of voice she'd perfected through her years of smacking desks with rulers. She'd told me she reserved it for answering questions that tested her patience and the validity of the phrase "there are no stupid questions." "Many people love the craft fair," she told him now. "Many of the craftspeople depend on their sales from weekend fairs like this one for the extras others of us take for granted—music or dance lessons for the children or grandchildren, for instance."

"I meant no disrespect."

"Of course you didn't. Ten has a booth at the fair this year," Ardis said, calling Joe by his childhood nickname for Tennyson, something she and very few others could get away with. "Did you know that? Flies, lures, and watercolors."

"I didn't know."

"Kumihimo braiding, too," I said. "He's really good at it and it's cool."

Clod gave me a look.

"It is. And it's not just a booth. He's in charge of all the booths this year. It's a big responsibility and a heck of a lot of work. You should stop by this weekend and check it out. Stop and say hey. I know he'd appreciate it."

"Coleridge will no doubt be on duty all weekend," Ardis said, "busy working on this terrible case. And that brings me back to your question, Coleridge. You asked what Hugh told me about being in town for Handmade Blue Plum?"

"Yes, ma'am."

"Doesn't it fall into the category of hearsay evidence?"

"It might be helpful to the investigation."

"Hunh."

"Ms. Buchanan, what did he say?"

"Not a blessed thing."

"Do you think he believed you?" I asked after Clod left.

"Possibly not."

"Are you okay? Do you need to take some time?"

"No, hon."

"I'm sorry about Hugh. He was ... he seemed ..."

Ardis nodded. "That's it exactly. We really don't know anything about Hugh beyond 'was' and 'seemed.' I only knew him 'when' and you didn't know him at all. And I wasted the time I spent with him over lunch yesterday wagging my own chin. Catching him up on people I *do* know something about."

"*Did* Hugh say anything to you about being here for Handmade Blue Plum?"

"Do you think I would *lie* to Deputy Coleridge Blake

Dunbar?" A glint of humor kindled in her eyes, then flickered out. She bounced the eraser end of a pencil on the counter as she became thoughtful. "No, he didn't. It's hard to remember if he said much of anything at all." She bounced the pencil a time or two more. "So, what is it about the fair, or what's going to be *at* the fair, that's interesting enough to bring Hugh McPhee back to town after all these years?"

"Or *who's* going to be there. *If* Deputy Dunbar is right—because we don't know why Cole thinks Hugh *did* say something to you about being here for Handmade. Asking you implies that he knows Hugh did come for the fair, but that he isn't sure *why* he came for the fair. But what if he just thinks that's why Hugh was here? What if he's assuming?"

"But why would he ask me if he didn't know for sure?" Ardis let the pencil bounce one more time and then tossed it in the air. "Did I just say that? Did I just assume that because Cole believes something and says it out loud, then it's true?"

The pencil had flown as far as the mannequin and stuck in the gray cowl like a dart. I went around the counter and carefully pulled it out. Ardis put out her hand for it. I didn't give it back. She put her hands flat on the counter.

"You're right, Kath. You're right, and we don't know if Cole is right. I'll tell you what we do know, though. And knowing this brings me to a place of calm." She took a deep breath in and let it out. Then she held out her hand again. "Please give me the pencil." I did. She flipped the notebook open and saw my *dabbling in detective work* note from the day before. "Cole's joke isn't really funny anymore, and yesterday morning seems like a long time ago." She turned the page. "We know the police at least *think* Hugh was here for the fair. That gives us another clue to work with." She poised the pencil over the page, then swiveled it in her fingers and pointed it at me. "Because we *are* going to find who killed him."

I nodded and watched as she jotted her own note. "You said that gives us another clue. What else have we got?"

"The slip of paper with my name. Why was it in his sporran?"

"Oh, right. How did I forget that?"

"You were distracted by Cole's pantomime—and its location—as he searched for the right word," Ardis said.

"Disturbed by it anyway."

"Also, what book did Hugh have in his sporran? Is it significant? Or was the slip of paper with my name on it merely a bookmark in a random book?"

"Lost in a random universe?"

"That has a lonely, existential sound to it." She made several more notes with slashing underlines, and then grew still. "I think Hugh was lonely. And now he's lost forever." She put the pencil down and stared at her hands.

"Ardis, I hate to say it, but maybe we should cancel the yarn bombing."

"No."

"Sneaking around so late at night, though? Out of caution, shouldn't we at least consider postponing it?"

"No. We're going to have a dozen people. We're working in groups. No one is going solo. It's perfect the way we've planned it."

"Postpone it out of respect for Hugh, then?"

"I asked him if he wanted to join us and he said yes. We need to do if *for* Hugh."

"Okay. I was just checking." I nudged her with my shoulder. "Here's another clue—the bagpipes and the midnight concert. When was the last time something like that happened in Blue Plum?"

"And his whole 'getup,' as Coleridge so ineptly called it. The kilt, the sporran, the pipes—that's not your typical east Tennessee 'getup.'"

"Not *upper* east, anyway. All the way west, over there in Knoxville, maybe. Or out in the hinterlands in Nashville or Memphis. Do we know where he's been living?"

"No."

"Or what he's been doing since—how long has it been since you've seen him?"

"I'll have to think."

I put the pencil back in her hand. "You should write down what you know and what you remember about him, Ardis. If the police are going to come pick your brain, the posse should get first dibs."

"Before the police pick it clean. Do you mind if I go in—" She nodded to the small office behind us.

"Good idea. I'll reheat your coffee and bring it in to you. Then you'll be able to concentrate." And for a little while she'd be able to mourn one of her favorite students in private.

It was a very little while. As I pulled the door shut after taking Ardis the reheated coffee, Geneva swirled out of the office—through the door—and stopped in front of me.

"There are tears running down her face," she said.

"I know. She'll be okay, though."

"What did you say to make my great-great-niece cry like that?" She crossed her arms and leaned in close.

"It wasn't anything I said. If you were in there, didn't you hear—"

"I was just passing through." She turned away with a flap of her hand and went to sit on the sales counter. "Passing through is one of the perks for those who have passed on. I would not have paid the least attention to her, except that I am so sensitive to tears and sadness."

"But you didn't want to ask her what's wrong? Or offer comfort?"

"I am too sensitive for my own good and did not want to risk being responsible for more misery." She kicked her heels a time or two. "What is her caterwauling all about?"

"I don't hear caterwauling. I think she's being dignified in her grief."

"Grief?"

"Didn't you hear? You were popping in and out all morning."

"Perks of being a ghost. I was feeling perky."

"Geneva, Ardis is upset because Hugh McPhee died last night. That's why Deputy Dunbar was here."

"Kilt?

"Killed, yes."

"No. *Kilt.* Are you talking about the man in the kilt? Was he the man Ardis was fawning over? With the bald spot, the scar, and bagpipes?"

"Yes. Why?"

"Argyle and I saw him last night before the hellish noise began and we had to take cover."

"Where did you see him?"

"Although, come to think of it," she said, "from the way Argyle sprang straight into the air, it is possible he was napping when the noise began. If that is the case, then he will not have seen anything more than one of his lives passing before his eyes like a comet. Poor dear. How many lives do you suppose he has to spare?"

"Geneva, where did *you* see Hugh?"

"The more interesting question would be with whom."

Chapter 8

"You know who it was? Oh my gosh." I couldn't believe the luck—Geneva had been looking out the window at just the right time to see someone with Hugh—to see the murderer? "Who was it?"

"That is the stumper."

"You didn't recognize him?"

"Or her. Between trousers and kilts, the fashion world was topsy-turvy last night."

"But can you describe the person? How tall? Or how tall compared to Hugh? The hair? Anything?"

"It would be helpful if I could." Her shoulders rose and fell on a moan. "I am a terrible detective. I know that is what you are thinking."

"No, I'm not. And don't be hard on yourself. There's no way you could've known we'd need to know anything about that person."

"But the best detectives are always on duty. My skills have deteriorated and I am no longer among their ranks." She paused. "Perhaps if I were allowed to refresh my memory by watching classic how-to documentaries such as *Cagney & Lacey*, my skill level would rebound. I could pick up tips to share with you, so that we can work better together as a detective duo. I might pick up hints for engaging in buddy-type banter. Also, any of the *Law & Order* oeuvre would be helpful for our ensemble work with the posse."

The posse she referred to was the small group of TGIF members with whose help we'd solved several crimes. Geneva, although she'd made valuable contributions to our investigations, was the most excitable member of the group. As she might say, "excitable" was a good word meaning "unpredictable" or "volatile." Because of that, and as much as it grieved her, it was probably best the others didn't know she was a member. Ardis knew now, but investigating Hugh's murder would be the first time they were both aware of working together. Given the uncertain chemistry between them, that could prove interesting.

Geneva hummed the theme music from *Murder, She Wrote* and smiled at me.

"If you throw in episodes of *Miami Vice*," she said, "I could give you pointers for piloting a powerboat seized from drug smugglers and teach you to drive your car in a sportier manner. Not to mention make suggestions for a snappier way of dressing."

"Sorry, no TV."

"In that case, I will only agree that you are disagreeable," she said, and she disappeared.

Bombing Blue Plum—yarn-bombing it—had been Thea Green's idea. Thea, in addition to being an active and avid member of TGIF, was the director of the J. F. Culp

Memorial Library—Blue Plum's public library with a name almost longer than the sign for it on the lawn in front of the building. Thea was constantly looking for ways to engage more teenagers and twenty-somethings in library activities.

"It wouldn't hurt to shake up TGIF, too," she'd said back at the beginning of September during a meeting of the TGIF challenge knitting group known as Fridays Fast and Furious. We were furiously working to meet our goal of knitting one thousand baby hats for newborns by the end of the year.

"We might actually get a few bodies younger than geriatric to join," Thea had said that afternoon. "Yarn bombing is cutting-edge stuff—or it would've been if we'd done it a few years ago. What could possibly be cooler than fiber graffiti? And it ties in perfectly with Handmade Blue Plum next month. And the kids will be out of school for the fall break with time on their hands. We can leave fun fiber surprises all over town for the visitors to find and enjoy. It'll be like a knitting and crochet scavenger hunt. And it'll help clear out everyone's stash closet. If we start now, we'll have time to prepare. It'll be exciting. Edgy, even, depending on how we do it, and if you think this town can handle edgy. And *if* we do it, we can still claim to be on top of the wave, because yarn bombing's never been done around here before. What do you think?" In her excitement, Thea stood up and waved her knitting needles so that she was in danger of losing stitches.

"Step over here and call me geriatric. That's what I'm thinking," Mel Gresham said. Mel and Thea were only a few years older than me, putting them in their early to mid-forties. Mel, with spiked lime-green hair, was slicing the tunnel of fudge cake she'd brought for refreshments, and she still held the knife.

"*Are* we geriatric?" Ernestine O'Dell—seventy-something—turned to John Berry—eighty-something. "Except for my eyesight, and a few more pounds, and a touch of stiffness first thing in the morning, and the occasional memory lapse, and shrinking an inch or two, and, of course, the white hair and wrinkles, I don't feel any different than I did at fifty. And one of my great-grandchildren told me they aren't wrinkles anyway. They're 'life experience lines.' 'Geriatric' doesn't sound as nice as plain old being old."

"I like the words 'spry for his age' better than 'geriatric,'" John said, "as long as they aren't on my gravestone."

Thea interrupted a growl coming from Ardis. "Relax, Ardis. And, Ernestine, you're fine the way you are. John, I *know* you can dance jigs around me. I was just making sure I had everyone's attention. Let me show you some pictures and everyone will feel better."

She'd brought her laptop and she set it up in front of Ernestine. Ardis, John, Joe, and I put down the baby hats we'd been working on, and Mel laid down the cake knife. We gathered behind Ernestine while Thea showed us two or three dozen photographs of yarn bombing projects from around the world that she'd gleaned from the Internet.

Zealous and imaginative people had created cozies for fire hydrants, car antennas, mailboxes, and bollards. They'd crocheted bikinis for nude statues and given others leggings, hats, ties, and warm sweaters. Whole avenues of trees wore garter-stitched stripes. A tree in California had turned into a giant blue knitted squid. Bike racks had become snakes and hungry caterpillars. Lampposts put on socks and grew bird and monster feet overnight. Potholes and cracks in sidewalks were filled with coils and loops of yarn in intricate, multicolored patterns. Bicycles and whole vehicles were covered in rainbows of knitted and crocheted panels.

"What do you think?" Thea asked again, after the last picture.

"About practicing anarchy in downtown Blue Plum?" Joe asked. "Using knitting needles and crochet hooks?"

"That's the general idea," Thea said. "You can do macramé, if you want. Weaving, tatting. Cut up old sweaters and use the pieces. Tie giant trout flies and hang them from the trees. That would look incredible. Are you in?"

"Sure." Joe handed her a piece of Mel's tunnel of fudge. "I'm hooked."

We all were—on yarn bombing and on Mel's cake.

"Can we produce enough material in a month?" I, the slowest knitter in Fast and Furious, asked.

"We won't need anything elaborate," Ernestine said.

"Unless I go in for the giant trout flies," said Joe.

"You just need to concentrate on the right activities, Red," Mel said with a wicked smile. "Spend less time on extracurricular diversions." She tried leering at Joe. He ignored her for a more meaningful exchange with his slice of tunnel of fudge.

Ardis said she would invite our weekend high school help, Abby. Thea told us she'd spring the idea on the next unwary teens to cross the library's threshold.

"But let's us go ahead and do it, even if you don't get the teenagers," Ernestine said. "I never heard of yarn bombing before today, but now that I have, I know it's something I've always wanted to do."

We all agreed. After telling us she'd report back, Thea left the meeting looking pleased.

A few days later, Ardis and I were closing up shop for the day when Thea stopped by, looking even more pleased. Geneva had been lying across the blades of the ceiling fan, listening to us and dangling her arm as though trailing it in water. When the camel bells at the door jingled, announcing Thea, she sat up. Thea came in, stopped near the door, and put her hands on her hips. Always a stylish dresser, she wore a mix of browns—from creamy to dark chocolate, including knife-creased trousers, a pair of killer heels, a creamy silk tunic, and what could only have been the stole she'd been knitting since spring.

"I am awesome," Thea said.

"Hold your arms out and let's see." Ardis motioned for Thea to twirl.

Thea's turn was more of a stately rotation than a twirl, but she spread her arms, showing off the lacy leaf pattern and her fine handiwork. She'd used fingering-weight wool in a rich chestnut brown several shades darker than her skin. "Welcome to the debut of my mocha mousse stole," she said, advancing on the counter and stopping with a shallow bow.

Geneva clapped.

"You're right," I said. "It *is* awesome. Will you think about letting the mannequin wear it for a week or two?"

"Oh, please, please, please, please!" Geneva said. "I know I will look fetching sitting on its shoulder."

Somehow I didn't think "fetching" would have been

the first word to cross Thea's mind if she'd been able to see Geneva preening on her beautiful stole.

Geneva was right, though. Her gray mist would look good against that almost edible brown. But her near swoon over the stole put a thought in my head—I'd never asked her what she saw when she looked in a mirror or saw her reflection in a window. Did she see the hollow eyes I saw when I looked at her? Or did she see blue eyes looking back at her, and were her cheeks blushed with pink? For that matter, what did she see when she looked at her hand or her sleeve or skirt? If I ever dared ask, I knew I'd have to do it carefully. It was the sort of question that might make her prickle.

"I'm kind of enjoying the mocha mousse too much myself right now," Thea said, "but I'll think about it. As for awesome, I wasn't just talking about the stole. I was talking about the teens I caught in our web of artistic anarchy. I snared them and I signed them up for the bombing of Blue Plum. I am awesome, and fiber awareness will be elevated to new heights in our younger generation."

"Do your recruits know how to knit or crochet?" Ardis asked.

"It doesn't matter," Thea said. "TGIF is equal opportunity, isn't it? We're here for people who can whip out a pair of double knitted mittens with their eyes closed and we're here for neophytes who don't know a crochet hook from a meat skewer. If the kids don't know how to do anything, we'll teach them. Or they can help put up and attach the stuff other people make."

"And do they know to keep quiet about the project?" Ardis asked. "Do *you* know to keep quiet?"

Thea pulled the end of her chocolate mousse stole across the lower half of her face in a fair imitation of Zorro. "We are a closemouthed cabal of anarchic crocheters," she said. "Quiet and quixotic. Watch and be amazed." She left through the front door without making the string of camel bells jingle.

"How did she do that?" I asked.

"She is a librarian," Geneva said. "They *know* how to be quiet."

"Mm-hmm," Ardis said. "When they want to be."

"You're right. Most of the time she is quite loud," Geneva said. "But knowing when to be quiet is like a code of honor to librarians. She has impressive skills and knows how to use them."

"But knowing and doing are two different things." Ardis went back to unpacking and checking in the newly arrived order of silk kumihimo cords and missed the look on Geneva's face. It had shifted from sunny—for Geneva—to scowling.

"In any case, I think Thea's idea is going to work out fine," I said. "Abby's excited and the other teens will be a fun addition to the group. Oh. We should've asked Thea if her crew is coming to the next meeting. I'll give her a call later."

"Ask her how many," Ardis said.

"Good thinking. We might need more chairs."

"And we'll definitely need more refreshments."

That had all happened at the beginning of September. Clod's news of Hugh's death came on the Wednesday morning before Handmade Blue Plum. We'd spent the intervening four weeks identifying and measuring bomb targets and preparing ordnance—"For our assault," as Ernestine delighted in saying. Her eyes grew huge behind her thick lenses every time she said it.

We had our final pre–bomb planning meeting that same Wednesday afternoon. I kept an eye on Ardis throughout the day, still concerned about her reaction to the shocking news.

"You're sure you don't want to take off early?" I asked her. "I can take notes and drop them by your place later. We really only have a few details to iron out."

"The devil might be in those details," she said.

"True. On the other hand, we know we're going to have to be flexible and ready to ad-lib, so if you'd rather . . ."

"I'll be fine, and this is important. *Both* meetings are important."

"Both?"

"Final plans for tomorrow night," Ardis said, "and initial plans for our investigation. We'll have a quiet word with the posse members during the planning meeting. Let them know what's going on."

"You're not planning to involve the teens or the others in the investigation, are you?"

"No. They can go on home before the posse meets."

"Okay."

"And then the posse can saddle up and ride again."

Chapter 9

"Two meetings?" Mel Gresham said when I told her the posse was back in business. She'd arrived early for the yarn bomb meeting, bearing her project bag, a bakery box, and an insulated carafe. Ardis hadn't been kidding when she said Mel was busier than any two of us combined, and I felt bad for making her green hair spikes droop. "I'm not thrilled. But for you, Red, and because I feel a sense of duty to the posse, to this town, and to anyone who finds himself dead in his kilt, I'll stay and hear you and Ardis out. Who's coming for the first meeting?"

"It's easier to say who isn't. Joe and Rachel can't make it. As far as I know everyone else will be here."

"Rachel Meeks," Mel said. "That tickles the tar out of me. Who knew Rachel the banker had a sense of adventure, much less a desire to creep around town committing fiber graffiti?"

We held our meetings in the TGIF workroom on the second floor of the Weaver's Cat. Granddaddy had made the airy space by taking out the wall between the two back bedrooms. Granny had filled it with oak worktables, half a dozen comfy chairs, and a parade of mismatched Welsh dressers for storage around the walls. The members of TGIF kept the room filled with all manner of fibers, fabrics, colors, textures, and a healthy amount of laughter. Mel generously kept any meeting she attended from going hungry by bringing treats from the café.

"Generous nothing," Mel said when I thanked her. She opened the bakery box, which smelled of apple and cinnamon. "My contributions are a totally mercenary gesture. This is advertising through free samples." She set a plate of something that looked crusty, flaky, and warm on one of the Welsh dressers. "But if you want to call my gesture 'spreading the love,' that's okay by me." She wore a pair of black-and-white houndstooth chef's pants, a white T-shirt, and an apron that matched her hair.

"Do you get your aprons dyed to match your hair or vice versa?" I asked.

"Trade secrets."

Ernestine arrived, puffing from the stairs, in time to catch and misinterpret Mel's answer. "Oh no, let's not trade secrets yet," she said. She held on to the doorframe with one hand and put the other to her chest as she took several gasping breaths. "I've kept a few bombs secret to surprise all of you. And I'd still like to be surprised by everyone else's secret bombs. So let's not trade secrets and spoil the fun."

"I was talking about my hair, Ernestine."

"Were you?" Ernestine peered at Mel, and Mel ran her fingers through her spikes, giving them extra lift. "Well, I've always liked your hair, so that's all right, then."

Ardis and John Berry had come up with the idea of secret bombs. After Thea's slide show and some Web surfing, they'd decided it would be fun if we each planned to hit extra targets on our own, with more than the basic strips and rectangles. That way, when the rest of Blue Plum woke up Friday morning and discovered the results of our creativity, the bomb squad could share the fun by looking for the touches and embellishments we'd added behind each other's backs.

"I can't tell you how much I'm looking forward to tomorrow night," Ernestine said. She let Mel take her project bag and her arm and walk with her to one of the comfy chairs arranged for the meeting. She settled in the chair and Mel handed the project bag back to her. Ernestine smiled sweetly at the empty chair next to her and flashed her thick lenses at the other empty chairs and around her. "Hello, everyone," she said.

Mel sat in the chair next to Ernestine's and took what looked like a striped scarf—or a psychedelic boa constrictor—from her own project bag. "I'm pretty sure I knitted fifteen yards of this stuff in my sleep last night," she said. "That's not good for my sleep or my baking. Plus, my baby hat production is suffering." She pointed one of her needles at me. "Not to worry, though, Red. I bet I still finished more hats this week *and* more yards of ordnance for the bombing than you did."

"Thanks, Mel. If someone has to make up for my deficiencies in knitting, I'm glad it's you."

"Baking, too. Don't forget that."

"No question."

"Glad we've got that straight. Now, where is everyone? Let's get this show on the road."

"Isn't Ardis here?" Ernestine asked. "She was coming up the stairs behind me."

"I'm here," Abby, our Goth teen, said from the door. "Ms. Buchanan said she'll be just a minute. She went on up there." She pointed toward the attic and the study.

Interesting—I hadn't seen Ardis go past the door and head for the stairs. Not that she wasn't welcome in the study anytime. And she knew that, but she considered the study my private space, as it had been Granny's, and she rarely intruded. If she'd nipped up there thinking she'd have a quick, friendly chat with Geneva, though . . . my glance ceiling-ward, toward the study, must have been uneasy.

"Have you got your trade secrets up there, Red?" Mel asked.

"My embarrassing mess, more like. Come on, Abby, let's surprise Ardis and start adding up this week's production. Joe's not here, so I'll take the pictures."

We were documenting the project from start to finish, so that we'd know what did and didn't work if we decided to yarn-bomb again. We kept track of the amount of material we produced and Joe took pictures of it. He planned to write an article about it for the paper in Asheville.

Abby took paper and a pencil from a drawer in one of the Welsh dressers and then sat on the edge of the chair opposite Mel and Ernestine. "Ms. O'Dell, what shall I write down for you?"

"Ten feet made from red acrylic leftover from some bygone Boy Scout project. If I remember right, that was the year a first-time den mother thought the boys would enjoy making poinsettias out of it, but they had more fun making reindeer with glue and Popsicle sticks. Your daddy might have been in that den, Abby."

"Gramma hangs the reindeer at the top of her tree every year," Abby said. "Ms. Rutledge, how much for you?"

"A fifteen-foot strip of random stripes," I said, trying not to sound as pleased as I felt for trumping Ernestine's output for once.

"That's wonderful, Kath," Ernestine said. "You were a real powerhouse this week. Abby, dear, jot me in for twenty-five feet of random stripes, too."

We'd decided our basic yarn bomb units would be strips—five inches wide and as long as we cared to make them. They could be knitted or crocheted. Stitch choice was anyone's fancy. I stuck to garter stitch for maximum efficiency and speed, and my output wasn't as shabby as Mel liked to joke, even if I didn't match Ernestine's. There were a dozen of us going at it, needle and hook, including some who were happy to knit and crochet, but who had no plans to join us after dark Thursday night for the actual deed. We planned to wrap the strips around lampposts and railings, and piece them together or hang them side by side to cover larger areas.

From idea to installation, we'd only had a month, but our mad preparations had put a serious dent in the yarn stashes all over Blue Plum. The colors showing up in our strips ranged from eye-dazzling, to appealing, to motley, to puzzling. It was no wonder Mel felt as though she'd been knitting strips in her sleep; we all felt as though we'd produced miles of the stuff.

"That old red acrylic was more fun than what I'm going to use next," Ernestine said. She pulled a large ball of grayish, yellowish chunky yarn from her project bag. "My daughter donated this to the cause. It'll work up quickly, but can anyone think why in the world she would have bought something this color? I have trouble making myself touch it."

"Does that color even have a name?" Mel asked.

"OMG," Abby said. "Old moldy gravy."

"Let's hope we never encounter its namesake in real life," Mel said. "Not in my café, anyway."

Goth Abby had a sudden bright spark in her kohl-lined eye. "If you knit something flat and kind of like an amoeba with that stuff, it could look like a toxic puddle on the sidewalk. A puddle full of pathogens. Ms. O'Dell, if you don't want to use it, may I?"

"Won't that be a cheerful surprise outside someone's door in the morning?" Mel said. "But"—she caught Ernestine's alarmed look—"Abby, if a puddle of toxic waste is your surprise, remember, we don't want to hear about it."

"Unless you tell us where you're going to put it so we can avoid tripping over it or looking at it," I said.

"Good point," Mel said. "And, Ernestine, don't worry. If anyone tries to spoil your fun by revealing any more secrets, I'll jab her with a knitting needle."

Ernestine handed the ball of yarn across to Abby, who thanked her with an un-Goth-like giggle, took knitting needles from her backpack, and started casting on.

We heard John and Thea kidding each other as they came up the stairs, and then Ardis greeting them as she came down from the study. They trooped in, and I tried to give Ardis a questioning look without being too obvious. The look wasn't obvious enough, though; she put her arm through John's and they brushed past me without a glance. But I saw her whisper in his ear, no doubt telling him about the posse meeting we'd called. John spoke quietly to Thea and then claimed his favorite comfy chair.

Ardis headed straight for the coffee carafe Mel had set next to the strudel. She poured herself a cup, standing with her back to us. More feet on the stairs distracted the others, and I didn't think they noticed her bowed head and silence.

Wanda Vance popped into the room followed by slouching Zach Aikens. Zach was one of the teens Thea had lured to our meetings with the triple enticement of outsider art, creeping around town after dark, and snacks. Zach and our part-timer, Abby, were the only ones who'd actually joined TGIF and stuck with us through the month of preparation—not the resounding success Thea had hoped for, but she declared it a good start. Several of us had gotten to know Zach, as much as one ever knows teenagers, when we volunteered for a high school history program at the end of the summer. He was whip-thin and inquisitive. He and Goth Abby got along well together.

Wanda Vance called herself "a member in lurking" of TGIF. She came to the membership meetings on the second Tuesday evening of each month and always had a knitting project with her—generally something small and unremarkable-looking. She blended into the group unremarkably, too, tending toward neutral colors in her clothes and not varying the simple cut of her mouse-brown hair. She never stuck around for the hospitality half hour after the meetings, and hadn't joined any of TGIF's small subgroups, but yarn bombing had piqued her interest. In her own quiet way she was almost as excited about it as Ernestine. Ardis told me Wanda had retired from a career in nursing and the Army Reserve Medical Corps. "Reserve" was the right word for her; I hadn't gotten to know her any better during our planning meetings.

"All right, listen up, people." Thea put her hands on Zach's shoulders and pushed him toward an empty chair. I slipped into the chair between Zach's and Mel's. "No Show Joe is busy with less important things like getting his booth ready for Handmade Blue Plum. Rachel's in her countinghouse counting out someone else's money. Tammie is babysitting the destructosaurus and the wailer, but was kind enough to not to bring them here. They'll be here tomorrow night. Tammie without the terrors."

Tammie Fain, an indulgent grandmother of two under the age of three, had made the mistake of bringing her darlings to a meeting only once. It was a meeting none of us was likely to forget.

"First point of business," Thea said, "when and where do you show up tomorrow night?"

"Excuse me, Thea," Ardis said, turning to face the room, "but the first point of business is a bigger question. *Should* you show up tomorrow night?"

"*What?*"

Ardis went on as though Thea hadn't just exploded. "My answer is yes, and I'll tell you why, but each of you will need to make your own decision. By now, I'm sure you've heard about the death that occurred here in town last night. *I* will show up tomorrow night *because* of that death, to honor the memory of Hugh McPhee. Hugh was a student of mine, way back when, and he planned to join us tomorrow night. But now, given the circumstances of his death, we'll understand if anyone would rather not participate in the yarn bombing. I'm thinking of our younger members in particular," she said, looking at Abby and Zach. "And of your parents who might be worried."

"Handmade Blue Plum hasn't been canceled, though, has it?" Thea asked.

"No."

"Then why—"

"The question had to be brought up," I said. "I agree with Ardis; we should go ahead with the yarn bombing, but no hard feelings if anyone has second thoughts before tomorrow night."

"Good," Thea said. "Let's get back to business. When and where do you show up tomorrow night? By ten minutes to ten, here. Back door only, though, right?" She looked at Ardis for confirmation, but Ardis was staring into her coffee cup.

"Right. Back door," I said.

"And here's what to bring with you," Thea said, reading from a list. "Backpacks with extra yarn, knitting needles, hooks, blunt needles with large eyes, scissors, and flashlights. If you have duct tape, that isn't a bad idea, either. We'll have the strips ready to go in black garbage bags. Any strips you haven't already dropped off here at the Cat, bring tomorrow night. In black garbage bags. No white. Wear dark colors tomorrow night. I won't call out the names of you with gray heads, but cover them."

"Are the tags ready?" John asked.

Thea turned to me. "Kath?"

"Joe said he'll have them."

Our pre-bombing research told us that yarn graffiti artists often tagged their work—as a way of claiming it without signing their names to it—just as paint graffiti artists did. Tags might be symbols, nicknames, or the name of the groups involved, and some bombers knitted or crocheted their tags right into their designs. We were working with so little lead time we'd decided to print our tags and tie them on like package labels. Joe had offered to design and make them, and he wasn't in the habit of letting people down, but he didn't always step into the same river of time as the rest of us.

"Have you *seen* the tags yet?" Thea asked me. Then she turned to Ardis. "Have *you* seen them?"

"He told me they'd be ready," Ardis said.

"If Ardis says they'll be ready, they will be," said Mel.

I couldn't help noticing that she hadn't said, "If Kath says they'll be ready, they will be." And I couldn't help wondering if that was a tribute to Ardis and her wise ways and the fact that she'd known Joe most of his life, or if it was a veiled comment about the solidity of my fairly new relationship with him.

"Moving on," Thea said. "Our targets are identified—"

"Except for our secret targets," Ernestine cut in.

"Aren't all the targets supposed to be somewhat hidden?" Wanda asked. "So that when people notice them, they'll go looking for more? Wasn't the point to let visitors search and discover?"

"The point is to amuse visitors and citizenry alike," Thea said.

"With the discovery of hidden delights," Wanda said. "Someone said that at the last meeting. I took notes."

Thea looked at Wanda over the top of her glasses.

Wanda didn't notice. She rummaged in her project bag, then switched to her purse. She shuffled the contents but didn't take anything out except for a snarl of embroidery floss. She scowled at the tangled floss and jammed it in her pocket, then glanced at Thea. Catching Thea's quelling librarian eye, she visibly startled. "Oh well," she said, "I don't have the notes with me, but I wondered—"

"Yes?" said Thea.

"I wondered why we added the courthouse at the last minute. The columns are lit up at night. That kind of defeats the purpose of sneaking around. Besides, the columns are huge."

Thea pointed a crochet hook at me. "Tell her, Kath."

"Neckties," I said.

Wanda looked confused.

"We're tying neckties on the columns," I told her. "Six yards of our five-inch stuff should be plenty for a tie on each column. By now we've got enough yards of material to work with for all the targets, and it shouldn't take too long to tie—"

"Windsor or four-in-hand?" John asked.

"Does it matter?"

"If you want them to look like neckties, yes. And if you know how, it won't take any time at all. Do you know how to tie a Windsor knot, young man?"

"I'm a knot kind of guy," Zach said without looking up from the strip he was crocheting. "Windsor knots are cool."

"Windsor it is, then," I said. "We can leave the necktie

tying to the cool ones, or if you want to become one with the knots, you can probably find a video on the Web." I made a mental note to look one up.

"Here's how you solve the visibility problem," Mel said. "Drape some of your strips over the floodlights before you run up the steps. The lights are right there in the grass. Cover them and you've got instant blackout. Then after you dude-up the columns, you grab the draping strips and head for the next target. Piece of cake."

"See?" Thea said. "No worries."

"And the reference to cake leads us straight to salivating for cinnamon sour cream strudel." Mel rubbed her hands.

"Superb." Thea paused to breathe deeply in the direction of the Welsh dresser.

Ardis, who hadn't moved from the dresser, stepped aside, to give interested eyes and noses an unobstructed view and a whiff of cinnamon.

But Thea held up a hand. "No strudel yet. Let's make sure we're all clear about how the bombing will work. We're hitting one big target—the courthouse columns— to get everyone's attention. Then we're hitting all the rest of the targets to tickle their fancies and encourage them to look around town. Feel free to call the other targets 'hidden delights' if you want, Wanda. In fact, that sounds so good that your notes must be right and *I* said that. But to stir up some immediate wham-bam excitement, our target needs to be large and obvious. Like me." She struck a pose and looked at the teens. "When I make a joke about myself, it's okay to laugh."

Abby did, along with most of the rest of us. A smile came and went on Zach's face, but he continued concentrating on the strip he was crocheting. It was brown and not more than an inch wide. I leaned closer to see it better.

"Why so narrow?" I asked.

"Not telling." He bared his teeth in a fake smile, then looked across at Ernestine and gave her a thumbs-up.

"I'd like to say something else." Ardis spoke quietly, cradling her coffee cup, shoulders drawn. When we were all looking at her, she spoke again. "For the record, I'd like to say that bombing the courthouse columns makes a statement."

"What record? What statement?" Wanda asked. "I'm not being contrary. I want to understand."

"I think I've got this." John looked to Ardis. She nodded. Then he turned to me and mimed writing.

"I've got a pencil and paper, Mr. Berry," Abby said.

"If you'll take this down, then, I believe it will be record enough. Although we want to be careful and not let that paper get away from us. You should find your notes, too, Wanda. A document with the words 'Blue Plum' or 'courthouse' and 'bomb' might raise eyebrows, even if 'bomb' is coupled with a word as innocent as 'yarn.'"

"I'll see your 'might raise eyebrows,'" Mel said, "and raise you the certainty of brown and khaki panties in a twist."

"Good point. We don't need 'bomb' or 'courthouse' for our statement anyway," John said. "How does this sound? Whereas Blue Plum is our town, and whereas we love Blue Plum, we therefore and hereby claim Blue Plum in the name of freedom for textile and fiber arts and for all other forms of creative expression.' What do you think, Ardis?"

She and Wanda both nodded.

"Wanda, you were here the day we added the court-house to the target list," I said, "but that was the meeting when Tammie brought her grand-terrors."

"Enough said." Wanda shuddered. "I dropped more stitches that day than I have in the last ten years. It's no wonder I lost track of any intelligent conversation."

"That's settled, then," Mel said. She put her needles down and stood up. "On to strudel."

"But first—" Ardis moved back along the Welsh dresser so she blocked our view of the strudel.

We waited. Her silence prompted Zach to stop cro-cheting, and he watched with the rest of us as she stared into her coffee cup again. She'd been subdued since Clod brought the news of Hugh's death, but even more so since coming down from the study. Unless I was imagin-ing that. But she worried me. I was about to go to her when she roused and spoke again.

"Right now. Especially now." Without turning to see, she reached behind to the dresser and set her coffee cup down. She stood straighter and looked at each one of us. "*Especially* now," she repeated, her voice stronger and full of conviction. "We'll be making the right statement. That Blue Plum *is* our town. That we'll stand together, we'll work together, we'll hold fast together. That we won't be cowed—"

The others might have thought Ardis finished her statement at the word "cowed." She did a good job of making it appear so—she closed her mouth, crossed her arms, and gave a single, sharp nod. And a look of satis-faction eased the strain that had troubled her face. Er-nestine, John, and Mel clapped. Then Mel got up and headed for the strudel, followed by Zach, Abby, and Thea. But I'd caught a momentary widening of Ardis' eyes just before the look of satisfaction smoothed her brow, so I knew that something else was going on.

Then again, I would have known something else was going on without the eyes and brow for clues, because someone whispered in my ear and put her ghostly arm around my shoulders, making me shiver.

Chapter 10

"Why is Ardent bellowing about cows?" Geneva asked.

I didn't answer.

"Her bellowing is not all bad, though. It made me think of a riddle. A paranormal puzzler, if you will. Par excellence, if I do say so myself."

She disengaged her arm from my shoulders and moved around in front of me. Seeing Ardis and the others through the vaporous form floating before my eyes gave me the feeling of disappearing behind a swarm of gnats. I was tempted to flap my knitting at her, but that wouldn't have been kind, and it probably wouldn't have helped. She was intent on telling me her riddle.

"Of course, you cannot give your answer without sounding batty," she said, "so I will be helpful and pretend that you give up. Ready? What did the bellowing bovine say when it gave up the ghost? What? You're giving up already? Okay, you asked for it." She leaned in close so that we were nose to nose. "Moo!"

After telling me her riddle and rocking with laughter,

Geneva sat on the arm of my chair "discussing" the others, who were enjoying Mel's strudel. Ignoring her running commentary was easier than ignoring the strudel. But I told myself that my wits and my waistline would both thank me for staying strong. I tried humming quietly to myself to drown her out. It rarely worked, and didn't this time, either. It also didn't drown out the oohs and aahs over the strudel.

Geneva didn't say what brought her down from the study. She didn't usually come to our "knit and natter sessions," as she called them. She didn't like the clicking of so many knitting needles. *If you will imagine a dozen mice clattering their tiny claws across a cold stone floor, you will understand my aversion,* she'd said. I assumed she'd arrived early for the posse meeting, and that that was why Ardis had gone to the study. Ardis smiled and waved at us, but stayed on the other side of the room. Giving Geneva her space, no doubt.

"Red," Mel called, "I can't help noticing that you're avoiding my strudel. Should I be affronted?"

"I'm saving my calorie splurge for the après bomb party."

"Good enough. Coffee?"

"No, thanks, I'm fine." After knitting the town red—and orange, yellow, green, blue, and all shades in between—we were all meeting back at the Weaver's Cat for debriefing, celebration, and refreshments Mel said she'd send over. She, being an early-to-bed and up-before-dawn café owner, wasn't joining us for the bombing.

"I wonder if her alert hair makes *her* more alert," Geneva mused, looking at Mel. "She is good at noticing things, such as your delusion that you will lose weight by eating tomorrow what you avoid eating today. Have you noticed that I am practicing my noticing skills and that I'm using them well, this afternoon? For instance, I have noticed three things about you. Would you like to hear them?"

I pulled my left earlobe. That was supposed to mean "no," but she wasn't paying attention.

"First, I noticed that you failed to compliment me on my paranormal puzzler. However, that was not your fault, because we are not alone, so I am not affronted. Although it was *udderly* fantastic."

I swallowed a sputtered laugh.

"The second thing I noticed is that you are finally knitting something other than one of those tiny hats you have been such a slave to. I applaud the fact that you are branching out, but now it looks as though you are using the dregs of someone's uninspired basket of leftover yarn, and it is not an improvement." She looked around at the work the others had set aside for coffee and strudel. "Good heavens. You all are. I think someone should warn you that you are likely to scare people with all these long, narrow, ugly scarves."

That comment threw me. Did she really not know what we were doing? But no, maybe she didn't. The yarn bombing was supposed to be hush-hush. Ardis and I had been careful not to talk about it in front of customers. Geneva had been avoiding Ardis for weeks, so even when we had discussed it, she would have taken herself off in a sniff. And she really *didn't* like the sound of many needles knitting, so she hadn't come to any of our planning meetings. With her slippery grasp of time, she seemed to think this was a meeting of Fridays Fast and Furious, the subgroup of TGIF dedicated to knitting one thousand baby hats for charity by the end of the year. I hadn't specifically asked her to join us for the yarn bombing because it was the kind of activity that frustrated her—she couldn't manipulate anything, so she couldn't help us. And she was a homebody, for the most part—although she would probably have something to say about the "body" part of that. But since moving in, she only occasionally left the Weaver's Cat.

"The third thing I noticed about you, other than your sudden and rude lack of attention to me, is that you are not downstairs keeping the dear Spiveys from bopping Debbie on the head. I would have thought—"

I didn't wait to hear what she would have thought. I was up and out of my chair and flying down the back stairs.

I leapt the last two stairs and landed in the kitchen feeling like a ninja juiced on adrenaline. Or a nut. Running recklessly around blind corners in a shop specializing in pointed sticks, hooks, and needles, when I might plow into someone holding one or a quiverful, wasn't the best plan. Besides, Shirley and Mercy Spivey might be irritating, but I'd never known them to be violent. Just irritating and sneaky.

I listened and only heard the pleasant murmurs of customers fondling merino or alpaca in the next room. No annoying Spivey voices. No cries of protest from Debbie or sounds of bopping. But had they bopped and left? Bopped and hidden? Bopped at all? Geneva hadn't come down the stairs with me—a big, fat clue that reports of bopping were exaggerated. She being a huge fan of bopping as well as bar fights. And yet.

I peered around the corner into the hall. No one lurked beyond the racks of patterns. Neither of the twins would be able to hide behind the coat tree draped with scarves and hats. I slid into the hall and along the wall, stopping where I could peek around the edge of the doorway into the old dining room where the fondling was taking place. I recognized the women. They had their hands full of alpaca. When they looked up, I raised my eyebrows in a "can I help?" sort of way. They waved me off with smiles and shifted their attention to gently mauling the merino. Shirley and Mercy were nowhere to be seen in the room. I sniffed the air. They were nowhere to be smelled, either, although traces of Mercy's terrible cologne lingered, evidence that Geneva was right; they had been in the shop.

I tiptoed to the front room and stopped at the edge of that door, too, my back pressed against the wall, the better to avoid detection or contact. Not that I detested Shirley and Mercy, but there was a prickly strand running through my relationship with them. The most recent chafing from that strand came when we invited them to teach a quilting class at the shop. Ardis had been leery. I'd been optimistic. And it hadn't worked out. To put it euphemistically. They'd alienated half a dozen of our longtime customers, a fabric sales rep with whom we'd been trying for months to get an in-shop appointment and who'd left the shop in tears, and a cake decorator in Asheville. That all happened on the first and last day of their class. The cake decorator didn't matter so much. The twins had only gone to Asheville because Mel had come up with an excuse not to deal with them. But as

Ardis had said, the incident with the decorator was the icing on the cake.

Shirley and Mercy were, however, kin. They were daughters of one of Granny's cousins, making them somewhat removed from her and more so from me. So they were kin, yes, but they were also . . . so Spivey. In my mind, "Spivey" was shorthand for snoopy, gossipy, and manipulative. They had a history of being unpleasant to Ernestine. But they had a sense of devotion to family and community that couldn't be overlooked. And they were artists when it came to embroidery and quilting. So they weren't all bad. Just . . . all Spivey. Geneva adored them. Because I preferred to avoid complications and conflict, I tried to avoid Shirley and Mercy.

Yet I'd pelted down the stairs, possibly straight into their beady-eyed sights. To throw myself between them and Debbie? Was I so selfless? Or was I thinking more of myself and how hard it would be to replace Debbie if they did something to make her quit? Those were complicated—and possibly revealing—questions I didn't want to answer. Instead I sniffed the air one more time for Mercy's cologne, like a nervous rabbit, and listened.

The only sound coming from the front room was Debbie humming "You Are My Sunshine." That wasn't the song of choice for someone beset by Spiveys. I pulled myself together, pushed myself away from the wall, and went around the corner.

Debbie was sitting on the stool behind the sales counter, a pencil in one hand, leafing through a yarn catalog and making notes. Granny had described Debbie to me as looking as though she belonged in a watercolor by the Swedish artist Carl Larsson. Today, with her blond braid coiled around her head and felt clogs peeking from under the hem of her long jean skirt, she could have stepped right out of the painting to man the cash register. She looked up, seemingly unbopped, as I came in.

"Meeting over?" she asked, putting the catalog aside.

I moved behind the counter. "Were Shirley and Mercy just here?" I sent a few more darting glances around the room and wondered if I would recognize paranoia in myself if it bopped me on the head.

"The twins? You're kidding. Were you really expecting them? I'm sorry. I thought they were spreading the usual manure and it would be better to say you weren't here." She looked miserable about her imagined faux pas, and for that, I knew I couldn't imagine what we would do if she ever did leave the Weaver's Cat. She was a great employee and a better friend. "It was an automatic reflex," she said. "They're gone. I'm really sorry."

"No, no, no. No need to apologize. I *wasn't* expecting them. Your automatic reflex was perfect, and I'm eternally grateful you can be so convincing. Do you give lessons?"

Debbie laughed. "I learned it from Bill. He can make the sheep stand on their heads if he wants to." Bill was her border collie, a no-nonsense guy who wouldn't see the humor in making sheep stand on their heads. He would do it for Debbie, though, and not ask questions. "It's all in the eyes," she said. "But your eyes spill everything, Kath. Shirley and Mercy know that. Everyone knows that." She cocked her head. "Weren't you upstairs at the meeting? How did you know they were here?"

"Mercy's cologne sure has a long afterlife, doesn't it?

Phew." I picked up the catalog and flapped it around, fanning it mostly in front of my face—in front of my blabbermouth eyes.

By the time I got back upstairs, the first meeting had adjourned. So had the strudel. Mel said she'd split what was left between Abby and Zach to take home. I hoped my blabbermouth eyes wouldn't tell her how unfair they thought that was. I'd said no when that flaky, buttery strudel called to me earlier, but now a slice would be most welcome. It could help restore my equilibrium, after sacrificing myself in the face of Spiveys, and surely my dash down the stairs had used calories in addition to adrenaline.

Wanda had gone, too, and the yarn bomb materials had been stowed away in project bags. Ernestine told me she'd volunteered to contact Rachel and Tammie to confirm the time, place, and final details. She had more spare time than most of us, but we were all grateful that she was willing to sacrifice some of it in case Rachel got started talking.

"And we all assume you'll be in touch with Joe," Thea said.

"As far as I know."

"Of course you will," Mel said. "Let's shift gears."

This was now a posse meeting, and although it was Wednesday and not Friday, posse members all belonged to Fridays Fast and Furious, so baby hats came out of the project bags and charity knitting went into full swing. Geneva had moved around behind Ardis' chair—in ghost stealth mode—where Ardis couldn't see her. She was floating far enough behind Ardis that Ardis wouldn't feel a telltale chill, either.

Thea was knitting another in the endless stream of red-and-white-striped hats that were her specialty—a nod to Dr. Seuss and part of her campaign to promote early literacy. Mel took three finished baby hats and another almost complete from her bag. All of them were bright red. She laid the finished hats on the low table our chairs were grouped around.

"Are you in your apple phase, Mel?" John asked. He'd retired from the navy and then spent years sailing in the Atlantic. He knitted hats that reflected the ocean's moody blues. Mel, on the other hand, knitted what she called "organics" and had already worked her way through a range of berry, melon, and lettuce colors. "Or is it your beet phase?" John asked.

"Fire engine," said Mel. "It's National Fire Safety Month. Say, Red, have you ever thought about adding a swath of fire engine red to your head? It'd be a nice highlight for your natural shade."

"If I did, you couldn't call me Red anymore. It'd be too obvious."

"Then I'd call you Sparky. What have you got to show for yourself this week?"

"Hang on." I looked for my project bag. Thea had taken the chair I'd catapulted out of, and she did her best now to look immovable. She kindly handed me my bag, though, which she'd had to move in order to sit down. Before dropping into another chair, I pulled out a pen and two notebooks—Ardis' and my own. I did have a baby hat in the bag. It lay at the bottom, and if yarn could sigh, I would have heard a small, sad exhalation from the half-finished and unremarkable pink beanie. Poor neglected thing. The posse and my notebook—an old-fashioned-looking leather journal with an elastic band that Ernestine had given me—were the primary reasons my hat output lagged (or so I told myself). I gave the hat a silent promise of quality time that evening and tucked the bag beside me. I slipped the elastic off my notebook, indulgently stroking the leather a couple of times.

"Ready to begin the case of the—what are we going to call this one?"

"Not until you tell us where you went jackrabbiting off to," Thea said. "We hadn't covered the schedule of operations yet."

"She wasn't a jackrabbit," Mel said. "More like the proverbial bat. Where'd you go?"

"To the rescue," I said. "I went to intercept Shirley and Mercy." That had the expected effect, including a muttered "Spivey" from Ernestine—more of a spit than a whisper. Ardis patted Ernestine's shoulder, then turned to me, eyes snapping.

"What did those twin plagues want? Are you sure they're gone?" She looked ready to launch herself down the stairs in a repeat of my performance.

"Debbie got rid of them," I said. "We're Spivey free, and the air quality downstairs has almost returned to normal."

"How did you know they were here?" Thea asked, echoing Debbie's question.

"Duh," Mel said. "Debbie has Kath's Batphone on speed dial."

Geneva hung upside down and made flapping motions behind Ardis. The others, thank goodness, thought I was laughing at Mel's joke.

"What *did* they want?" Ardis asked again. "I find it highly suspicious that they showed up today. This afternoon. At the exact time we're having our final strategy meeting. Highly, *highly* suspicious."

"They were up to something, but I don't know what. They told Debbie I was expecting them. She handled it, though. She told them I wasn't here and they left."

"And *that's* suspicious, too," Ardis said. "Since when do they give in so easily? That's part of the pervasive Spivey problem. They don't know when to quit."

"Perseverance isn't all bad," I said.

"Pigheaded poltroonery is," said Ardis. Behind her, Geneva had been shaking a finger at phantom Spiveys, then pounding a fist into her hand. When Ardis planted her fists on her hips, Geneva did, too, with a clear "nyah, nyah" wiggle to her hips. It was also clear that she and I needed to have a chat about manners and mocking.

"Anyway, they're gone now," I said.

"Although not permanently," Ernestine murmured, "and more's the pity. Oh my goodness, did I say that out loud? I am so sorry." She tried to fix a contrite frown in place, but a smile got the better of her.

"Nothing to be sorry about, Ernestine," Ardis said. "You're right, too. They might come back. Slip in the back door, like as not, like a pair of noxious and obnoxious eels. Then they'll eel their way straight up the stairs."

"We'll hear the bleat of electronic sheep, if they do," Mel said. "Baa-aa-aa. I love it."

"Boo-oo-oo," Geneva said in her own version of a bleat. "You'll hear *me* if the darling twins return." She circled Ardis' head once and then swooped out the door. Ardis turned a moment of wide-eyed surprise into a show of concern. Thanks to her lifetime membership in the Blue Plum Repertory Theater, she was masterful and convincing.

"On to the reason we've called this meeting," she said, "the tragic death of Hugh McPhee. I think we should call this the case of the—"

"One more interruption, please, before we set sail in a new direction," John said. "About the timetable for to-morrow night."

"We've already been over it," Thea said.

"Yes, but this is about the timing of events."

"John, we covered it," Thea said. "We'll pass timeta-bles out tomorrow night, not before."

"I'm sure Kath agrees with that. Don't you, Kath?" Ardis asked. "Especially after your near miss with Shir-ley and Mercy. From this point forward, we need to be extra cautious. No chat in public and the timetable stays under lock and key so that it doesn't fall into the wrong hands. I hope we emphasized that strongly enough with the kiddos, considering the way they text every thought and heartbeat these days. But everyone here is clear on the importance of secrecy—am I right?"

"Clear," Ernestine said, raising her hand.

She looked so solemn and earnest that my hand went up, too. So did Mel's and Thea's.

"John?" Ardis prompted.

"Military time," he said with crisp enunciation. He'd set his knitting aside, something he rarely did during dis-cussions, and his eyes were the color of a winter sea. "It is easy. It is precise. That is all I was trying to say."

"All righty," Thea said, drawing the words out as though she hoped enlightenment would strike before she got to the end. It didn't. She tried raising her eyebrows at him and waiting another few seconds before giving in. "What, John? That's all you're saying about what?"

"Ah. Sorry. I thought you were following me." John hitched forward, his hands ready to illustrate. Drawn in, we all leaned forward, too. "I suggest we use military time, tomorrow night, for the timetable and for any telephone and text communications between our teams of operatives. You know that I don't usually pull rank—"

"I don't think you've ever pulled rank," Ardis said. "It's not like you."

"But as a former naval officer, one who is experienced in campaigns, covert and otherwise, I know what I'm talking about," John said. "While secrecy is important, precision is key." He looked at each of us in turn, then sat back and took up his knitting.

"Thank you, John," Ardis said. "That's very helpful."

"Not really," Thea said. "That isn't going to fly. Or sail, either. We're knitters, John, not Navy SEALs. We're going out at night. Everyone knows it'll be dark. If I tell people to be here at ten minutes of ten, no one's going to be confused and show up in the morning."

"Point taken," said John. "I only wanted to be heard and to help."

"It was a good suggestion," Ernestine said.

"And much appreciated," said Mel. "You can talk about bells and zero hundred hours and avasting at the café any time you want." She watched him knitting and we all listened to the clicking of his needles, as crisp and precise as the advice he'd offered. "And bring Ambrose," Mel said, still watching him. Ambrose was his brother.

"You're kind, Mel." John acknowledged her with a

quick smile. "And delusional if you think that will be a pleasant experience for anyone." As a young man, John had followed his whim to a life at sea. As an old man, he'd answered a need and come home to look after his even older brother. I'd never met Ambrose, and although I'd heard enough to make me curious about him, I trusted the general, quiet consensus of the group. Mel had summed it up best and bluntly with *John's a saint; Ambrose ain't.*

"John, if you need to back out of tomorrow night, everyone will understand," Ardis said. "There is no dishonor in the burden you've undertaken."

"I will be here," John said. "At ten minutes of ten." His needles flashed as something flashed across his face. "And so will Ambrose."

Chapter 11

Silence met John's announcement of the impending Ambrose. It wasn't necessarily an uncomfortable silence, and no one appeared to be stunned, so I decided it was the silence of mental gears shifting. My own shifted first one direction, then another as I wondered how Ambrose would add to or gum up our work. Maybe he wasn't as bad as I'd been led to imagine. Or were we all afraid we'd hurt John's feelings if we told him that he shouldn't or couldn't come if it meant bringing Ambrose along?

Ardis didn't give me any help in deciding which of those options was more likely. She smiled and said, "That's fine, then, John. We'll see you both tomorrow night." But the warmth of her smile and the kind tone of her words might have been her stellar repertory skills coming into play.

"We'll be here," John said, no longer looking anyone in the eye. "Ten minutes of ten."

"Precisely," Ardis said. "And now let's move on to the new case at hand. I have to tell you, this case sorely grieves me. I don't even want to give it a name."

"We don't need a name for it," Mel said. "We don't even need to get involved—"

"Yes, we do," Ardis and I said in unison.

"Just checking," Mel said. "I'm all for it, but we need to be realistic, too. These cases create stresses. Unevenly shared amongst us. But that's the nature of working on something like this. And the nature of stress." She looked sideways at me. "Are *you* up for this, Red? You never talked much about what happened with the last case."

And I probably wouldn't. Geneva and I had talked about it, and I'd told Ardis some of what had occurred, but as for the rest of the posse and the rest of the story . . . They'd been there, but they couldn't see Geneva. They hadn't seen what I had. Joe was amazingly understanding about my silence. He'd asked a few times, more as a way of letting me know that he would listen, and he hadn't pressed. He didn't seem to resent being kept outside that strange patch of my life. And he had quietly run interference for me, deflecting questions from the rest of the posse, and from his brother, in the weeks afterward.

"I'm fine, Mel. Thank you for asking. The stress is something we should all consider. But speaking for myself, I say we go ahead."

"Good. He deserves it," she said.

"You knew him?" I asked.

"Knew of more than knew. He was the kind of guy in high school who left a lasting impression."

"A good one?"

"Oh yeah."

'We'll need to know more about that."

"And that's bygone Hugh," Thea said. "We need to know about recent Hugh, too."

"The man left a generous tip for his lunch," Mel said. "That's about the most up-to-date you'll get."

"Except for the bagpipes," Ernestine said. "He was quite good. I was enjoying his concert last night."

"You were?" Thea asked.

"I jumped right out of bed when I heard them." Ernestine laughed at the memory. "I couldn't help myself. I threw my bathrobe on over my nightgown and went to sit on the front steps—a sight to behold, I don't doubt, except I didn't turn the porch light on so maybe no one saw me. But that's what the sound of pipes does to me. Caution to the winds!" She threw her hands up. "Oh dear." She looked at the stitches she'd lost in her fling. "But that's the way it is with me. There's no telling what I might do when I hear the pipes calling." Ernestine, round as well as wrinkled, looked about as unrestrained as a grandmother mole, but she obviously had hidden passions. "I'd like to have a piper at my funeral," she said, settling back down.

"Hugh was piping at his own funeral," Mel said.

"Is that when it happened? When the pipes stopped?" Ernestine bowed her head. "I put myself back to bed feeling cheated. I feel terrible."

"You didn't know, and there wasn't anything you could have done at that point." I thought about her sitting on her steps in the dark. If it hadn't been dark, if her eyesight were better . . . I'd stood on her front steps one day, in the summer, and admired the view of the creek running through the park behind the courthouse. "You couldn't have done anything at that point, Ernestine, but now . . ."

Her head came up.

"Think back over last night," I said. "Take your time, though. See if you remember noticing anything else while you were sitting on your steps."

"Start with waking up," John said. "Imagine yourself waking up and getting up."

"Even better," I said. "Thanks, John. Ernestine, he's right. Start with waking up. Think about what you heard. Think about throwing on your robe, walking through the house, going out onto the porch. What did you see from your steps before you sat down? What did you hear? Or smell? Were there any other sounds besides the bagpipes? And when the piping stopped, it must have seemed quiet all of a sudden. Was it?"

Ernestine, knitting in her lap and eyes closed, moved her head as though trying to bring a sound or the memory of one into better focus. She ended up shaking her head. "I don't even remember what tune he was playing."

"Don't sweat it," Thea said.

"I'll try it again when I'm home. Tonight. I'll lie down on my bed and go through all the motions. And if a vehicle backfires, then all the better. That might help jog something loose."

"Pesky things, those backfires," Ardis said. "When did you hear it last night?"

"After the pipes quit and I realized how chilly it was. I pulled my bathrobe closer around me, and I pulled myself up with the railing to go back inside. Then I wondered if I'd been a ninny and locked myself out, but the doorknob turned, and as I went inside, I heard a backfire. I thought the piper must be on his way home to bed, too. And that he ought to take his car to my grandson at Ledford's for a tune-up."

"I can't think when I last heard a backfire," John said. "Modern engines and all."

"Plenty of older vehicles around," said Mel.

I could think of one in particular—a monstrosity of fuel inefficiency and pollution belonging to a handyman named Aaron Carlin. I liked Aaron; hated his green pickup. He didn't live in Blue Plum, but he and Mercy Spivey's daughter were a bit of an item a few months earlier. And he might have other business in town.

"Do you ever go hunting with your grandsons, Ernestine?" Thea asked.

"You don't need to pussyfoot around, dear. If you're asking whether I know the difference between a backfire and a gunshot, I suppose I could be fooled. But do we know if he was shot?"

The others looked at Ardis. Then all of them looked at me.

"Huh. Well, I guess that's a good enough place to start the official case file." I slipped the elastic off the leather journal with a satisfying snap and turned to the first blank page. But I didn't put pen to notebook yet. I had a question for Ardis. "Do you think if we'd asked Cole how Hugh died, he would have told us?"

"There's no telling, but I'm surprised at us for *not* asking him."

"Shock," Ernestine said. "You couldn't be expected to think straight."

"You're too kind, Ernestine." Ardis wasn't being kind to herself. She beat the arm of her chair twice with her fist; it might have been her breast. "No. I made Cole tell me when and where Hugh died. How he died should have followed."

"But we were distracted," I said. "He told us about your name on that paper in Hugh's sporran."

"Whoa. Stop. Hold it," Thea said. "What paper in Hugh's what? This reminds me of some of the worst questions we get at the library. You two are treating information like flotsam and jetsam." She smiled at John. "I threw in some nautical jargon for your sake, to show no hard feelings over your martial arts time zones or whatever. You should be threatening to keelhaul someone over this lack of precision. We're sliding into the investigation sideways."

"She's got a point," Mel said, "overexcited though she be. Arrrrdis, you start from the beginning with the facts. Kath, you write them down. Then let's figure out a preliminary round of questions we need to answer, and let's finish up so we can get out of here. Not that I don't love your company. *But.*"

"Fish to fry and cakes to bake?"

"Falafel," Mel countered. "And black rice pudding with coconut milk."

"Ooh." I clicked my pen and smoothed the page. "Ardis already made a start on questions this afternoon."

"And when were you going to tell us that?" Thea asked.

"Right now. I just did. You haven't missed out on anything. I haven't read through them yet myself. Let's get the facts down. Are you ready, Ardis?"

The facts didn't take much ink. Fact: Hugh had arrived in Blue Plum. Fact: He'd played his bagpipes on the lawn at the courthouse. Fact: He was presumed to be the midnight bagpiper. (We wrestled over whether we could call that a fact and decided that, although we didn't know for a fact that Hugh was the midnight piper, we did know for a fact that someone had piped, and we knew that Cole Dunbar presumed the piper was Hugh.) Fact: Hugh was found dead, partially obscured by reeds along the creek, in the park behind the courthouse. Fact: A piece of paper was found in a book in his sporran. Fact: Cole Dunbar wondered why Hugh was in town for Handmade Blue Plum. Fact: Ernestine heard a presumed backfire after the bagpipes went silent. (Ernestine made me go back and add the word "presumed" before the word "backfire.")

"Our facts aren't much to go on," Ardis said.

"Since when have we let that stop us?" I turned the page with a flourish, hoping it would have a bolstering psychological effect for her.

"And it probably isn't all we know. I'm proof of that," said Ernestine. "I'll go home as soon as we're through here, and I'll try my best to bring back any other visual or auditory clues from last night that are stuck up here in my little gray cells." She tapped her forehead. "In my case, though, the cells are old as well as being little and gray, so we'll see how well that works."

"I might be able to dredge something up," Mel said. "Chopping onions usually does it. It's amazing how onions and a sharp knife free the mind."

"The library has old yearbooks," Thea said. "I'll troll through those."

"And we all need to talk to customers and library patrons," I said. "Casually, though, and we'll see what people know or remember about him."

"Customers, patrons, and casual go without saying, don't they?" Thea asked. "As part of our usual bag of operating tricks?"

"I'm just keeping to this afternoon's theme of being precise," I said, "which moves us nicely into what we should do next—come up with specific questions. What do we need to know about Hugh McPhee to help us figure this out?"

"Read what you've got, Ardis," Mel said. "It'll prompt other questions, and there's no point in duplicating your efforts."

I put her notebook on the table and gave it a shove toward her. Ardis stared at it but didn't reach for it.

"That's okay. I can do it." She watched me pull the notebook back across the table; then she looked at her lap. I opened the notebook and leafed through it to find the questions—found the "dabbling" page—found several pages of close writing past the "dabbling" page— none of it in the form of a list, not a question mark in sight. I started reading it—to myself, thank goodness. Ardis hadn't written questions about Hugh's death. She'd started an almost stream-of-consciousness story about a child, a class, a teacher . . . There were three or four unreadable splotches where her ink had blurred.

"Waiting, waiting, waiting," Mel said.

I tucked Ardis' notebook beside me in the chair and picked up my pen.

"Kath?" Mel asked. "Time is ticking."

I watched Ardis for some kind of reaction. "That was a different assignment, Mel. A personal one. Let's go ahead and brainstorm the questions."

"We know so little," Ardis said to her hands in her lap. "The unknowns are almost too much."

"Then we'd better get started," said John. "Top of the list is how did he die? After that, here are my prelimi-

nary questions. *Was* he here for Handmade Blue Plum?
If so, why? In what capacity? As a craftsman? Who's in
charge of Handmade who can tell us?

"They asked Joe to step in and oversee booth setup,"
I said. "If he doesn't know anything about Hugh, he'll
know who to ask."

"And who did he still know in Blue Plum?" John
asked.

"He recognized Cole as a Dunbar," I said after I'd
gotten John's questions down. "And he remembered that
the brothers have unusual names, but he didn't remember what they were. He didn't know Cole was a deputy."

"There might be a lot of people in town he knew once
or knew in passing," John said. "But who did he know
better than that? Who did he keep in touch with? What
about family?"

"It was never a close family," Ardis said. "Olive
Weems is a cousin, but she's never had news to pass on.
The grandfather outlived Hugh's parents and Olive's, but
of course he's been gone for decades. Anyone else I
might have stopped in the grocery to ask about Hugh,
over the years, and what he was up to . . ." She shook her
head. "You know how people come and people go. Hugh
asked about a few names, yesterday, when we had lunch."

John turned to her. "That's very good information.
Who?"

She shook her head. "You'd think I'd remember. I
talked my fool head off and I can't tell you who he asked
about and who I threw at him thinking he might be interested."

"Was he interested?" I asked.

"Was he interested, or was he being polite?" Ardis

pressed her lips into an annoyed line. "I don't know. I wasn't polite enough myself to notice. And the names he asked about? Gone."

"The names will come," Ernestine said. "Try the imagination thing, like I did. Did he say how long he was staying in town?"

"Did he say *where* was he staying?" Mel asked.

"Oh, that's a good question," Ernestine said, "and it makes me wonder. If I were to wear my Miss Marple, do you think I could convince whoever's in charge of wherever he was staying to let me have a look at his room and belongings?" Ardis might be a lifetime member of the repertory theater, but Ernestine was a born-again Golden Age sleuth.

"Let's hold off on entering places under false pretenses," Thea said.

"At least for a day or two," I added. "What other questions have we got? What else do we need to know?"

"Does *his* vehicle backfire?" Ernestine asked.

"Where *is* his vehicle?" John asked.

"And if it's old enough to backfire, is it also old enough that we can use a coat hanger to unlock it?" Ernestine asked. "I used to get such a kick out of that."

Thea tsked.

"It isn't all that hard," Ernestine said, "and it's very satisfying being able to get yourself out of a pickle."

"Or into one," Thea said. "I'm trying to be the voice of reason and responsibility here."

"I appreciate that. But you can find out a lot about a person by what he keeps in his car and how neat or messy it is. And I wouldn't mind having a chance to practice with a coat hanger again. It was a useful skill."

Ardis hadn't said anything more. I glanced at her a few times as I caught the questions bouncing back and forth around the circle and got them down in the journal. From the furrow between her eyebrows and the return of thin lips, she was either thoughtful or unhappy. But if she was thinking, or trying to remember something, the usual energy of her thought process was missing—there was no jostle of knee, no pencil, foot, or finger tapping. None of the wrestling between one point and another that might be going on in her head was visible on her face. I tried to catch her eye, but she continued to stare at her lap. During the next lull, I nudged my way into her silence.

"Ardis, after you and Hugh had lunch together, you came back here to the shop alone. Did he say where he was going? Anything about his plans for the afternoon?"

"No." The single syllable was a tangled knot of frustration and self-recrimination that she had to force out.

"Take it easy," Mel said gently. "If he didn't tell you, he didn't tell you. Lots of people don't volunteer their plans to me. I only know Kath's plans for tonight because I asked Joe. *She* didn't tell me."

"I could have asked Hugh," Ardis said. "I didn't. I don't know why he was here. I didn't ask how long he was staying. I didn't even ask him to come for supper. I wanted to. I meant to."

"You aren't the prying type," Ernestine said.

"I thought I was."

"You're the caring type," Ernestine said, "sometimes mistaken for the prying type. But you care, and that's why you're beating yourself up now. Please don't. You were happy to see him again and to know that he re-membered you."

"He remembered some of the lines from the play I wrote for the class. After all these years, he remembered that. I could've asked him if he'd ever done any more acting. I didn't."

"Because you're also the perceptive type," Ernestine said.

"You'd know that if you were more perceptive, Ardis," said Thea.

Ernestine shushed her. "If he'd wanted to let you past his facade, you would have known, Ardis. That's what I'm saying. But he hadn't been back to Blue Plum for years. There was a reason for that, and whatever the reason was, it wasn't something he was giving away over lunch with a favorite teacher."

"It was lunch," John said. "You were happy. He was happy. You didn't need to know more to be enjoying yourself. He wasn't letting more out. Equilibrium. Stasis. Let's move on."

"Wait." Ardis' chin came up. "Was he happy?"

I jotted that question down and watched her lips shift left and then right—her thoughts creaking back into motion.

"Okay." She rolled her shoulders and neck. "Yes. We need to find out what Hugh did yesterday afternoon and evening. And yes, let's break that down into specifics. Where did he go? Who did he see? Who saw *him*? Did he spend time with anyone?" She gained momentum and my notes began to sprawl. "The bagpipe incidents—both of them—what prompted them?"

"We can't get inside his head," Thea said. "That's a good question, but we need another entry point."

"His car or his hotel room." Ernestine's eyes lit with the possibilities of coat hangers and tweed skirts.

Ardis wasn't finished. "The piece of paper with my name on it. Was anything else on the paper? What kind of paper? A whole piece? A scrap? And the book where they found it ... they found it in his sporran ... what book? Does that even matter? And you—" She pointed at me. "You said something about him being a tourist. What made you think that?"

"The camera around his neck."

"A camera, not a phone. Does that tell us anything? And where is his camera? And who, and/or what, did he take pictures of?" She stopped talking, but her eyes—not focused on any of us—moved as they prodded each corner of her memory.

I shook out my writing hand, ready to begin again.

"That paper ... there's something else about that piece of paper. You were there, Kath. What is it?"

"Name, book, sporran." I shrugged.

"His sporran," Thea said, rolling the word out. "What else does a man keep in his sporran?"

"Very good question," Ardis said. "Cole wouldn't necessarily tell us everything they found in it. In fact, he *wouldn't* tell us. But it might be important."

"It's definitely important if we're going to get a full picture of the man and the situation," John said. "Whether or not it has anything specifically to do with the crime. We need to talk to someone."

"Idiot," Ardis exploded. "No, sorry, John. *I'm* the idiot. Not you. Cole said they'd send a deputy around to interview me about the paper. That's what I was trying to remember, and they haven't done it yet."

"Low priority," Mel said.

"No priority, as far as I'm concerned," Ardis said. "I have no idea why my name was in the sporran."

"I think I'll try penning a naughty Nancy Drew," Thea said. "The Clue in the Splendid Sporran."

I scribbled a note in the margin about Thea's fascination with sporrans. If I could find one that wasn't too expensive, it would make a good Christmas present for her.

"As long as the sheriff hasn't already sent a deputy over," Ardis said, musing in her own way, "I wonder if I can request one. A *specific* one. A woman one."

"One who's almost one of us?" I liked where this was going. "One who has come over to the fiber side?"

"Yes, indeedy." Ardis rubbed her hands, then mimed putting a phone to her ear and said, "Calling Deputy Dye. Calling Deputy Dye."

By weird coincidence, my Batphone buzzed in my pocket. At the same time, we heard a light step in the hall, the floorboard at the door creaked, and the newest member of the sheriff's department, and the only one with an unshakable enthusiasm for everyone she met, stepped into the room. Deputy Darla Dye smiled at us. "Hey, ya'll. You rang?"

Chapter 12

The buzz of my phone was a text from Debbie letting me know Darla was on her way up. It wasn't much of a warning, but for Darla it didn't need to be. Argyle liked her, too. He trotted down from the study and gave her ankles an extra circuit.

"Deputy Darla, come on in and sit yourself down," Ardis said. "I was just about to call Sheriff Haynes and see if I could track you down."

"Then I've had a nice walk on this beautiful afternoon *and* I've saved you a call. What's your pleasure, Ardis? Official business of the peace officer type or official business of the knit and crochet type?"

The pleasure and interest Darla took in her job and the people around her had a reflective quality to it. What radiated from her smile and the laugh lines at the corners of her eyes was returned in kind. She wasn't a member of TGIF—she said her work schedule was all over the place and she didn't like to join an organization and then never show up—but she was a passionate knitter of long, bulky scarves. Ardis told me that as far as she knew, no one ever saw the scarves again after they were wrapped and presented to their new owners. I liked Darla even more for that. We'd had a hard time making ourselves keep the yarn bombing a secret from her, but we thought it best, considering the organization she owed her paycheck and bulky yarn money to.

Darla dropped herself into one of the comfy chairs, making it look as though she'd come home and was happy to be there. The only thing out of place about her was the lack of needles and yarn in her hands. That and the holster and gun on her hip. Her khaki and tan uniform and regulation footwear weren't typical knitting circle couture, but they didn't call any more attention to themselves than Mel's chef pants and aprons. Or Thea's holy terror heels. Darla was single, mid-thirties, had a teenage son more interested in NASCAR than needlework and, if rumors could be trusted, a crush on Clod Dunbar. She nestled her shoulders into the chair, planted her elbows on the arms, and clasped her hands across her midriff. Argyle invited himself onto her lap and she helped him settle with a few strokes down the back of his neck.

"What can I do for you, Ardis?"

"It concerns Hugh McPhee's murder, and a piece of paper, one with my name on it, that someone in your department found with his body."

"In his spittoon?"

All eyebrows rose, even Darla's.

"I'm sorry," she said. "I'm so sorry. That just slipped out. It was an insensitive and uncalled-for joke at the deceased's expense and the expense of anyone who knew and loved him. I don't find it funny myself, but the boys in the department, well . . ." She chuckled softly. "They will be horses' patooties, God love 'em." She marveled at her fellow deputies' patootiness for several more seconds, then burst into another smile. "But, Ardis, this works out perfectly. I saw Debbie downstairs and she said you might still be in a meeting, and did I want to wait? She offered to show me some of your new Incredible Bulk yarn, but I said no, I'd just come on up. And the reason I did is that piece of paper."

"Wonderful!" Ernestine said, caught up in the sunny bubble surrounding Darla. "And you certainly don't mind if the rest of us—"

"Take off?" Darla said. "Not at all."

"Sorry?" Ernestine said.

"I'm sorry you have to go, too," Darla said. "We don't see enough of each other these days, do we? John, Thea, Mel, Kath." She nodded to each one of us. "I'll see you another time."

Between us we gathered project bags, notebooks, and Mel's coffee carafe, and trooped out of the room—Ernestine looking confused by our eviction. At the door, I looked back to catch Ardis' eye. I caught Darla's, too. As soon as we'd left, she and Argyle had moved over to the chair next to Ardis'.

"Debbie and I'll lock up, Ardis. See you tomorrow."

"Bye, now," Darla said with a wave.

"She's a trip," Mel said on the way down the stairs. "And if the rumors are true, and Cole is of the opinion that she makes khaki and tan look cute, then he'd better watch his step. He's dallying with someone smarter than he is and, I bet, someone who knows what she wants and knows how to wrap it up, tie it with a bow, and send it to herself."

"It might be the best thing that ever happened to him," John said.

I looked for Geneva before I left the shop for the day, but didn't see her. She often made herself scarce at closing time, though. She'd told me she didn't like good-byes because she'd had too many permanent ones. I'd invited her home with me, any number of times, but she'd never taken me up on it. I was just as glad of that, since Joe and I were seeing more of each other, both figuratively and literally. Having a doleful, gray, canoodling-averse ghost hanging around could only put a damper on a budding relationship. Even if—or maybe especially if—only one of the pair knew of the ghost's existence.

My phone buzzed on the walk home. I expected it to be Ardis with an update. Instead it was Joe breaking our dinner date. The floor plan used to assign spaces for booths at Handmade Blue Plum—agreed upon by the craftspeople as they registered for the weekend—was being called unfair by half a dozen newcomers. Joe had spent the day making calls, making assurances, making changes, and making no headway on putting together his own booth. Considering he was usually more of a booth-half-built person than a booth-half-in-a-shambles guy, he sounded pretty down. To take his mind off his own worries, I told him mine about Darla questioning Ardis.

"You didn't find a way to eavesdrop?" he asked.

"Nope. Not even tempted."

"And you didn't need to be. Ardis will fill you in."

"True enough. I'm willing to bet I couldn't have done it and gotten away with it anyway. Not without Darla finding out. She doesn't miss much. Hey, you know what might be fun? We should double-date with Darla and Cole."

Joe must have taken a drink as I said that. I hoped his phone was spatterproof.

"They're dating?"

"You didn't know that? Actually I don't know for sure, but Mel and I have each heard it and John thinks it'll be good for Cole. If it's true."

Joe was quiet and I could picture him thinking over that new information, a finger of his left hand stroking the beard on his lean face. "Do you really want to?"

"Double date? No. Well, maybe, but only if Darla drops Cole off at the Burger Barn and meets us at Mel's on her own. How much more do you have to do tonight?"

Joe was quiet and I could picture him gesturing with a finger at the Handmade Blue Plum floor plan. "You'd better go ahead and eat without me."

Being civic-minded, I didn't say anything; I was passing a young couple pushing a stroller, and no G-rated thoughts were rolling around on my tongue.

"You still there?" Joe asked.

"Yeah."

"What I just said?"

"Yeah?"

"It was said pathetically."

"If I bring something by in half an hour or so, will you be able to take a break and eat?"

"Can you bring it by the school? To the gym? If I'm going bombing with you tomorrow night, and spending all day tomorrow holding hands with a hundred crafts-people putting up their own booths, I'd better get mine set up tonight."

We closed out the conversation, him sounding less pathetic, me beginning to worry about Ardis. How long could it take Darla to describe the paper for Ardis and then ask a few perfunctory questions? Ah, but maybe silver-tongued Ardis had charmed enthusiastic Darla and they were having one of Ardis' patented chin-wags. And even now, while I needlessly worried about Ardis being cautioned that what she blabbed might be used against her—even now, Darla might be passing along information vital to the case. Information that, although it was being withheld from the general public, was willingly being entrusted to a strategic, completely trustworthy few. At least, I hoped my worries were needless.

I tried calling her, but got her voice mail. "Call me," I said, and went back to worrying. Maybe she was down at the sheriff's office helping with their inquiries, leaving her ancient daddy to get his own beer and change channels for himself.

The call from Joe and my return to worrying about Ardis took most of the walk home to the yellow frame house on Lavender Street. I'd inherited the house from Granny along with the Weaver's Cat. I loved walking home to that house where I'd spent happy summers with Granny. I was an incredibly lucky person to have the house and the shop, and to have people I cared about in my life. I knew that. I did. But I repeated it to myself as an antidote to the slow seep of uneasiness that made my feet pick up their pace.

I exchanged a hurried "nice night" with the woman

two doors down from me who spent as much time in her garden as her garden gnome did.

The days were growing shorter, but it wasn't dark yet. More like twilight, or gloaming. "Glooming," Geneva would probably say. She didn't like going out at night. She said she was afraid of the dark. I wasn't usually afraid of the dark, but my uneasiness had me feeling jumpy—and remembering a few surprises I'd found waiting for me on my front porch. Surprises in the form of Clod Dunbar or Shirley and Mercy Spivey. But despite the gloomy gloaming, I didn't see anyone sitting on the porch swing or standing in the shadows and trying to blend in like twin chameleons.

The lid to the mailbox screeched hello when I lifted it, and I marveled over a day without junk mail. I let myself in, shed purse and shoes, and pulled the drapes at the front window. If I changed without dawdling and hopped into the car, then I could swing by Mel's, grab something tasty, and still be at the school within the half hour I'd promised. If I called Mel's and asked for a to-go order, even better.

A pair of jeans and a long-sleeved tee later, my taste buds were yammering for some of Mel's new lentil salad and a side of flatbread. While I called the café, I went through to the kitchen. Mel's was hopping. I said I'd hold and congratulated myself for calling ahead. While I waited, I took a pitcher of tea from the fridge and poured a glass. Sweet tea made with honey and mint from Granny's— my—herb garden in back. I looked out the window over the sink toward the garden. There was less light in the twilight now and not many features visible in the yard.

Except . . . a strange car backed up near the garage so

that it was facing the house, but in such a way that it couldn't be seen from the street.

And there I was, standing in the kitchen window, lit up as though onstage. If I'd been smart, I would have doused the lights or moved away from the window. But I was too busy squinting at the car. I could only make out a silhouette, but it looked as though someone was sitting in the passenger seat. Did that mean someone else was prowling? In the yard? Around the house? *In* the house? But I hadn't noticed anything missing or out of place. I hadn't heard noises, stealthy or otherwise.

That was when the voice speaking into my ear scared the bejeebers out of me and I screamed.

And I lost the connection to Mel's, because the guy taking phone orders had answered and then wisely hung up when I screamed into his ear. In my defense his *"how can I help you?"* had sounded exactly like *"don't move or I'll slit your throat"*—to my hyperventilating imagination. In addition to screaming, I'd whirled around, sloshing sweet tea in a wide arc as I went.

As someone who'd grown used to a ghost floating up behind her and saying "boo" (and as someone who should have remembered she had a phone pressed to her ear), I shouldn't have been so startled. But there was still a strange car backed up to my garage.

And a face, framed by two hands, peering in the window over the sink.

Chapter 13

Someone else was rattling the knob on the back door. I thought about mopping up the tea and ignoring them—the window peerer and the doorknob rattler. But the latter sounded frantic and the former looked—oops. She suddenly disappeared, dropping out of sight with a squawk, having fallen off whatever she'd been standing on. The knob rattler abandoned the back door—to check on the window peerer's condition, no doubt. Against my better judgment, I turned on the light over the back door and went out to check, too.

"You okay?" I asked from the back steps. Checking was one thing; going closer and getting involved was another.

"Her foot went through the bottom of the flowerpot. She'll need a bandage."

I couldn't tell, from where I stood on the steps, which Spivey twin was sitting on the ground wearing a flowerpot on her foot and which stood over her with her hands on her hips. Both looked annoyed.

"Why'd you scream bloody murder?" the one on the ground asked.

A question I didn't want to answer. "Did you come in that?" I pointed to the car. It was a black two-door sedan, not their beige Buick.

"It's Angie's," the standing twin said, referring to Mercy's daughter. "Ours is in the shop. Mind if we come in?"

"I was on my way out."

"Mercy's ankle is bleeding pretty good."

Mercy wasn't applying pressure and didn't seem overly concerned, but better safe than sued.

"Come on in." I should have tried to sound less grudging and more gracious. It would have been wasted effort, though. Mercy swatted at Shirley when she helped take the flowerpot off her foot, and Shirley fussed at Mercy when she pulled herself to her feet by grabbing on to Shirley's arm, nearly toppling her as she did. Mercy didn't leave a trail of blood as she limped to the back steps.

"What's Angie driving while you have her car?" I asked as we trooped inside. "Aaron's pickup?"

"That old hunk of junk," Mercy said, which didn't tell me yes or no, but told me Angie and Aaron were still together. Mercy sat down at the kitchen table with a credible wince, then looked at the tea I hadn't mopped up. "What kind of accident did *you* have?"

"Tea." It was my turn to wince as Shirley walked through the puddle to sit opposite Mercy.

"Tea?" Shirley said. "Why, thank you. We'd be delighted."

"Go ahead and pour it," Mercy said, "and then you can bring that bandage. A dab of gauze should do it."

"Then, after we're all settled, we'll tell you who we saw with Hugh McPhee yesterday afternoon." Shirley's statement was followed by a yip and a glare for Mercy, who must have used her good foot to kick Shirley's shin.

"I'd like to hear about Hugh first," I said. "Is that why you stopped by the shop today?"

They both glared at me.

Choose your battles, Granny used to tell me, *and learn to know who's vexatious enough to turn around and bite you in the bottom if you win.*

With a deliberately slow blink, I disengaged from the twins' stubborn challenge. Then I took a moment and looked around at Granny's kitchen cupboards, her worn countertops, the floor I'd tracked mud on. She and I had made innumerable batches of cookies at that table. She'd taught me how to wash dishes in her chipped porcelain sink. Shirley and Mercy were about as vexatious as they came, but if sweet tea and gauze were all it took to get information about Hugh McPhee's last afternoon in Blue Plum—and to keep their overly white teeth at bay—then I could play nice. The tea and gauze didn't come with a smile, though.

While I looked for gauze and adhesive tape in the bathroom, I called Joe and told him I'd probably be another half hour. "Sorry about the delay. I'll tell you about it when I get there."

"I'm getting nowhere fast," he said, sounding like a man who wanted to sigh but didn't believe in it. "I'll be here."

I decided to get dessert from Mel's, too. We both deserved it.

"Good tea," Shirley said when I returned. "And if

that's what's on the floor, you might want to wipe it up. Sweet as it is, it'll be a terrible, sticky mess if you don't."

"It is good tea, though," Mercy said. "And wouldn't it go just right with a cookie or slice of cake?"

"Wouldn't it? Sorry. I haven't got any." I handed her the gauze and tape. "Too bad. But I was I was on my way out for something when you *dropped* in."

"Pun intended," Shirley chortled. And got another kick from Mercy.

I wet a paper towel and handed it to Mercy for her ankle, then wet a few more and wiped tea from the floor.

"Any antibacterial ointment?" Shirley asked.

"I thought I had some," I said to the floor near her feet, "but I didn't find it."

"You didn't get that spot over there." Mercy pointed to the place. My trajectory had been far and wide. "Ointment is something you should always keep in your medicine cabinet," she added.

"I'll put it on my list." Instead I pictured getting a pair of socks and putting one in each vexatious mouth. That cheered me and I finished the floor with another wet towel, and then joined them at the table. "More tea?" I topped their glasses. "How's the ankle, Mercy?"

"Not as good as new, but it doesn't throb nearly so much. Thank you for asking." She'd put the rest of the gauze and tape in her pocketbook.

"So, tell me about Hugh McPhee." I didn't ask why they thought I'd be interested. I'd never told them about the posse and they'd never asked. It was one of those situations—they knew; I knew they knew; and they knew that no member was ever likely to ask them to be part of it. But in their own subtle and often irritating Spivey way, they had contributed to our investigations. And whether it was a way of saving face or not, they made it look as though they preferred their outsider status.

"We'd have told you this afternoon," Mercy said, "but you were conspicuous by your alleged absence."

"You didn't leave a message."

"Of course not," Mercy said. "Too dangerous."

"And you can't let anyone know we told you what we're about to tell you," Shirley said.

"You'll be painting bull's-eyes on our backs if you do," said Mercy. "That's why we parked so no one could see us."

"And why you were sneaking around, looking in my kitchen window?"

"We had to make sure you were alone."

Their hushed voices and uneasy glances over their shoulders were infectious. I found myself leaning toward them and looking left and right. "Who did you see with him?" I asked quietly.

"Al," Shirley whispered.

"Who?"

"From Chicago." Mercy stared at my face, then threw herself back in her chair. "I knew it. A waste of time and good skulking. I told you, Shirley. Didn't I tell you? She doesn't know Al from a fire hydrant."

"And you should have listened," Shirley said, "because it was *me* who told *you*." She scooted her chair back, taking a layer of linoleum with her, but avoiding another kick.

I avoided pinching the bridge of my nose. To me, that would have been a sign of holding it together—barely. To the twins it might have been a sign of weakness.

"Shirley, I'm at your mercy. Mercy, surely you can tell me what you're talking about."

"Now you're making fun of us," Shirley said.

"I wasn't—"

"A fine way to thank us," said Mercy. "And after we came to warn you. Come on, Shirley."

I held the door so they couldn't slam it. After they took off with a spatter of gravel against the garage, I dialed Mel's again.

Mel manned the café counter when I ran in to pick up the order, her apron crisp, her hair alert.

"Date night?" she asked, handing me a bag with two Reuben sandwiches, two of orders of sweet potato fries, and a box with two pieces of what she called Chocolate Cubed—a cube of two dense layers of chocolate cake filled and topped with dark chocolate ganache studded with dark chocolate chips. After the day and evening Joe was having, and after my unexpected Spivey Time, I'd changed my mind about lentil salad. We both deserved calories and comfort. "Don't go passing this off as your own cooking, though, Red. Joe might be moonstruck by your charms, but he won't fall for that baloney."

"You know what you need, Mel? Music for people to listen to when they're on hold instead of silence that lets their own thoughts run away with them. Merely a suggestion." I plunked two bottles of root beer from her cooler on the counter. The plunk might have sounded more aggressive than it needed to. I probably needed those calories and comfort more than I'd realized. "No offense meant, though, Mel."

"None taken, Red, though I do wonder why you bring

that up this evening. Apart from your obvious case of nerves. But do you know what we really need? Caller ID. It'd be helpful for business purposes, and it might also cut down on prank calls. We had a screamer tonight. Scared the new guy out of his wits. He might never be the same." She looked at me with assessing eyes. "You know anything about that, Red?"

"Your guy's voice came out of dead silence and Mercy Spivey was looking in my kitchen window."

Mel flinched. "Say no more. Your reaction is totally understandable. You aren't the first one to suggest hold music, either. I've toyed with the idea of reading the menu into a tape recorder, you know, describing each item in sultry, salivating detail and using that instead of music."

"I think it's all digital now, Mel."

"Whatever."

"So, why don't you do it? It'd be great."

"Because I don't do sultry, Red. But if I did, it *would* be great and then we'd have people calling from who knows where just to be put on hold and I don't have time for that kind of nonsense."

"Can I ask you a quick question?"

But she didn't have time for any more chitchat, either. She flapped me away with her apron and turned to help the next person in line. I'd wanted to ask her who Al from Chicago was. I saved the question for Joe.

Joe was capable of many things and good at what he enjoyed doing. Herding rabid craftspeople—even if only over the phone—wasn't one of those things. I drove over to the school and called him from the parking lot. He told me the door at the far end of the building, under the security light, was unlocked. I found him inside, sitting on the stage, knitting. A long snake of garter stitch spilled from the stage to the floor below. It was striped in an amazing range of colors. He must have put every odd inch from his stash in it.

"Is that helping?" I asked.

"Fishing would be better. Not an option right now. Just taking a short break. Steadies the nerves. Never knew my nerves could be so easily shot."

"Is it really that bad?" I shouldn't have asked. It was like hitting a man when he was feeling down because the big one had slipped the hook. I put the bags and box from Mel's on the stage and boosted myself up next to them. "Put your needles down and scoot over here." He did and I gave him a kiss. "Now we eat. And then, if things aren't looking better after Reubens, fries, and Mel's Chocolate Cubed, we'll call the whiners and the bullies and tell them we're refunding their money and they should take their crappy crafts and go away. Do you have the authority to do that?"

"I have authority over many rolls of painter's tape for marking booth spaces on the floor and numbering them consecutively. I ran out of the allotted number of rolls this afternoon and had to buy more. Now I have an extra roll. I could use it to bind and gag the most obnoxious of the crap people, but I don't have authority to do that."

I shushed him with a finger over his lips. "If you don't have the authority to dump those losers, then we'll call whoever's in charge of the whole caboodle and toss the problems in his or her lap. Who *is* in charge?"

"Olive."

One of the charms of small-town life—that everyone knew everyone else—could also be one of the problems. People often assumed I was on a first-name basis with everyone, too. "I don't think I know an Olive."

"Pokey's wife."

That name I did know. There was only one Pokey that anyone talked about—Mayor Pokey Weems, son of Gladys the Blue Prune who'd kicked Clod's shin and been as pleased as Ardis to hear that Hugh McPhee was back in town. I wondered how Gladys was taking the news of Hugh's death. "Did you know that she and Hugh were cousins? Ardis mentioned that at the meeting."

"I should cut her some slack."

"Probably, but Ardis said they weren't close. And anyway, being the mayor's wife, Olive should be used to dealing with all kinds of situations. Doesn't she have a committee and know how to delegate?"

"She does." Joe nodded. "And when she called last week and asked me to do this favor for her, because the person who *was* in charge of logistics suddenly backed out, that's what she was doing—demonstrating how she deals and delegates by rolling the two up into one f—one freaking mess and slam-dunking the whole thing into my lap." He stopped and held up a hand. "Not that I'm bitter. I'm not. Want me to show you how much I'm not bitter?" He pulled me to him and he was right. Aggravated he might be, but his kiss was gentle and sweet and not bitter at all. "It's my fault," he said, letting me go. "I should've asked more questions before I said yes."

"You think she knew these people were going to cause a fuss?"

"At this point, whether she did or not doesn't matter. Besides, what happened to 'Now we eat'?"

I opened the bag and handed him his sandwich, fries, and bottle of root beer, and we sat with our legs dangling from the edge of the stage. Joe and I had eaten supper in the gym once before, when we both went to the Historical Trust Annual Meeting and Potluck in the spring. We hadn't been a couple then, but we'd ended up going through the supper line together. Joe, noted local potluck connoisseur, had been the perfect tour guide through the various pots, bowls, casseroles, and cake and pie plates. The gym looked bigger without the ranks of folding tables that had crowded it for the potluck. The blue rectangles Joe had spent the afternoon taping and numbering on the floor looked like a quilt, or an odd game of hopscotch.

Mel's Reubens came on grilled pumpernickel with beef she corned and sliced paper thin. The smell alone had calories. Salty, tangy, cheesy, warm—Joe was lucky I hadn't pulled off to the side of the road between Mel's and the school and eaten my sandwich and half of his. It was a messy sandwich for takeout, but so worth it. And Mel, knowing the habits of her sandwiches, included an extra wad of napkins in the bag. The sweet potato fries were caramelized from the hot oven and sprinkled with a nicely balanced combination of salt, garlic powder, and smoked paprika.

"I'm guessing Olive—"

"No more about Olive," Joe said. "I'm enjoying Reuben."

"You'll enjoy this, too. I was just going to say that I guess Olive isn't anything like her mother-in-law." I told him about meeting Gladys, and about Gladys' pocketbook meeting his brother's diaphragm. It was good to hear him laugh when I described her new superhero status as the Blue Prune.

"Gladys is a pistol," he said.

Pistol. "Have you heard anything about how Hugh McPhee died?"

"No."

"Tell me about him. Ardis and Gladys were happy he'd come home. Your brother seemed excited, too."

"Someone wasn't. Did you guys come up with anything at the meeting this afternoon?"

"A lot of questions and not much else, but that's the way we usually start. Did you know Hugh?"

"By reputation," Joe said. "He was enough older that he wasn't on my radar."

"Cole seems to think he was in town for Handmade."

Joe chewed that over with the last bites of his sandwich. "No one from the sheriff's department has called to ask if he was registered for a booth. No one's called me, anyway. But they'd probably talk to Olive."

"Was he registered for one?"

"No, but the committee only took one name for each booth registration. That's been part of the problem. They should have taken the name of every person associated with a booth, but they didn't. So I've had people calling and complaining about how the booths are arranged, and where their booth is, and they're not on my list, so I don't know if they're legit or trying to pull a fast one or trying to screw someone else over."

"They'd do that?"

"Crazy, isn't it? But these folks are serious, and to

them, you're nowhere without location. No one wants to be buried back by the restrooms."

"So who is?"

He looked away and raised his hand.

"You're too good."

He shrugged. "I have a trick or two up my sleeve. People will find me."

"Isn't there a master list of craftspeople, though? Didn't they all have to pay a fee, separate from the booth fee?"

"Olive said she'll be here tomorrow afternoon and she'll bring the list with her."

"She couldn't send you a copy? Wouldn't that have helped you deal with the irate calls this afternoon?"

"She's a technophobe. Only has a hard copy, and only the *one* copy." He wadded his sandwich wrapping, squeezing it into a tight ball. "She would have brought the list this afternoon, but she had other commitments and no time to 'share the information.' Those were her words, 'share the information.'"

"You should have given everyone who called her number."

"She switched her phone off. Her voice mail is full." He added my sandwich wrapper to his. I hadn't picked the last scrap of salty beef from my paper, though, and watched sadly as he compacted it, his knuckles turning white. It was probably good therapy, but I was glad I wasn't one of those sandwich wrappings.

"Calm down, there, hotshot."

"Sorry."

"Here." I handed him his share of the Chocolate Cubed. "And when Olive calls next year, say no."

I blessed Mel for the ameliorating effect of her cake. And while we benefited from it, I remembered that I hadn't told Joe about the Spivey invasion or asked if he knew Al from Chicago. One or the other of those tidbits should take his mind further off Olive and her cantankerous craftspeople.

"I forgot to tell you why I was late."

"I should have asked." He put his empty cake plate aside. "I've been selfish. Thank you for bringing supper. I feel better."

"Supper can do that."

"You do that. Thanks for coming. So go ahead, tell me why you were late."

He looked so calm. At peace. Maybe I shouldn't disturb the good-natured curve of his lips and the tranquil blue of his eyes by mentioning Shirley and Mercy. But I'd spent too long thinking. His eyebrows rose.

"Did Ardis get back to you?" he asked. "Is everything all right?"

Ardis! How could I have forgotten? "No, she hasn't called. Wow, I'd better try her again."

"If anything were really wrong, we would've heard."

"Would we?"

"If it'll make you feel better, go ahead and call, but first, why *were* you late?"

He was still calm, but only in the way strong, silent types appear calm on the surface when they're trying to keep everyone around them from panicking. I wasn't exactly panicking about Ardis, but niceties, such as easing into the topic of Shirley and Mercy, were right out the window.

"The twins were skulking around my house," I said.

"Not very gracefully, though. Mercy put her foot through a flowerpot and cut her ankle. They were being all Spivey and dramatic." I waved my hands to capture the full Spivey effect, and thought I detected a smidge of a twitch in Joe's calm strength. "They had Angie's car and pulled it around the side of the garage so no one could see it from the street. Then they peeked in my windows."

Definitely a twitch that time.

"They said they had information about Hugh Mc-Phee."

That was met with a minor eye roll.

"That's what I thought, too." I handed him my root beer bottle, sacrificing the last of it to help him bear up. "They were keen to tell me who they saw with Hugh yesterday afternoon. They obviously thought it was significant, but when I didn't know who they were talking about, they got all snooty and left."

"Who'd they see?" It would have been better if he'd waited for my answer before swigging the last of the root beer.

"Some guy named Al. Al from Chicago."

Chapter 14

"**W**ho *is* this guy?" I grabbed the extra napkins Mel had put in the sandwich bag. "Should I be worried about him? Hey, wait a second—" If I'd thought Joe was blindsided by the mention of Al from Chicago and coughing to clear his lungs of aspirated root beer, I was a hundred and eighty degrees off. He wasn't shocked or shattered. He was laughing. Although still coughing. But coughing meant he was breathing, so I didn't pound him on the back. I waited for an explanation.

"Al Rogalla," Joe said. "And yeah, he is from Chicago—twenty-five years ago. At least."

"Okay, so what's the big deal?"

"Nothing. He's a nice guy. An accountant. Volunteer fireman, too."

"So why would anyone care if he spent time with Hugh McPhee yesterday? Why were the twins acting like it was earth-shattering news and they were in danger for breathing his very name?" And why did the name suddenly sound familiar?

"Consider the source," Joe said. "Behold, they are

Spivey. The thing is, after all these years, Al does still sound like he's from Chicago."

"And there's a *problem* with that?" I might have said that with narrowed eyes and a hint of hypersensitivity, having been told on more than one occasion, by people who thought they were being helpful or informative, that I "talked funny."

"I hope you know that I don't think so."

I nodded.

"And it was kind of you to snarl on his behalf."

"Thank you."

"But again, you have to consider the source. To Shirley and Mercy, and others of the Spivey ilk, Al's still 'not from around here,' as silly as that is. There are also some who've never forgiven him for being a big, muscular kid who excelled at football for the two years he played on the high school team."

"That sounds illogical, even by Spivey standards."

"Doesn't it? But he had the bad grace to break a long-standing record. Two, really. Rushing touchdowns in a single game, and then rushing touchdowns in a season. And he didn't just break the records—he tore them to shreds, mopped the field with them, and tied the rags to the goalposts. If a local boy had done that, it would've been a different story and hailed for all time. But Al was bigger than the other boys, and a better player, and he hadn't paid his local-boy dues."

"You mean he hadn't been playing here for years? That was hardly his fault if they'd just moved here."

"Of course it wasn't his fault. And I don't want you to get the wrong idea; not everyone felt that way. But it wasn't just Al, who really was, and is, a nice guy. It was his father. He came down here, big man from the big city, with a management job at the paper mill, and arrived with all the worn-out myths about benighted, impoverished, uneducated southern Appalachia firmly in place. And he thought he could lend a hand up."

"Lord Bountiful?"

"With his lady. I'm sure they meant well. They were joiners and they wanted to be movers and shakers. That's what I remember hearing, anyway."

"People like to talk as if they know all about someone, and if they don't know it, they'll make it up. Granny used to say that."

"Ivy was another pistol," Joe said.

I'd never thought of Granny quite like that, but as soon as he'd said it, I knew she would have liked the label. At some point after I'd gotten busy with my preservation career at the museum in Illinois, and didn't make it back to see Granny as often, she and Joe had become good friends. It had turned out that there was a lot of Granny's life I hadn't known about. That was only natural, I knew. But sometimes I wished I could have been a fly on the wall—or like Geneva, a ghost on the ceiling fan—and watched Granny and Joe and listened to what they talked about.

"I wonder if Al's mother was a knitter. I wonder if Granny knew her."

"No idea if she was into any kind of needlework," Joe said. "They joined every organization they could. Happy to help, happy to donate money when asked. But it wouldn't have mattered if Al's father had come down here and given folks the honest-to-God and verifiable secret to spinning straw into gold. An awful lot of them wouldn't have listened. Some would've listened, but after they'd spun their fortunes, they still wouldn't have liked Mr. Rogalla." Joe ticked off a string of unflattering adjectives off on his fingers. "I heard every one of those applied to that family."

"Al's still here, though."

"Yeah, because he *was* that big, muscular kid, and he had an incredibly thick hide. His folks and younger sister moved on. Al never had his folks' attitude. He probably could have gone anywhere he wanted after college, but he liked it here. After graduation he came back and made a place for himself."

"But some memories never let go?"

"W-e-e-e-e-e-l-l, there's still the matter of the long-standing records he rushed right into the ground."

"Oh, come on."

"People like their grudges. There but for Al Rogalla stood a record they or their boys might have knocked down. And no one's busted that record since."

"Wait a second. Now I know where I heard that name. Your brother. Yesterday morning. He asked if I'd been talking to Hugh McPhee at the courthouse. I told him I didn't know, and he said he'd find out—before Rogalla found out. What kind of rivalry have they got going?"

"Pfft. There's always been something between the firefighters and the deputies. That tug-of-war they have across the creek every summer? No playacting involved."

"You're not serious."

"And Cole?" Joe said. "Captain of the varsity team junior and senior year. Starting quarterback both years. Had his eye—they all had their eyes—on breaking Hugh McPhee's record. And Cole got it into his head that but for Al from Chicago, he would have been hailed the next Hugh McPhee."

"That's so . . . wait. It was Hugh McPhee's record? You might have mentioned that sooner."

"Didn't I? But what difference does it make? How could that record have anything to do with Hugh's death? Hugh was the hero and Al was the villain. Years ago. But he was the villain for killing the record. Why would he kill the hero, too? Especially at this late date?"

"You said there were long memories," I reminded him.

"But long, lethal memories? And why kill Hugh? Rogalla's the one who broke the record and destroyed the myth of invincible Hugh McPhee."

"Yeah, I guess if the long memories came into play, either Cole or Rogalla would snap and one of them would kill the other."

"It wouldn't happen, though," Joe said. "Al's never had anything against Cole, personally, and by now Cole's gotten so used to hating Al that if he stopped to think about it, he'd realize they're friends. What? You don't believe that?"

"I'll have to see them out for a beer together before I believe it."

"It could be true, though. It makes a nice story, anyway."

"You only think that because you're a booth-half-built kind of guy. Cole's more of a single-minded mule playing tug-of-war."

That reminded him that he had to get back to assembling his booth, and I wanted to call Ardis again.

"Why don't you call her now?" Joe asked.

But I wanted to wait until I was home, surrounded by Granny's things, her comfortable memories, in case there was any reason to fall apart. Not that I was really worried Ardis had been arrested. Or detained for hours. Not really. But where was she? So I told Joe I didn't want to distract him from his work, and he wiggled his eyebrows in a distracting way, so that it took a few minutes to say good-bye. Then I drove home, hoping to find no one there.

All appeared to be well as I rolled cautiously down Lavender Street. No cars lurked at the curb under the maple in front of the house. None waited for me down the driveway when I turned in. The house looked quiet. It sounded quiet, too, when I stopped outside the back door before going in. A stale whiff of Mercy's cologne brushed past my nose when I opened the door, but it dissipated when I fanned the door a time or two. I went into the living room and sat in one of the faded blue comfy chairs, letting my head rest in the hollow Granny's had made and left for me. Except for my nerves, all was peaceful. I called Ardis, and she finally answered on the eighth ring.

"Don't you check your messages?" she asked. "I sent you a text a couple of hours ago."

"It never showed up."

"I wonder who I sent it to. It's this new phone. Well, never mind. All is well and I'll see you tomorrow."

"Wait! Did you learn anything from Darla? About the paper? The book? The sporran? How he died? Anything?"

"Darla was being cagey," she, the Queen of Cage, said.

"So nothing?"

"Well, now, I wouldn't say it was nothing. I'll tell you all about it tomorrow. Good night, hon."

"Wait! Ardis?"

"*Daddy,*" she shouted, though not directly into the phone, "I'll be there in two shakes. Keep your shirt on. That was not an idiom, Kath," she said, speaking to me again. "He's been stripping off and prancing around all evening and here he goes again. All I can say is thank goodness he sleeps through the night and God bless the in-home day care ladies who let me out of this nuthouse during daylight hours. I'll talk to you tomorrow."

I dreamed that night that I was juggling bombs. Bombs that fell whistling toward my hands, and the whistle turned into the wheeze of bagpipes. I was a good juggler until I got cocky. Then I dropped one of the bombs. But it vaporized before it hit the ground, and became a misty, gray ghost. That startled me and I missed the next one. As I watched it fall to the floor, it turned into a pair of pants, and when I looked up, Ardis' daddy pranced by.

"If I were able to make a pot of coffee for you, I would," Geneva said when I let myself in the back door of the Cat the next morning. "Your disguise does not help."

"Good morning to you, too. What are you talking about?"

"Slender black skirt, snug-as-a-bug emerald green sweater with the *plunging* neckline."

"It's called a V-neck, and in this case it isn't much more than a lowercase *v*."

"But meant to attract and distract. Do you see how

well I am noticing? You dressed up because you are feeling down."

"Close. Tired, though, not down. I didn't sleep very well last night."

"The distraction isn't working. Have you looked at your eyes in the mirror? I am sorry, but I believe that even I look livelier than you do this morning. Perhaps I should keep Ardent company in the shop this morning so you can take a nap in the window seat upstairs with Argyle. He has not come down yet, because neither of us expected you this early."

"Ardis would be happy to see you in the shop."

"She's happy and yappy and you look crappy." She slapped her hands to her mouth, then took them away. "Have you noticed that I am helpless in the face of a snappy rhyme? But really, *do* think about taking a nap. You might be surprised how improving they can be."

"I'll be fine."

"Argyle and I slept quite well in the absence of midnight bagpipes. What was your problem? A guilty conscience?"

"A bad dream. It had a bagpipe in it, though. Why would I have a guilty conscience?"

"Because," she said, floating closer and whispering, "you're sneaking in here to talk to me before Ardent shows up. Keeping things from your business partner could easily lead to a guilty conscience. And bags under the eyes."

"I do want to talk to you, but this is something that Ardis knows about. It's not a secret from her; it's a secret from almost everyone else in town."

"So you and I are having a hush-hush rendezvous?"

"A hush-hush rendezvous *about* a hush-hush rendezvous. It's about something a group of us is getting together to do, later tonight, and I wondered if you'd like to come along. The whole thing's been top secret. That's why you haven't heard us talking about it."

She leaned close. "*Top* secret?"

"Yes. It's called a yarn bombing."

She mouthed the word "bomb" and a shiver ran through her. I wouldn't have thought it possible, but her hollow eyes grew wider. "Tell me all about it," she said. "Spare no details."

I spared most of the details because I figured either they didn't matter or they'd bore her. Although maybe I didn't spare enough of them. When I got to the part about everyone coming back to the Cat afterward, for refreshments, she drew back.

"I don't get it," she said. "How does this tie in with our investigation?"

"It doesn't. It's more like an art project."

"Then I am getting it even less. How is it that you have time for frivolity and yarn spewing when there is a murderer on the loose?"

"Sometimes what looks like fun and games, or what begins that way, turns out to yield the best clues. It's a strategy of blending in and observing. You're good at both of those, you know."

"Yes, I do know. They are two of my strengths."

"The yarn bombing is something we've been planning and looking forward to. We think it'll add extra zest to the town and the arts and crafts fair this weekend."

"And nothing says 'zest' like yarn and bombs?"

"Something like that. Besides, when we've worked on cases in the past, we haven't spent every second investigating. The rest of life goes on."

"Easy for you to say."

"Sorry. That was insensitive."

"I forgive you. But I do see what you mean. Death goes on, too. And on and on. Do you know what has occurred to me? You and I are always in a life-and-death situation. We are the yin and yang of existence." She wafted back and forth—miming yin and yang with her arms, first one on top, then the other—in a watery, ghostly ballet.

"Did you believe in ghosts when you were alive?"

She froze, left arm cradling her imaginary yin-yang orb, her right arm curved over its top. I froze, too. The question I'd asked was the kind that had so often made her howl, in the past, or sent her into a huddle of gray mist. She'd mellowed over the months we'd known each other, though. Mellowed somewhat. I held my breath.

"Death was not such a stranger to us then, as it is to people now," she said. "Although you and I seem to attract more than our share."

"Deputy Dunbar would agree with you on that. But did you believe in ghosts?" I hesitated. "Did you see them?"

She stared at me and swayed. I thought I might have pressed my luck. She didn't swell or look thunderous, though. "Have you ever seen a wreath made from human hair?" she asked. "Mourners weave them from the hair of deceased loved ones."

"We had a few of them in the museum's collections back in Illinois. People don't make them anymore."

"I'm glad." She wrapped her arms around herself. "Someone put one in my hands when I was a child. It didn't feel like hair."

"The ones I saw were fairly intricate. From the way they were braided and woven, I can imagine they wouldn't feel much like hair anymore. Not like the hair on someone's head."

"The wreath felt cold in my hands." She held her hands out as though they carried a great and sorrowful weight. "The cold sucked at me like a breath. The wreath felt like death in my hands, and I dropped it." She rubbed her upper arms to warm herself, or to scrub the memory of that feeling from her hands. "I dropped it, because in my hands it was no longer a wreath. It was a ghost. Do you know what I mean?"

I didn't say anything. I didn't know *what* to say.

"You do know what I mean," she said, "because you see ghosts and you feel them the same way I did. That's what is happening when you touch people. You feel something, don't you?"

"Not always. Sometimes." She was talking about that other weird "talent" I'd developed after Granny died— the ability to "feel" a person's emotions by touching a piece of clothing. Love, hate, confusion, fear. But not always, thank goodness, and not when I touched a person I'd come to know, trust, and love. "Only sometimes," I said. "And not everyone."

She was suddenly directly in front of me, her eyes pulling mine in. "You do feel ghosts, though, and when you do, they come like a jolt out of the blue."

"No. Not ghosts."

"Not like me, but ghosts all the same. Ghosts of feelings. Ghosts of emotional energy. And that feeling—that connection—gives you the willies."

She was giving me the willies.

"Don't turn away," she said.

I couldn't. She was right. Or her words for the weird sensation were as good as any—ghosts of feelings. "When you felt the wreath, you felt—"

"The agony of a woman dying in childbirth."

"And was that the only time you felt emotional energy?"

"No."

"What did you do?"

"As you said, it was only sometimes."

"But what did you do? How did you deal with it? You're right; it comes like a jolt. How did you handle it?"

"I do not remember that I did. Although a child will learn not to touch a hot stove."

We hadn't moved from the kitchen. I could hear someone coming up the back steps, probably Ardis, but I didn't turn to see.

"Geneva, quick, why do I see you? Why do I feel whatever that energy is? Why did you? Do you know? Now that you're dead, have you found out why?"

She stopped midshrug as Ardis put her key in the lock. "I've told you before. I'm only dead; I'm not an expert. But if your granny was still here, and if you could ask her, what do you think she would say?"

The back door said, "Baa," Geneva echoed it and disappeared, and Ardis blustered in, already talking.

"I might as well admit it front, right, and center," she said. "I know, I know. This isn't how we planned to do it. But *you* know how carried away I get, especially when emotions are running high, so let me just confess and get it over with." She stopped for a wide-eyed breath, then rushed on. "It's out of the bag and it won't go back in."

"And, um, I think I might still be outside this conversation trying to get in."

"Really? I thought for sure you were getting suspicious when you finally got hold of me last night."

"Mm, no. There were several layers of worry going on, with a heavy infusion of angst about your interview with Darla, but no suspicion. I'm suspicious *now*, though." I tried a Geneva maneuver and took a step closer.

"Oh." She glanced at the door, as though there might be time to slide back out of it and come in again, minus the confession. But that wasn't like Ardis. She turned back to me, squared her shoulders, and pasted a large repertory theater smile on her face. "I told Deputy Darla about the yarn bombing and guess what. She's decided to join us."

Chapter 15

"It's a bit of a bombshell, isn't it, hon." Ardis might as well have said *there, there* and patted my cheek. She didn't pat; she fixed her repertory theater smile back in place and brought her hands together in a single loud clap. "And here we are. B-day at last. That's catchy, don't you think? B for *bombshell*. B for yarn *bombing*. B for *Blue* Plum. B for I am *beyond* excited. Let's go with what we've got. No, let's *run* with what we've got—and *who* we've got—and see what happens."

I hadn't really moved past suspicion yet, so I almost certainly didn't look as excited about a sheriff's deputy joining us as Ardis hoped. Not that I had anything against Darla, but we'd discussed and agreed not to . . .

"Ardis, why—"

"Why don't I go open shop for the day? That's what I was about to say myself. I'm glad we're on the same wavelength." With that, she turned tail and very nearly ran for the front room.

Speaking of tails, Argyle trotted down the stairs from the attic with his tail held high and a trill on his lips. He twined around my ankles to let me know he was happy to see me and would also be happy to have breakfast.

"And how happy would you be," I asked him as I tipped his favorite fishy kibbles into his dish, "to have a sheriff's deputy joining you while you're covering the town in graffiti?"

Argyle said, "Mrrph," which was noncommittal but sounded calm and practical. I hung around in the kitchen while he ate, waiting to see if Geneva would reappear, and practicing a calm and practical acceptance of our evolving bomb squad.

"The more the merrier, right, Argyle? Although, after hearing John describe Ambrose as 'mean as snakes' more than a few times, I think we have to wonder if anyone will end up being merry with him along. And how many more surprises do you think we'll have before we're finished tonight?"

He asked for a few more kibbles.

"Sure, why not? Here's a better question. How many more surprises do you think we can stand?"

He finished breakfast without offering any further advice, and I followed his calm, practical tail down the hall to join Ardis in the front room. She and a customer, whose back was to us, were standing next to the mannequin, chatting as though the three of them were old friends. The *four* of them. The air above the mannequin's left shoulder rippled and—surprise, surprise—Geneva appeared.

Ardis, bless her self-control, acknowledged Geneva with a barely perceptible nod. When she saw me, she used some of her pent-up enthusiasm to wave me over.

Argyle naturally assumed he was welcome, too, and leapt onto the counter, inviting everyone within reach to scrub him between the ears. The customer declined his pretty invitation and took a step back.

When she did, I saw her face and recognized her as the woman who'd called me Kathy at the courthouse Tuesday morning. Calling me Kathy was an easy and common mistake. Joe and Clod Dunbar's parents had graced them with star-studded literary names, but my mother had been frugal with many things, including names. I'd only ever had the names Kath and Rutledge, with no other syllables tacked on or taking up space between them.

"Hello again," the woman said, twiddling her fingers at me. She looked to be somewhere in her sixties, but the twiddled fingers didn't seem to match her particular style of being sixty. Hers were the kind of sixties it took a fair amount of time and money to maintain, with hair that was coifed and colored, not merely cut and blown dry. It had more of the poodle look to it than might be currently fashionable, but she had the legs of a woman with the self-discipline to regularly run or dance—and the guts to wear leggings and ankle boots. A dark gray lightweight cowl sweater (angora?) hit her at mid–muscular thigh. "I told you I'd be in later this week, Katie," she said to me, "and here I am."

"*Kath,*" Ardis said, "do you know Olive Weems? Olive is Mayor Weems' wife. You've met Pokey a time or two, I'm sure."

A prick of irritation, no bigger than a gnat's whisker, came and went on Olive's face. At her husband's nickname? At receiving second billing as Mrs. Mayor? She must be used to both, but I got the feeling Ardis played them broadly on purpose.

"I hear you're in charge of Handmade Blue Plum," I said. "That must be a huge undertaking."

Olive nodded her appreciation of the recognition. "A labor of love," she said, one hand on her heart, "and I wouldn't have it any other way. I hope you'll stop by the fair, *Kath*." She smiled at getting my name right. "I know it's a busy weekend for merchants, too, not just the craftspeople and visitors coming in for the fair. That's why I take the time and make the effort to come around and personally invite all of you. This weekend is always a fun time for Blue Plum."

"Is Pokey opening the fair this year?" Ardis asked. Without waiting for Olive to answer, she turned to me and asked, "Have you ever seen Pokey attacking a ribbon with his giant pair of scissors?"

Geneva, sitting on the mannequin's shoulder, appeared to be nodding off. But when Ardis mentioned the giant scissors, her eyes popped open wide.

Olive didn't wait to hear if I had or hadn't seen Pokey wield his scissors. "As long as I'm here," she said, "I might as well take a look around and see if there isn't some little thing I can't live without." She twiddled her fingers again and went around the corner into the other room.

Ardis maintained the full wattage of her repertory theater smile until Olive was out of sight, then gave her face a rest.

"When I came in and saw you two together, I thought you were good friends," I said, keeping my voice low.

"Friendly enough. But she isn't a CC." She glanced at

me. "Sorry. CC is shorthand Ivy and I used for people like—" She nodded in the direction Olive had gone. "CC stands for constant customer, something she most definitely is not. Her visit here today is exactly what she said it is."

"An invitation to see giant scissors," Geneva said. "It was friendly."

"No," Ardis said. "She wasn't doing anything more than drumming up business for the fair. I'll give you this— she always makes a point of buying 'some little thing' she can't live without when she comes to issue her Handmade Blue Plum invitation. She also makes a point of shopping locally during mayoral campaign seasons. But otherwise she does most of her shopping online or in Asheville and Knoxville. That's where she goes for her angora and mohair and silk blends, too."

"She knitted the cowl she's wearing?" I asked.

"If she didn't, she could have. She's that good."

"Excuse me." Geneva raised her hand.

Ardis raised her eyebrows, clearly wondering about the change in Geneva's behavior. I wondered, too.

"Is there something wrong, Geneva?"

"Is there ever anything wrong with good manners?" she asked. "I thought I should point out that Olive can still be called a CC. If she shops locally during campaigns, then she is a campaign customer, and that, also, is a CC."

"No," Ardis said. "That just means her status can be described as OOPS—only occasional paltry sales."

"I guess something *is* wrong, then," Geneva muttered. "Me." She started to billow, glanced at me, and stopped. She muttered something else, then drooped over to the counter and sat next to Argyle. He'd stretched out to take up as much acreage as possible on the counter, and greeted her with a lift of his chin and another luxurious stretch.

Olive didn't take long to find what she couldn't live without. Although why she couldn't live without a hank of orange cotton embroidery floss was beyond me. She stopped short of the counter.

"Oops," Ardis said.

"I should think you'd say that a lot with a cat in a wool shop," Olive said with a laugh. "It's a twist on the bull in a china shop, isn't it? And you'll never believe it, but this orange is the exact color I was looking for to finish a bib for the first grandbaby. It's 'Go, Vols' all the way with his daddy."

"Isn't that nice?" Ardis said. She took the floss from Olive and made a production of ringing it up and putting it in a bag.

"And I guess I am wrong again," Geneva said with a heave of her shoulders.

I wasn't sure I wanted to know what she thought she was wrong about, but figured it was better—and possibly safer—to find out. I moved closer to her so she couldn't miss my sign language, and so we'd be less distracting to Ardis; then I tilted my head and touched my right ear.

"You are not much of a detective, if you need to ask," she said. "It is as plain as the nose on your face, and as plain as the small pimple on your nose that I was not going to mention because I thought minding my manners was the *right* thing to do."

I touched my ear again, but she turned her back on

me. When I turned back to Ardis and Olive, it was obvious I'd missed something.

"I'm not sure what it will be, or when," Olive said, "but I'll let you know when I find out."

"I'd appreciate it, Olive. Thank you." Ardis handed her the small bag with the hank of floss. "You haven't heard anything about how he died, have you?"

"It's a terrible thing to have happened," Olive said. "I hadn't heard from him in years, but it's still so completely shocking. If Palmer has heard anything about the case, he hasn't shared it with me. What was Hugh thinking, though, playing those things at that time of night? Especially after he'd been asked to stop playing them that afternoon, when some people might have actually enjoyed them. He never did consider other people, though."

"Who asked him to stop that afternoon?" Ardis asked.

"Lonnie, the poor man. He looked like that noise gave him one heck of a migraine. Or like he'd seen a ghost."

It was an expression, of course, but it startled the two of us who were aware of the ghost on the counter not two feet from Olive's elbow. It startled the ghost, too. Geneva, Ardis, and I looked at each other out of the corners of our eyes. Rather awkwardly, I thought. The obvious question for me was, who was Lonnie? But Geneva asked hers first.

"Why did she say that?" she whispered.

"Why did you say that?" Ardis repeated, not sounding entirely natural. "About seeing a ghost?"

"Well, you know," Olive said. "Because no one had

heard from Hugh or seen him for so long. I suppose that was it."

"Because no had seen him for so long? No," Geneva said, shaking her head, "that was not it."

Ardis, still listening to Geneva, nodded. "I think you're right."

"You do?" Geneva said. "Will wonders never cease?"

"Yes," said Olive, "the shock of seeing him after so many years—I'm sure I'm right."

"Um, Olive?" I thought I'd better get her attention and give Ardis a few seconds to refocus on the here and alive. "Someone said Hugh was here for Handmade Blue Plum. Do you know if that's true?"

"That's what I was telling Ardis. Some of the crafts-people knew him. Maybe way back when? I really don't know. They heard about his death, though, and they've asked if they can do something by way of a memorial for him at some point this weekend. I won't forget, Ardis. I'll give you a call as soon as I know anything."

"Thanks."

"Who's Lonnie?" I asked after Olive left.

"A sensitive creature," Geneva said.

"He's about as sensitive as Olive's bull in a china shop," Ardis said. "He'd rattle the shop, but nothing rattles him. There's no way that just seeing someone, Hugh McPhee or anyone else, after umpteen years would make him look like he'd seen a ghost."

"But who is he?" I asked.

"You and most people know him as Sheriff Haynes. And some call him Leonard. But only a select few call him Lonnie."

"Olive is one of the few?"

"She's proud to think so. At a distance," Ardis said. "But to his face? I'm not so sure. Even though she is Mrs. Pokey Weems."

"Maybe she does it because she *is* Mrs. Pokey Weems. Compared to 'Pokey,' what's wrong with 'Lonnie'?"

"Perhaps nothing is wrong with poor Lonnie," Geneva said. "Even if he is as strong as a bull, you are forgetting about the ghost. Seeing one can be quite disturbing."

"She meant wrong with the name, not with him," Ardis said. "Better make a note of that, though, Kath. I don't know how we'll follow up on it, but we need to find out why he had that reaction when he saw Hugh."

"Maybe it really was a migraine." I added *migraine* to the note. "Or Olive's imagination?"

"Or the kind of exaggerated memory that sets in after a sudden death?" Ardis said.

"Or it was the ghost," Geneva said, enunciating each word.

"No, really, that's unlikely," Ardis said. *"Oh."*

"What?" I looked up from writing.

"She stuck her tongue out at me and disappeared."

"If she is so sure that seeing ghosts is unlikely," Geneva said when I found her stewing in the study window seat, "then I want you to take that green braided bracelet you made away from her. She does not deserve to see any ghost at all."

"Sticking your tongue out was childish."

"She does not deserve good manners, either. She was being rude to the mayor's wife. I *thought* I was being friendly and helpful."

"So did I. So did Ardis."

"She told me I was wrong every time I turned around."

"She didn't mean to hurt your feelings."

"I *did* mean to hurt hers. She made me feel like a scolded child."

"Will it help if I ask her to apologize?"

"It will help if I am allowed to enjoy my death in peace and quiet."

Running investigations on the QT out of a profitable yarn shop wasn't easy. The profits *would* keep walking through the door—as they should. As gratifying as the brisk business was that morning, it kept me from cornering Ardis and making her tell me what she'd learned during her interview with Darla. She took every opportunity to personally guide customers to their destinations, thus keeping out of my clutches. Shortly after noon, she said she'd run to Mel's and pick up a couple of salads.

"I'm having a hard time keeping a lid on my B-day excitement," she said, speaking behind her hand so the customers browsing the display table didn't hear. "The fresh air will do me good. Might knock the edge off."

"Do you mind if I go instead?"

She stooped, peering into my face. "Are you all right? Here I am, all hyped up, and I just realized that you've been awfully quiet. Problems with Her Highness upstairs?"

"No." That came out more sharply than I'd meant and I tried to soften it. Hard to do after the fact, though. "I might be more keyed up than you think. Sorry, Ardis. I didn't mean to sound snappish. You can go if you need to get out."

"You go on, hon. I'll expend my extra energy flinging a dust rag around."

"Thanks."

I went out the back door, the baa sounding troubled and melancholy to my ears. That sound and kicking a stone down the service alley toward Mel's back door suited my mood. I didn't know what I was going to do about my two mismatched, peas-in-a-pod friends. What if they couldn't learn to get along? Geneva's interpersonal skills had improved over the months we'd known each other, but they were still rusty from more than a century spent in the limbo of haunting a house where no one knew she existed. And that put the burden of compromise on Ardis. Strong, stable, sure-of-herself Ardis—who didn't seem to be getting it right.

I waited in line at Mel's counter wondering if there was such a thing as a family therapist who specialized in normal and paranormal families, and if so, where I'd find one.

"Order, please," Mel said when it was my turn at the counter. "I'd engage you in pleasant banter, Red, but Ardis called ahead to warn me that you're feeling contemplative." She pointed at the man behind me in line. "You don't mind stepping back, do you?" she asked him. "We're having a private moment here." She made shooing motions at him, then crooked a finger at me. "Ardis hopes you're working out an intricate part of the case," she said almost under her breath. "But she's worried that what's really going on is that you and Joe are having problems."

"What? Why?"

"She hasn't seen you two together much lately. She thought it might be preying on your mind."

"He's busy with Handmade Blue Plum. You had time for this conversation with her during the lunch rush?"

"She talked fast."

"She could've talked to me."

"She wanted an impartial opinion. I told her not to worry, that you two are fine, and that if there were problems, I'd probably know about them before you did. But going with her first thought, that you're in a detecting haze, she ordered lunch so you wouldn't have to waste brainpower wondering what to get. Roasted beet and radish salads à l'orange and a couple of lemonades are waiting at the pickup window."

I handed her my credit card.

"Sorry I can't join the fun tonight," she said.

"We are, too, but we'll tell you all about it in the morning."

"You'll find something extra in your bag you're going like. Now move along and quit holding up the line."

"Thanks, Mel."

I picked up the bag with the salads and something extra, visions of another new menu experiment dancing in my head. I didn't look to see what it was, deciding to let Ardis have the pleasure of discovery. Mel would have made a good bartender, I thought. What kind of commonsense advice would she apply to my paranormal friend and family situation? Could I discuss it with her, using the clichéd "friend with a problem" ploy? Would the identity of the friend surprise her?

I pushed through Mel's back door, juggling the bag

and the caddy holding the lemonade, feeling more hopeful. Not looking for Spiveys lying in wait.

"There you are," said the unscented Spivey to my left when the door snapped shut behind me.

"Oops," the scented one said. "And there goes your lemonade down the steps."

Chapter 16

"We thought we'd give you an update," Mercy said. "It's a good thing the lemonade missed your shoes and tights," Shirley said. "You might want to let Mel know it's there, though, or people will be tracking it into the café all afternoon."

I might want to vault over the lemonade—or their heads—and run down the alley to get away from them. "What update?"

"On the McPhee-Rogalla rendezvous."

"On Tuesday afternoon."

"We know where they went."

"Who they saw."

"You look like a metronome," Shirley said. "Does this help?" They'd been standing on opposite sides of Mel's back landing. She moved over next to Mercy, giving me a single focal point. It did help.

"Where and who?" I asked.

"The courthouse," Shirley said. "The Register of Deeds."

"And then the bank," said Mercy. "Rachel Meeks."

That was so interesting that I looked the twins in their eyes and thanked them—sincerely. Their surprise at my sincerity said something about the usual tone of our interactions. Their surprise wasn't quite enough to make me feel bad about that usual tone, because I was still suspicious of their motives. But when they shooed me along, saying they would tell Mel about the lemonade, I thanked them again, avoided the worst of the spill, and headed back to the Cat.

"Don't worry about the lemonade," Ardis said. "I'll make tea. There's nothing wrong with tap water, either, although with the twins on the loose, something stronger wouldn't go amiss."

"Amen."

"Ivy used to keep a bottle in the office."

"Granny?"

"For after hours only."

I glanced toward the office. "Bottle of what? I haven't found anything like that in there."

"The last was a bottle of dry sherry. We finished it one memorable night last spring. She didn't get around to replacing it before she passed, and I didn't have the heart to."

"Maybe we should replace it now."

"Not a bad idea."

"Ardis, what do you know about Al Rogalla?" I hadn't told her about Shirley and Mercy's visit the night before, or about the update they'd sprung on me at Mel's back door. Ardis' feelings for the twins were visceral, and I wanted to hear her views on Al unfiltered through her Spivey senses.

"I'm not sure I've ever trusted him," she said.

"Why not?"

She screwed her mouth sideways to give the question serious thought. "I don't suppose I have a good reason. He's a volunteer fireman, and that speaks well for him. He's an accountant. There's nothing intrinsically wrong with that."

"Joe says he's a nice guy."

"Well, Joe is Joe, and that doesn't make him the best judge of character, does it." She said that with the kind of offhand chuckle that suggested this shouldn't be news to me.

"But you like Joe." Her statement *was* news to me. Except for the first time we'd met—when I'd caught him in a house he had no business being in—I hadn't seen or heard anything that would lead me to think he or his judgment couldn't be trusted. Nothing concrete. Nothing specific. But this "old news" played into some of my questions about him that I'd found it easier to bury since we got together. "You like Joe and you trust *him*, right?"

"In every way that matters." She said that without hesitation, with sure conviction.

"But not Rogalla."

"I feel like we're overthinking this," Ardis said. "Allegiances aren't always rational. Humans are funny that way, as I know you've noticed. It might be something nebulous that comes down to familiarity and comfort level. But why do we care about Al Rogalla? He knows how to put out a fire and he doesn't do our taxes. Two pluses in my admittedly irrational human worldview. And that leaves you still holding the bag." She pointed at the lunch bag.

"Do you want me to tell you why we care about him before or after lunch?"

She sighed and dropped onto the stool behind the counter.

"I'll be quick. First, Cole mentioned Al Rogalla Tuesday morning. Like he has a competition going with him. That makes Al interesting right off the bat. Second, the twins told me they saw Hugh and Al together Tuesday afternoon."

"Busybody snoops."

"Hold on. Believe it or not, you and they are on the same wavelength where Al Rogalla is concerned. If you'd told me that you like and trust him as unequivocally as you told me you like and trust Joe, I'd take their information with more than a grain of salt."

"I think we'll still take it with a grain of salt."

I nodded. "My thinking, too. But they say they found out that Hugh and Al went to the Register of Deeds together, and then to meet with Rachel Meeks."

I handed her the lunch bag. "Here, you eat first."

"And I'll chew over that bit of news while I do."

The phone rang while I was ringing up a substantial purchase of the kumihimo silk cord. I apologized to the customer and picked up. It was Thea.

"I'm with another customer. Do you mind if I call you back?"

"I'm not a customer. I'm reporting case information."

"Text it?"

"You know I won't. Story time starts in five minutes. This won't take thirty seconds."

I apologized to the customer again. She was the best

kind of patron; she took the delay as an opportunity to resume shopping.

"Hugh McPhee played his pipes at a funeral for Walter Jeffries in Knoxville on Monday."

"Do we know who he was?"

"No. I'll find out what I can after story time. We're doing *Extra Yarn* by Mac Barnett today. The kids get to decorate boxes and take them home with a ball of yarn. See you tonight."

Ardis' eyes were red when she came back out front after eating.

"It's the downtimes that are hard," she said. "I find it very easy to make myself cry. Maybe I shouldn't eat lunch for a while."

"Or not alone. Geneva used to cry a lot when we first met."

"And that breaks my heart, too. All that time, all those years and years she spent alone. She must have been a very strong person to have held her wits together through all that."

"She still is a person, Ardis. Just extremely differently abled. Did you know that she used to draw?"

"Speaking of which." She handed me a piece of lined notebook paper folded in quarters. "This was in the bag with the salads."

"Just the salads? Mel said she put in something extra."

"That must be it." She mimed flipping the paper over, where Mel had written *Dish. I think you'll like it.*

"Have you looked at it?" I asked as I unfolded it.

"I thought I'd read over your shoulder."

I unfolded the paper, revealing a couple of paragraphs

in rounded cursive, followed by a small stick figure. But no sooner had I smoothed the paper on the counter between us than the camel bells at the door jingled. I refolded the paper and handed it back to Ardis. And in walked a man Ardis was beginning to warm up to, but not much.

"I'll go on upstairs and do that straightening I didn't tell you about that I really must do immediately," she said. "Call me if you need me. Or send smoke signals."

Her comment wasn't the politically incorrect remark it sounded like. And if Ardis hadn't been warming up to Aaron Carlin, she would have made the crack about smoke signals loud enough for him to hear. She didn't, though, and he stepped inside with a wave and his sweet smile in place. Aaron was the handyman whose pickup truck I'd thought of when Ernestine told us she'd heard a vehicle backfire late Tuesday night. His truck was leprous, and backfiring might be its least toxic trait. Ardis was of the opinion that Carlins in general were toxic. They were known as the Smoky Smokin' Carlins, because they had the bad habit of starting fires in the national forest down around Newport where they lived. More than a few of them had spent time as guests of the federal government. Aaron himself had stood trial on arson charges, but had been acquitted. That was before he and Mercy's daughter, Angie, got together. I didn't know Aaron well. Joe trusted him, though ... dang.

"How's it going, Aaron? Haven't seen you for a while."

"Fine," he said, rocking a time or two on his heels. "Yeah, yeah, fine."

"And Angie?"

"Oh yeah. She's, you know, fine." He stuck his hands in his pockets.

Aaron never did have much to say, and that generally seemed to suit him. But that afternoon he didn't sound or look as copacetic as I'd come to expect. In fact, he looked as though he might develop a twitch any minute. By the way he kept turning around and looking over his shoulder, I might have thought his unease came from being surrounded by so much yarn. But a fear of fiber seemed unlikely for a man who wasn't afraid to tickle a rattlesnake under the chin—and I had firsthand knowledge of his delight in doing that.

He sidled over to the front window, possibly to admire the kumihimo loom. But he stopped short of the window, and seeing him slowly and carefully peer around the edge to scan what he could see of the porch jogged a memory. I'd seen a few others behave like that. It was taking a chance, but I decided to test a two-word theory.

I took a deep breath and enunciated clearly, "Spivey twins." And I was immediately sorry.

I took him into the small office behind the desk and made him sit with his head between his knees. He wasn't quite hyperventilating, but it took a good five minutes to calm the poor guy down. He told me that, yes, Angie was fine, Angie was more than fine (which, by the way he said it, sounded like too much information to me), but her mother and aunt—the Spivey twins—were more than he had bargained for.

"Did you know that neither one of them has been a Spivey for decades?" he asked. "One of them, and I don't even know which one it is, has been married two times, and that makes her twice removed from the blighted name, and they still call themselves the Spivey twins, and so does everyone else. *And*," he said, dropping his voice to a whisper, "I can smell them before I see them." He took a few tentative sniffs and shuddered.

I commiserated and told him I wished I had Granny's bottle of dry sherry to offer him.

He shuddered again. "I gave up drink after I met the twins. Can I tell you why I came? Then I'd like to leave out the back door if you don't mind."

"I'll check it before you do. Trust me, it's a good idea."

"I believe you, and boy howdy, I'd appreciate it. I have a, uh, a person I do business with from time to time. Sort of a . . ."

"A client?"

"Yes, ma'am. Client is what we'll call it. This client—I'm not saying he or she because the client doesn't want anyone to know who—durn. I almost said it."

"Your client wants to remain anonymous?"

"Bingo."

"We could agree to use 'he' to make it easier."

"Okeydoke. That'll work. He says he was in the park the other night when that feller got killed."

"Whoa."

"Yep. That's about what I said."

"Did he see—"

"Maybe. Maybe not."

"Why are you telling me this?" That and a few dozen other questions flew through my head. Some that it might be better not to ask.

"My client told me to tell you he might or might not have useful information."

"But—"

"He can't go to the police."

"Okay." Why he couldn't was probably one of the questions I shouldn't ask.

"I got him to agree to talk to you," Aaron said.

"May I ask why you or your client think I can help?"

"No need to, is there?"

"Huh. So, how does your client want to do this? Do we pick an out-of-the-way place or some kind of neutral location—"

"Tomorrow morning's good. And here's good, too. My client's been in here and liked it. I told her I'd bring her and stay to lend moral support."

I could see a load lift from Aaron when I agreed to meet. So much so that he'd relaxed and slipped—he and his female client would be at the Weaver's Cat around midmorning. He'd told *her* he'd bring *her* and stay to lend moral support. Angie Spivey?

Ardis laughed when I filled her in. She thought the idea of a Carlin lending moral support to anyone was hilarious. Geneva, maybe attracted by the laughter, floated into the room and huddled on a shelf near the ceiling between a box of rarely used display stands and another of never-used tablecloths. If she'd noticed the labels, she might have chosen that space because it made a statement and suited her mopish mood. Or she might have chosen it because I could see her but from where Ardis stood, she couldn't.

"It *could* be Angie," Ardis said, "but why would he call her a client and say he did business with her? Not much of a romantic, your Mr. Carlin."

I thought back. " 'Business' could've been a euphemism. 'Client' was my word. He was trying to be careful and I fed that word to him to speed things along. Geneva's right. I need to improve my interview skills. I bet she knows which TV shows I can watch to pick up tips and techniques."

"You'd be better off getting hold of a textbook from a police academy. Thea can find one for you."

I glanced up at Geneva. She'd turned her wispy gray back and looked like something else forgotten on the top shelf.

"For a well-rounded education, I could try both. A book for the nitty-gritty; TV for the dramatics. That reminds me, though. Thea called while you were eating. She found out that Hugh was in Knoxville on Monday, playing his pipes at a funeral for a guy named Walter Jeffries."

"The name means nothing to me."

"She said she'd dig further after story time. Judging from the book and craft they're doing, it sounds like she might be indoctrinating the kids so they can organize and go out and do their own preschool yarn bombing."

"Trust Thea for the literacy tie-in. I'm not sure preschoolers can learn to purl, but they can sure get things into knots. But here's another thing, Kath—if Aaron wasn't talking about Angie, then what in heaven's name kind of client does he have who hangs out in the park at midnight, seeing but not being seen? What exactly is Aaron Carlin's 'business'?"

"Being in the park at midnight might not have anything to do with being his client. Don't you think we should just be grateful they're coming to talk to us?"

"You're right. And if Aaron is that afraid of the twins, then we know he has his head screwed on at least half-way right. Now let me tell you what this is that Mel sent. I read it while you and Aaron were in conference." She held up the piece of lined paper. "What we have here is proof that Sheriff Haynes is not the only who looked as though he saw a ghost after catching sight of Hugh on Tuesday."

The paragraphs and stick figure turned out to be from one of Mel's waitresses. Mel had asked her to put down in writing what she'd seen happen Tuesday at the café while Ardis and Hugh were there eating lunch.

"I think it's accurate," Ardis said. "I had my back to the front door and Hugh was facing it."

The waitress had been delivering orders to a table near the one where Ardis and Hugh sat. She looked up when the front door opened, ready to smile as Mel had taught her. She saw a woman walk in, freeze, and "literally do a total physical double take." Then she turned around and left. The waitress was sure the woman was looking at the man sitting with Ardis. She was also sure the woman wasn't just startled to see him, but also upset, because she had called in a to-go order. The order was waiting for her at the pickup window.

"She never did pick it up," Ardis said. "She never called to apologize. It was only a sandwich, but it's a telling point. She could've gone back later."

"Or sent someone else. If there was an order, then we know who this is, right?"

"In a minute. This part is brilliant. The stick figure was

the waitress' idea, in case we couldn't picture how the woman looked when she saw Hugh. When you know that, it doesn't matter that it's a stick figure. Big round eyes, tiny *o* for a mouth. And the hair nails it."

"Who is it?"

"Mrs. Pokey Weems."

Chapter 17

"We have a lot of names all of a sudden," I said. "With no idea how they fit in."

"These investigations are like some of the more intricate embroideries I've worked on. Here—" Ardis looked through our plastic "hospital" bin behind the counter. It was where we kept the projects tearful customers brought in that needed the ministrations of experts—sometimes including surgery or the laying on of last rights. She brought out a piece of linen, flosses dangling. "In this state, it looks hopeless: patterns and images you can almost see, but not quite because they have no definition; a border that looks like it's going nowhere, which it might be, because she got way off on her counting; and threads tangling into a rat's nest."

"But we've fixed worse."

"With time and patience. These things always look worst when they're partway finished—needlework and investigations." Ardis put the linen back in the bin. "Go get your sleuthing notebook, and let's make a list of these names we're collecting."

"It's in the study. Be right back."

Geneva must have followed me up the stairs. She drifted into the study and slumped onto the desk. While I rummaged for the leather notebook in my shoulder bag hanging on the back of the desk chair, she traced figure eights on the desk with a finger. Neither her tracing nor her heavy sighs disturbed a single speck of dust.

"Penny for your thoughts?" I asked.

"Which would be useless to me, not to say worthless in today's economy. Here is a valuable tip for you, though. You should keep a small notebook in your pocket at all times. Patrolmen on the best shows keep them in a breast pocket."

"I could keep one in a hip pocket."

"That would look better on someone with your figure. You will find one in the kneehole drawer. Also your grandmother's drawing pencils. Your grandmother was talented. That waitress could never be a police sketch artist."

I laughed. "She wouldn't even make it in the door of sketch artist school, would she?"

"I was not making fun of her."

"I didn't think you were." I watched as she continued tracing with her finger, now working on something more elaborate than an eight. "Geneva?"

"Hmm?"

"Which do you miss more, turning the pages of a book or drawing?" Borrowing recorded books from the library had made a difference in the quality of her life— her afterlife. But I couldn't see any way around her problem of not being able to touch or hold anything.

She curled her hand into a fist, and then stretched her

fingers and used her whole hand to erase the tracings that neither of us could tell were there. "Before you go, will you please put the next disc in the machine? *The Lovely Bones* is a sad book. I am enjoying it."

"Call this list 'People of Interest,'" Ardis said, "and put Olive's name first."

"I don't know."

"Oh, sure. She likes to think of herself as rising to the top of any social occasion."

"I mean about a title for the list. It makes me nervous to call a list 'People of Interest' and then put the sheriff's name on it. And we have to add Cole's name, too. He was practically foaming at the mouth to find out if Hugh was in town, and to find out before Al Rogalla. We need to find out what that was all about."

To please Ardis, I wrote Olive Weems at the top of the list, then added Sheriff Haynes, Cole Dunbar, Al Rogalla, Walter Jeffries, Aaron Carlin's client, and Rachel Meeks.

"Who's the Register of Deeds?" I asked.

"I forget. Easy enough to find out, though. And this thing with Rachel introduces a bobble to the event tonight, but it'll work out perfectly. We can get the information about her meeting with Hugh and Al while we're bonding over bombing."

"You think she'll babble the information so freely?"

"We won't know until we try. We'll fit questions artfully into casual conversation while we're fitting casual art into bare spaces all over town."

"With the help of a sheriff's deputy."

"Has that got you worried? She promised not to wear

her uniform. As a group we *did* talk about asking her to join us. Our main objection was worry over how it could affect her job if something went wrong, and if she's fine with it . . ."

"No, you're right." I waved off that concern. "If she's fine with it, so am I. But what else did you and she talk about yesterday? Did she tell you anything?"

"Precious little. And still not how he died."

"Maybe they don't know."

"Do you believe that?" Ardis asked.

"No. I think there's something significant about how he was killed and they aren't releasing the information."

"Hoping someone will slip up. Doggone it, Darla is a tougher nut to crack than I gave her credit for. She must be taking lessons from Cole."

"But what *did* you learn?"

"It's so puny I feel like a failure."

"Stop talking like that, Ardis. Puny is better than nothing. What is it?"

"Only that there might have been other names in his sporran."

"But that could be huge."

"But I don't know it for a fact," she said. "And I don't know that it means anything if there were more names. And I definitely don't know what the other names are *if* there were any."

"And nothing about the piece of paper itself?"

"Or if it was one paper or two dozen."

"What gave you the idea there might be more names?"

"That's the worst of it," she said. "I was trying to be clever. I didn't want Darla to think I was pumping her for information. I didn't write anything down. Now I can't remember what she said." With each statement, Ardis pounded a fist on the counter. When she was quiet, I took her hand and held it in my two.

"It's okay, Ardis."

"It's the curse of an old head. I'll be going downhill like Daddy and prancing in my altogether before you can blink."

"Not for another twenty years, and nobody will mind if you do."

She tried not to laugh.

"And you know you didn't just dream up the idea of more names. If you got it into your head that there were more names in the sporran, then that's probably what you heard."

"Maybe. And maybe I can get confirmation of that out of Darla tonight—that and more."

"That's the spirit."

"It is." She took her hand from mine and thumped the counter one more time. "Good, because despite my poor showing in counterinterview techniques, I have a good feeling about this evening. About the art itself and the bonding. Bonding over bombing—it has a real ring to it. I'm surprised we didn't think of that sooner for our slogan. Bonding with the teenagers, bonding with a banker, bonding with the local constabulary. At the risk of sounding bombastic, I think the evening will be fantastic. What's not to like about supporting public art? And with all our plans in place, all our maneuvers mapped out, what can possibly go wrong?"

Chapter 18

Before I walked home that evening, I went back up to the study to see Geneva. The disc I'd put on for her had long since finished. She would have been happy if I ran up to the study throughout the day, continuously feeding discs into the player. It had taken a combination of cajoling and firmness before she'd grudgingly agreed to a pace of two discs per day. Argyle was in the window seat, sizing up several crows bragging in the tree across the street.

"Be glad you're in here and not out there with them, old man," I told him. "They look big enough to carry you away. He said, "Mrrrph," and turned his back on the hooligans. "Is our girl in her room?" I crossed the room and knocked on the panel that hid the cupboard she claimed as her own room. With a yawn and a shiver, she drifted out through the panel.

"Boo," I said.

"That is only funny when I say it."

"You're right. Sorry. Will you come with us when we go yarn bombing tonight? I'm going home now, but we're all meeting back here at ten minutes of ten. I'd enjoy your company, and you can be the lookout and let me know if anyone's sneaking up on us."

"And look for clues?"

"Sure. What do you say? Will you come?"

"Or are we looking for a ghost?"

I hesitated. "I don't think so. You and I saw ghosts that one time, but—"

"Special circumstances?"

"I kind of think so."

"I do, too. But there is the other kind of ghost. We were talking about them this morning. Or perhaps I imagined it."

"It was this morning."

"I know. I was giving you a chance to pretend we hadn't."

"Ghosts of feelings. What about them?"

"What if you were able to touch something Hugh Mc-Phee wore? His sporran everyone was so excited about."

"The kilt would be better. The sporran is probably made from fur and leather, and the thought of knowing an animal's feelings when it—"

"Then do not think about that," Geneva cut in. "Think about asking the darling Deputy Darla to let you in the evidence room. Do you think the sheriff's department has an evidence room?"

"It must."

"Then I think you must reach out and touch something."

"I'll think about it. If nothing else, I'd like to see everything they found in the sporran."

"You can make a list in the notebook you're going to carry in your hip pocket."

"And take pictures with my phone. Hey, I've never tried taking a picture of you. That could be interesting."

"I don't think so."

"Why not?"

"Do you like looking at pictures of yourself on a bad day?"

"No. Oh."

"Yes. Oh."

"Will you come with us tonight?"

"I'll think about it."

The night smelled like October, with a mix of chilly air, brown leaves, and wood smoke from a few fireplaces, when Joe and I crept downtown after dark. We didn't really creep, and it wasn't terribly late. But on weekday nights Blue Plum tended to roll up its streets by nine o'clock and sensible people already slept soundly in their warm beds. Dressed in head-to-toe black, wearing backpacks armed with crochet hooks, knitting needles, scissors, flashlights, and the universal emergency multipurpose tool—duct tape—we felt positively . . .

"Crafty," Joe said.

That carried us on suppressed snorts of laughter the few blocks between my house and the Weaver's Cat. Joe had left his pickup in my drive, pulled up to the garage. We'd left lights on and a movie playing on the television to make it look and sound as though we were in and occupied, in case of wandering Spiveys. We'd also made popcorn for olfactory verisimilitude, in case wandering

Spiveys went so far as to sniff at the cracks of doors. Joe thought of that detail.

By plan, we were the first to arrive at the shop. The back door greeted us with a warm bleat. A sleepy Argyle came to see if visitors meant snacks. I gave him a few kibbles. He crunched them and thanked me by leaving ginger fur on our black ankles for good luck. Then he leapt to the counter and took a sniffing tour of the black garbage bags holding our knitted and crocheted strips. The bags were only interesting in passing, though, and he jumped to the top of the refrigerator, where he settled into a loaf shape next to the huddled mist of Geneva. In the dark, I hadn't realized she was there.

I went over and reached up to rub Argyle's chin. "How are you?" I asked. "We're going to have a blast tonight. Don't you wish you could come with us? What are your thoughts on that?"

"It will take more thought," Geneva said. "I have had several life-altering experiences out there in the dark. I do not want to make the decision lightly."

Argyle said, "Mrrph."

"Maggie likes to be part of a conversation, too," Joe said. "Interesting, though, that she responds more to talk about yarn and colors than trout flies and fish. I think she still misses Ivy."

Maggie had been Granny's cat. She'd never liked me and had moved in with Joe after Granny died. They were a good fit, cat and man, but I didn't doubt she still missed Granny. We all did.

"Ardis found a sitter for Hank?" Joe asked.

"She did."

Geneva perked up at mention of Ardis' father. He

was tottery, half deaf, and Geneva referred to him as Ardis' old-as-dirt daddy. When she was in a room with him, he thought the lights were flickering or that he saw fireflies. He was Geneva's great-nephew and he shared her love for old cop shows.

"And you heard about John bringing Ambrose along?"

"He can't be that bad," Joe said.

"Ardis thought about offering to pay the sitter double, splitting the cost with John, and letting him park Ambrose with Hank for the evening."

"He might not be that good, either."

"That's what she's afraid of, so she didn't say anything to John after all. I don't know whether I'm looking forward to seeing what he's like or not. 'Mean as snakes' conjures all kinds of images."

"What snakes?" Geneva asked. "They do not like me and I do not like them right back."

"Not real ones," I said. Oops.

"Not real images?" Joe asked.

Geneva snickered.

"Not real *snakes*," I said, with a moment of inspiration. "After hearing about Ambrose all these months, he's taken on mythic proportions, so the snakes are mythic, too."

"I'm not sure that makes them any better," Joe said. "Mythic snakes are probably huge. We'd have to call Aaron and half his snake-handling kin to charm them."

"Speaking of Aaron, he's bringing someone by tomorrow who was in the park Tuesday night. Someone who won't go to the police."

"That's—"

"In confidence," I said as we heard feet on the back stairs. The door said, "Baa," and Ernestine and Zach came in, Ernestine apologizing for wearing dark gray instead of black.

"But my pack is black," she said, turning in a circle as she tried to catch sight of the pack on her back. "And I want you to know that this young man is an excellent driver. He was kind enough to pick me up and he said that if his brother will let him borrow his motorcycle, he'll take me for a ride sometime."

Zach's black hoodie set off his blushing cheeks nicely. He'd brought a black garbage bag with him, in addition to his backpack.

Tammie Fain, the indulgent grandmother who'd missed the last meeting because of babysitting duty, arrived next, minus her grand-terrors, I was happy to see. Wanda Vance was close on her heels. Neither of them had come in the back way before, and the electronic sheep surprised them. Wanda, the retired nurse who was usually so reserved, broke into a fit of nervous giggles and opened the door twice more to hear it again. She stifled a scream the second time when she found Abby on the other side. Abby came in with a polite but uneasy smile for Wanda, and immediately went to stand with Zach and Ernestine. Goth Abby fit the covert color scheme without special effort on her part. Ernestine admired the Batman backpack Tammie had borrowed from her grandson. I was happy Tammie had brought the backpack and left the grandson at home. Rather than a backpack, Wanda brought her tools and supplies in a split-willow basket.

Wanda nudged Tammie with her elbow, said, "Baa," and leaned against her, giggling.

"I should've turned the sound off for the night," Joe said, "so we don't attract attention with repeat baas."

"Is it easy?" I asked. "Can you do it now?"

"I can take a look."

"Or if someone will keep an eye on Argyle, we can hold the door open." I looked at Argyle and Geneva, still sitting next to each other on top of the refrigerator. He showed no interest in moving.

Zach went over and stationed himself in front of the fridge, at the ready.

"Thanks, Zach," I called.

Geneva leaned over and whispered something in Argyle's ear. He stretched one paw out and put it lightly on Zach's hair.

Joe leaned down and gave me a kiss.

"What was that for?"

"Keeping it simple."

"All right, you two," Thea said, coming up the stairs, "save that stuff for your own time." She slung her backpack on the table, looked at the clock, and rubbed her hands. "The time is ten minutes of ten. Are we ready to detonate? Oh—" She looked around. "After all that talk about precision, John isn't here on time? And Ardis? And bankers can't keep time? Where the heck are they?"

"I'm here." Rachel ran up the stairs. "Sorry I'm late. I ran into Ardis and John."

"Where are *they*?" Thea asked.

"On their way. Ardis said go ahead and start your pre-bomb pep talk."

"Good enough. Joe, close the door so I'm not announcing this to the whole neighborhood."

"Aye-aye."

"Whoa there, Joe." A hand stopped the door, mid-bleat.

"Oh, hey there, Darla," Joe said. "Um—"

"I'm late," Darla said, "but ready, willing, and able to tie knots with the best of them." She slid in past Joe and he closed the door. "Hey, everybody. Thanks for letting me join you. I hope ya'll are as stoked as I am."

Thea looked at me and I mouthed, "Ardis." She shrugged and turned to Darla. "Glad to have you. I think I can speak for the entire bomb squad—"

"Hear, hear!" Tammie said, prompting murmurs of agreement from the others.

"Thank you, thank you," Thea said with a bow. "Darla, having a needlewoman of your caliber with us tonight, who is also a daring deputy, adds another layer of excitement to our mission, as well as a sense of security. Welcome."

"I am off-duty, though, you know."

"Yeah, your yoga pants gave you away," Thea said. "No problem."

"And there's nothing more dangerous in my backpack than embroidery snips and the biggest crochet hook I could find," Darla said.

"We wouldn't have you any other way." Thea glanced at the clock again. "Joe? You want to check out there for Ardis and John?"

"Be right back." He ducked out the door.

"The rest of you gather around the table here and we'll get started while he's checking on our fashionably late members." She took a sheaf of papers from her backpack and held them up.

"Timetables—"

"I'll hand them out," Tammie said, reaching for them.

"That'll be great, Tammie." Thea put the stack on the table and her fist on the stack like a paperweight. "But let me have my shining moment first. Then you can pass them out. Our goal this evening—"

The back door baaed and Joe slipped back in. "The stairs," he said. "Difficult. Best if they wait outside."

"Is this about John's brother?" Tammie asked. "He looked unsteady, but between a few of us we ought to be able to get him up the stairs." She started toward the back door.

"They'll be fine," Joe said. With an interesting look on his face, and a curious lack of eye contact, he crossed his arms and leaned his back against the door. He did it oh so casually, making me oh so much more curious. He couldn't be in two places at once, though. So while he kept curious me from opening the door to see for myself, and while Thea started back in on her shining moment, I moved so I could see out the window over the sink. Joe noticed, but when our eyes met, his cut away again, and the interesting expression on his face made a subtle shift toward amused.

"Our goal this evening," Thea was saying, "is to perform the world's first yarn bombing in Blue Plum, Tennessee."

The alley wasn't terribly well lit—a situation the merchants had been lobbying the town board about for years, according to Ardis. I couldn't see much beyond the pool of light at the bottom of the back steps, but I could pick out Ardis and John standing in the shadows at the back of the garage across the alley . . .

"We will move like shadows through our fair town,"

Thea said, "garnishing it with garter stitch graffiti. We'll start at the courthouse as a group and finish at the foot-bridge over the creek in the park as a group. In between those two group efforts, teams will work separately, bombing our designated targets."

"With a few surprise targets along the way," Ernestine piped up.

"Yes, we'll have our surprises," Thea said.

I saw movement, and a thin figure next to John stepped out of the shadows. Ambrose, no doubt. John put a hand on his shoulder. Ambrose shook it off but stepped back into the shadows. What was Ardis standing next to? I didn't remember garbage cans in that spot . . .

"Joe, have you got the tags?" Thea asked.

"In my pack."

I still couldn't make out what was going on in the al-ley, if anything *was* going on. When I turned away from the window to see Joe's tags, I "bumped into" Geneva. She shrieked and put a hand to her heart. I congratu-lated myself on not shrieking, too, and hoped no one had seen my eyes fly wide.

"You should warn people before turning around sud-denly like that," Geneva said. "You frightened me nearly deader than I am. 'Boo' isn't a good joke word for some-one like you, but it is a good warning word. Remember that for next time, please. What are you staring at out there, anyway?" She knelt in the sink and looked out the window. She could have floated through it for a better look, but floating out into the dark on her own wasn't something she was likely to do. I left her to the puzzle out the window and turned to watch Joe unveil the yarn bomb tags he'd made for us.

He took his backpack off, unzipped the smaller of two front compartments, and took out four flat black packets. "A dozen tags for each team."

"Nice touch with the black envelopes," Thea said. "They match our chic special ops outfits."

"Nothing but good old construction paper," he said. "The tags are cotton canvas, three inches by three, big enough to read, but still small enough to be unobtrusive. The edges are pinked to avoid raveling and they're perforated for easy attachment with yarn or thread. Or you can staple them if you brought a stapler. Duct tape'll work, too, but it won't look as good, unless you've got a flair for duct tape." He handed the envelopes to Thea, then took a single square of canvas from his shirt pocket and handed that to her. "There's what they look like."

Thea cradled the tag in her hand, then looked at Joe. "How'd you do it?"

"Came up with the design. Made fabric transfers. Easy enough."

"Easy enough for you. Thank you. This is perfect. I knew you'd come through."

Joe snorted.

"Well, after Ardis said you would. It's a quote from Albert Einstein," she said to us. "It says, 'Creativity is contagious, pass it on.' And below that he added, 'First Annual Blue Plum Yarn Bomb.' This is great. Our yarn bombing is going to explode all over Blue Plum and it's going to blow people's minds. The whole thing is going to be excellent." She stopped to catch her breath before rushing on. "Okay, each team gets a dozen tags. Each team is equipped with black garbage bags. Make each installation as quickly and quietly as possible, attach your tag, move on to the next target—boom, boom, boom—just like that. All teams should meet at the footbridge no later than midnight. Ardis would like to take a few minutes there to remember the life of Hugh McPhee. He had plans to join us tonight, and as you probably know, he was tragically killed two nights ago."

There were murmurs, nods, and a few bowed heads.

"We'll bomb the footbridge as a group," Thea said, "and afterwards, we'll creep back here to the Weaver's Cat. That's still right, isn't it, Kath?"

"Everyone's invited."

"We'll have a quick celebratory nosh of refreshments," Thea said, "courtesy of Mel's on Main. In the morning, anyone who can be up and competent at eight will meet at Mel's for an après-bombing breakfast and debriefing. Joe is our official event photographer. Are you really going to be out there taking pictures before eight?" she asked him.

"The pictures and I will be at Mel's."

"Good," Thea said. "Now, final instructions. There are four teams. Assignments have been made. For safety's sake, please stay with your team. Look out for each other. Younger members, see that our older members make it over uneven ground. Watch out for broken pavement. Heaven knows we have enough of that around town."

"Thank you," Ernestine said.

"We'll communicate between teams by phone. Am I leaving anything out, Kath?"

"Timetables and team assignments?"

"Right. Each of you gets a copy of the timetable. You may keep them, but please don't share them outside the bomb squad and don't lose them. On them are the basic instructions we've just gone over, main targets, teams responsible for them, and approximate installation time—very approximate—and you'll need to factor in time for the targets you've been planning in secret. Also on the timetables are team rosters and phone numbers. Teams are as follows—"

Darla raised her hand and waved. "Why are you handing out the entire game plan with names and numbers? It makes it all not really secret. Which is what we're aiming for, right?"

Thea opened her mouth and shut it on an un-librarian-like word. She scooped up her stack of timetables and shoved them back in her backpack. "The curse of the anal librarian; I'm too thorough for my own good. Okay, hold it, hold it, rethinking . . ."

"Read the phone numbers out and we'll save them in our phones," Rachel said. "That makes sense, doesn't it?"

"Right," Thea said. "Phones out." There was minor shuffling and some digging as we located our phones. Thea went through the list of phone numbers—twice in most cases—and with an increasing edge to her voice. When Wanda asked her to repeat John's number for the third time, I interrupted.

"I think we're good enough, Thea. Some of us have all the numbers and all of us have some of them." I checked the time. "We aren't going to be calling back and forth much, anyway, and we're getting behind schedule."

"*And*," Geneva said, "the natives are getting restless in the alley."

"Four teams, then," Thea said. "They are Knit, Purl, Hook, and Needle. Team Knit is Kath, Ernestine, and Tammie. Team Knit, you are responsible for freestanding signs—meaning stop signs, other street signs, business signs, et cetera. Team Purl is Joe, Zach, and Rachel. Team Purl is responsible for trees. Please don't break your necks if you climb up into them. Team Hook is Wanda and yours truly—a small team, but excellent. We will do a strafing run on streetlights in the two-block area around the courthouse. Team Needle is Ardis, Abby, and John. Team Needle will bomb bike racks and benches. Darla, because John might be somewhat tied up with Ambrose, do you mind joining Team Needle? And will you give Ardis and John the gist of the pre-bomb pep talk?"

"I'll be happy to."

"Good. Any questions?" Heads shook as Thea looked around the kitchen. "Comments before we take off?"

"Bomb's away?" Ernestine said. "It seems appropriate."

"Thank you, Ernestine," Thea said. "I couldn't have put it better myself. Three key words to keep in mind for our cause—quick, quiet, and creative. And here we go; bombs away!"

A chill trickled down my back as Geneva put her arm around my shoulders. "Good news," she said. "Watching the shenanigans of the ancient hooligans outside our kitchen window made me realize how dangerous this yarn explosion you've dreamed up might be. Snakes or no snakes, I think it is best that I come with you, after all."

Joe held the back door open. With suppressed excitement, the rest of the bomb squad grabbed garbage bags of yarn bomb ordnance and trooped out. Geneva didn't bother with the door. Shouting, "Bombs away," she shimmered straight through the wall.

Chapter 19

"**A**rdie? Ardie, girl, when are they bringing my beer?" I knew that voice — Hank Broyles, Ardis' ninety-three-year-old daddy. He was across the alley, sitting in his wheelchair, with Geneva floating next to him. Ardis, John, and a crooked old man who must be Ambrose were there, too, waiting for the bomb squad as we spilled out the back door of the Weaver's Cat.

"Hank's sitter fell through," Joe told me as I locked the door behind us. "Ardis got him in the wheelchair by telling him they were going out for a beer. She apologized profusely."

"Eh. No big deal. What's one more with this crowd? Holy cow." I surveyed the milling group below. "We probably should've rethought bombing the courthouse as a mob."

"Where we lack inconspicuousness, we'll shine in ... um ..."

"Being chaotic?"

"Being colorful," Joe said. "In every sense of the word."

"Teams to the courthouse!" Tammie shouted.

"To the courthouse *silently*," Thea shouted back, except her shout had a husky quality that gave it the illusion of being a whisper. "Honed through years of shushing library patrons," she said when I complimented her on the skill. "I'm ace at shushing. Wanda? Let's go."

Thea and her Team Needle disappeared down the alley in the direction of the courthouse. After Ambrose shook his cane at them, Team Purl—consisting of Joe, Zach, and Rachel—headed for the courthouse, too. Tammie jogged in place, anxious for Team Knit to be on its way. I was beginning to see where her grandchildren got their barely controlled energy. She looked ready to take off running without us. Ernestine came to the rescue by latching onto Tammie's arm.

"Isn't this exciting?" Ernestine said. "Thank you, dear. I'm not quite as blind as a bat, but I appreciate your help getting down this dim alley." Behind Tammie's back, Ernestine gave me a wink much exaggerated by her thick lenses.

"Ardie?" Hank quavered. "Are you sure this place is even open?"

"Danged if you aren't right, Daddy," Ardis said. "Let's get out of here. John? Ambrose? Are you coming? Well, hello there, Kath. And Darla and Abby and Ernestine and Tammie. Why, it's a regular party."

"Let me get that." Darla took the wheelchair from Ardis and started the general movement down the alley.

Geneva popped up in front of me. "Her old-as-dirt daddy thinks he is in a beer garden," she said. "I will stick with him and the darling Deputy Darla. It will be the whole package—a family outing, a crackerjack crime investigation, and superior police protection. I will let you know if I find any clues. I will miss nothing with my eagle eyes."

I used our sign for "good," but she missed it in her hurry to join Darla and Hank.

"Once we get him moving, he'll enjoy himself," Ardis said, falling in step beside me. She didn't remark on Geneva's presence.

"How's John making out with Ambrose?" I watched the two old men walking ahead of us. Neither had ever been tall, but until he'd become bent, Ambrose would have looked down on John. If the stories were accurate, he looked down on John in more ways than one. John was still able to hold himself like the ex–navy man he was, though, and Ambrose walked with a drunken gait . . . "Ambrose hasn't been drinking, has he?"

"John says his legs are going. John is far more patient than I could be with that ungrateful old galoot. He got a walker for Ambrose, but Ambrose refuses to use it. Won't hear of a wheelchair."

"He probably likes shaking his cane too much."

"Fussing might be his only joy in life these days. It might be the only joy he ever had. I thank my stars Daddy's a cheerful old soul. I am sorry to slow us down tonight, though."

"Don't even worry about it. I know we're claiming a higher purpose, opening minds to art and creativity, but isn't our real main goal to have fun?"

Up ahead, Ambrose whacked a garbage can with his cane. "Crazy fool son of a—" The rest of what he said was lost in a muffled garble.

"His upper plate falls down," Ardis said. "Cuts off half

of what he says. John says he doesn't like to repeat himself. And of course he refuses to get it fixed."

"Oh dear. Well, if Ambrose doesn't bring some kind of fun to this, I don't know who or what will."

Ambrose continued swinging his cane as they walked, and John put a hand on his shoulder. Ambrose flinched, but John held his course, keeping his hand where it was. A few yards farther along, Ambrose shifted his cane to the other hand and slung his arm around John's shoulders. Down the alley they went, a couple of ancient buddies out for a night on the town.

We neared the cross street and heard Hank cackling at something Darla said as they went around the corner toward Main. I heard Geneva cackling, too, but again, Ardis said nothing. At Main Street we cut diagonally across the intersection. Darla hopped on the back of the wheelchair and rode it down the slight incline to the opposite curb. Abby ran alongside giggling and Hank and his great-aunt Geneva cackled as they went.

As planned, someone had draped strips of knitting over the floodlights aimed at the face of the courthouse. Activity around the columns and on the steps was still obvious, but we at least had the illusion of working in secret. Ernestine and Tammie had made good time, despite Ernestine's ploy to slow them down. They were already tying a knitted "necktie" on a column. Ambrose held a garbage bag open while John pulled a strip of knitting from it and worked on wrapping the central stair rail in a striped spiral.

"You go on up there and do a pillar, Ardis," Darla said when we caught up. "Abby and Hank and I have plans for bombing the pillory."

"Bomb, bomb, bomb," Geneva sang, "bomb-bara Ann."

"Haunted Beach Boys," I said as Ardis and I climbed the courthouse stairs to join the others, "sung by a goofball of a ghost."

"Beg pardon?"

I turned to her and held up a hand, stopping her on the step below mine. We were almost eye to eye.

"What is it, hon?"

I took her left hand and looked at her wrist. "Push your sleeve up?" Her eyes were only curious, not clouded by guile. She wasn't wearing the bracelet I'd braided and dyed for her with Granny's recipe. "Where is it? Did it break?"

She pulled her hand back and pulled her sleeve down. "Geneva's here?" She drew her shoulders in. "Didn't she say she wasn't coming?"

"Ghosts," I said with a shrug. "First it's no and then it's yes. What they'll do you cannot guess. As she would say, that's haunted humor."

"Don't tell her I took it off, will you, Kath? I don't want to hurt her feelings." Her eyes showed nothing but guilt now as she glanced left and right. "She isn't—"

"She's with Hank and Darla. What's wrong, Ardis?"

"I was afraid," she whispered, "so I took it off. I was afraid to wear it out here tonight, in case ... Kath, honest to God, if I saw Hugh's ghost in the park, if I saw him die, the way you saw that happen to Geneva out there at the Holston Home Place, I would not be able to stand it. It'll be bad enough when Daddy dies, but to see murder? I'd go out of my mind." She put shaking hands to her lips.

"Hey, hey, Ardis. Don't think about it. It's okay."

"But you and Geneva are strong."

"No, we're not. We just made it through a hard experience. Besides, do you want to know why she had to think twice about coming with us? It's because she's afraid of ghosts, too."

Ardis laughed, then covered her mouth again.

"She's counting on Darla to protect her," I added.

Ardis spluttered some more. "From things seen and unseen. Well, anyway, don't tell her I took the bracelet off. We're on the wrong feet these days, and she's bound to take it the wrong way. And now we'd better get up there and get busy with a column or Thea will fire us."

"Do you know how to tie a tie?" I asked as we climbed the rest of the steps.

"I've been working on something better." She opened her garbage bag and started pulling out a length of something hot pink and so fluffy it was frothy. "The other pillars are going to look like stuffy men with their neckties. This one"—she handed me an end of the pink froth—"is going to have a feather boa." She'd knitted yards of marabou to make her boa, enough to circle the pillar twice before knotting it.

"Looks great," Thea said, coming over to admire it. "But it should've been me who thought of that. I'm the one with class around here." She cocked a hip and put a finger to her cheek.

It was then I noticed. "You're wearing heels? In the dark? Through the park? After giving specific instructions about what and what not to wear?"

"They're black."

"They're heels, Thea. Toeless."

"And I am unapologetically fashionable. Besides, I didn't say anything about type or style of footwear. You already know I don't do ewe poo. I also don't do duck muck. You can go run along back there through the park. I am not leaving paved areas, and that makes my heels perfectly fine."

"They're fine and you're a nut. Although yes, a certifiably fashionable nut."

"Thank you." She curtsied. "What are you doing to the column now, Ardis?"

"Adding the pièce de résistance." She took a crocheted red bundle from her bag and held it so we couldn't see what it was. "Duct tape, please? Two six-inch pieces folded back on themselves so they're a double-sided loop will do nicely."

She took the pieces as I handed them to her, pressing them to the pillar above the boa and about a foot apart.

"Ready?" She shook out the red crochet and smoothed it. Then she pressed it to the tape on the pillar and stood back. Two scarlet lips pouted at us above the hot pink feather boa.

"We are *excellent*," Thea said. "Come see what Zach the wonder boy made. Then we need to break up this party and move on."

The narrow brown band Zach had been knitting had metamorphosed into the iconic Groucho Marx glasses, eyebrows, and nose. Rachel and Joe were behind the column stitching it in place. Zach was stuffing the nose with batting to give it the correct protuberance. Below the nose was a black bow tie and a white wing collar.

"Genius, Zach."

He gave me his quick smile, then grabbed the garbage bags at the base of the column and moved in his patented teenage slouch to join his teammates.

"Thea, do you mind if we rearrange the teams a bit?" Ardis had Darla at her disposal for casual information gathering, but the way the teams were set up, neither of us had easy access to Rachel. "Can we ask Tammie and Rachel to switch places?"

"Mmm, not without ruffling feathers—Tammie's to be exact. She asked to be on your team."

"Really? When? And why?"

"I didn't ask. To hazard a guess, she likes the A-list. You own the shop."

"Huh. What about Rachel and Darla changing teams?"

"Mmm, not without prompting questions—mine to be exact. What's up?"

I told her about the purported bank meeting between Rachel, Hugh, and Al Rogalla, but didn't mention the Spiveys as my source of information.

"It seems like there'd be an ethics line she wouldn't—or shouldn't—cross to tell you anything. On the other hand, if business or real estate was involved, there might be a public aspect to it with records available. In any case, you're too late. There goes Team Purl, slinking off into the night."

She was right; loping Joe, slouching Zach, and upright Rachel were on their way down the stairs—off to bomb Main Street's benches and bike racks. Ardis had rejoined her team, too, and Ernestine and Tammie were putting the finishing touches on crocheted leaves and flower petals they'd made sprout from uprights of the center stair rail.

"You know, you could let the investigation take a back burner for a few hours, Kath, and just enjoy the bombing."

Thea grinned. "Don't you love this? How often do you get to say something like 'sit back and enjoy the bombing' in Blue Plum? See you at the footbridge at midnight. And if you trip over a vital clue while you're traipsing through the park, pick it up and bring it with you."

Before joining Ernestine and Tammie, I took a chance and called Joe. He didn't mind contributing ideas and concrete actions to help our investigations along, but interrogating witnesses tended to be beyond his comfort range.

"You don't need to ask her specific questions," I said. "Just lead the conversation around to Hugh."

"Already done."

"You're one in a million."

"Not me. Zach. He said he wanted to know more about Hugh so he'd be in the proper state of mind for Ardis' memorial at the footbridge."

"Do you think that's true, or is he playing boy genius?" Zach asking a question to satisfy his state of mind was one thing. But he knew about our occasional detecting. He'd been present when we uncovered the truth about a previous murder. And he was bright, independent, and more curious than any cat I'd known.

"I'll keep an eye on him," Joe said.

"And—"

"And I'll ask Rachel when she last spoke to Hugh."

"And be careful, because you're at least one in a thousand." I disconnected and pushed a tickling strand of hair behind my ear. Or I thought it was the hair that annoyed me. It might have been a niggling strand of dread.

*   *   *

"When was the last time you strolled down the middle of Main Street?" Tammie asked. "I tell you what. This'll be something to tell the grandkids."

"She isn't strolling," I muttered to Ernestine, "she's standing. She's standing while we're over here stitching. And it isn't like downtown Blue Plum is devoid of life at this time of night. Someone is bound to see her."

Tammie's thrill at "strolling" down an empty Main Street was lasting longer than her attention span for bombing signs had.

"Someone's bound to see us, too," Ernestine said. "Isn't it funny how little light the streetlights seem to give on an ordinary night? Tonight Main Street feels like Rockefeller Center."

"It does. Have you ever been there? Rockefeller Center?" I tied off the strip I'd wrapped around the post of a crosswalk sign and moved a few yards to a speed limit sign.

"I never have." Ernestine was fitting a giant beret onto a mailbox.

"Neither have I."

"You should toss that beret in the air like Mary Tyler Moore," Tammie called.

"I'll go get her," Ernestine said. "I've got giant chicken feet in my pack she might like to play with."

"How many giant things have you got in your pack?"

"Some of them are Mel's special contributions," Ernestine said. "She enjoyed herself *immensely*." On a soft chuckle, she trundled out into the street to get Tammie.

"What a hoot," Tammie said when Ernestine gave her the giant yellow feet. "Are you sure these aren't owl feet? They look like owl feet to me, and they're a hoot. I know, why don't we put them on the 'Welcome to Historic Blue Plum' sign down the way? I'll go do it."

"That's in the next block," Ernestine said.

"And we're supposed to stick together," Tammie said in a singsong voice. "You'll know where I am and I know where you are. You'll be able to see me, for goodness' sake. We've got our phones. Ardis and her crew are already strung out along back there. We'll never get this done if we don't spread out, too."

"Sure." I stood up to give my knees a rest. "Go ahead, Tammie. Good idea."

"Do you think it is, Kath?" Ernestine asked.

Tammie didn't care what I thought. "Yahoo," she said. "Bombs away."

"You've heard of loose cannons," Ernestine said, coming back to the sidewalk. "She's a loose bomb."

"But if we try to keep her reined in, she'll drive us nuts."

"And then we'd be knit wits, wouldn't we? Now, would you like to see what else I have in my pack?" She tugged on a corner of turquoise crochet that grew and grew until it popped out, leaving her pack looking like an empty husk. "It's a moray," she said happily.

We'd told the teenagers to stick with their teams—not because any of us believed a random murderer was loose in town—but because it made good sense for general safety's sake. It also made sense in case we were seen and reported or stopped. The kids, on their own, might have a harder time explaining what they were doing. Especially if they were stopped by Clod. Especially if Zach were stopped by Clod—I knew Clod's opinion of Zach and his family and could easily imagine Zach's bright, independent mouth igniting downtown fireworks.

What hadn't occurred to me was how hard it would be to keep the adults with their teams. Tammie was the first to disappear.

Chapter 20

"She's a grown woman," Ernestine said. "Although she doesn't seem to be the kind of grown woman who follows directions." She peered up the dark street as though she'd be able to see anything closer than the five-foot moray eel we'd just attached to the windows of the electric company. Tammie was no longer in sight. "Did she attach the chicken feet to the welcome sign, or did they march off with her?"

Ernestine and I went to check the welcome sign, enjoying the image of Tammie and a pair of giant yellow chicken feet marching off into the distance. But we found the feet standing proud as part of the WELCOME TO HISTORIC BLUE PLUM sign.

"Try calling her phone," Ernestine said.

She didn't answer and her voice mail was full.

"I could call the others," I said, "and ask if they've seen her, but I kind of hate to admit we've lost her, you know? Do you think we should be worried?"

"If we don't see her somewhere along the street, and if she doesn't show up at the footbridge, we'll call her again." Ernestine bent to wrap more striped knitting around a NO PARKING sign. "She's a grown woman," she repeated.

The courthouse clock rang eleven o'clock. A freight train rumbled through, the engineer leaning on the horn through all four of the crossings in town. The dark and the late hour made the rumble and half-mile *hoooooooooooonk* seem bigger and closer than they would have if they were surrounded by the ordinary bustle of noontime. Ernestine's energy and good humor began to flag and I made her sit on one of the benches Ardis and team Needle had bombed. She stroked the crocheted seat.

"It's comfy," she said. "I could curl up right here and take a nap."

"Why don't I take you home, Ernestine?"

"Absolutely not."

"You've put in a good night's work."

"And I'll see it finished, too."

"Good. Me, too. Say, did you try your experiment? Trying to remember more about Tuesday night?"

"I remembered the name of the tune he was playing. "It was 'Flowers of the Forest.'"

"You don't sound happy about it."

"Because there are superstitions about the tune and I don't like believing in superstitions."

I sat on the bench beside her. "What are they?"

"One is that you should never play the tune indoors."

"That's pretty much true of bagpipes in general, isn't it?"

"Only for the unenlightened, dear. Another is that it's bad luck to play the tune unless it's at a funeral."

"Thea says Hugh played at a funeral in Knoxville on Monday."

"He did?" That seemed to lift her spirits, but a few seconds of thought flattened them again. "But does that funeral count if it happened the day before you play the tune? Do you see what I mean? No, no, no." She batted her words away with her hands. "Don't even try to see what I mean. I sound like a first-class ninny."

"Wondering how a superstition works doesn't mean you believe in it, Ernestine."

"But the last one is the worst—the tune shouldn't be played unless someone has died. If you do play it, and someone hasn't died, then playing it will bring about the death of a person close to the piper. Isn't that a nasty thought to put in someone's head? As soon as I realized what tune he'd been playing, I felt like I shouldn't have been enjoying Hugh's music at all that night. He played the tune and now he's dead."

"But Hugh was the piper, not someone close to the piper."

"You can't get much closer to the piper than *being* the piper," Ernestine said.

"You don't believe he piped himself to death, though, do you? You don't, Ernestine. You know you don't."

"But has anyone told us how he died? Why haven't they?" She looked at her knees, muttering.

"Hey, are you all right?"

"I'm giving myself a good talking-to for being a ridiculous old woman. Imagine, letting that—that—that irrational *worm* wiggle into my head."

"Think about it this way—anytime anyone learns to

play that tune, they have to practice. Probably over and over and over, right? So, have you ever heard of mass die-offs among the friends and families of bagpipe students? Of course not. Do you need another minute before we move on?"

"No." Ernestine patted my knee. "I needed your common sense and a good dose of reality. Let's go attach a lion's mane jellyfish to the porch of the County Extension."

"You've got one of those?"

"In the garbage bag, there. A medium- to small-sized specimen, inaccurate colors. I thought John would appreciate it and the eel. A touch of the deep blue sea in downtown Blue Plum."

We wrapped the posts of a few more street signs on our way to install the lion's mane, and stopped to do the same for the sign at the Methodist church, too. The church, set well back from the street in its tree-studded lawn, had already had a visit from Joe and team Purl. The Purls had left the sign for us, but had wrapped the trunks of the larger trees in spirals of rainbow garter stitch and hung one of the smaller trees with the giant knitted trout flies Thea had hoped for, and a few knitted trout, as well. The lawn had also sprouted a fairy circle of red-capped toadstools. We looked, but didn't see Tammie anywhere.

My phone buzzed as Ernestine opened the garbage bag and unfurled her jellyfish. It was Thea.

"Thought you'd like an update," she said. "First about how hard it is to keep a team from unraveling, if you will."

"Oh, yeah, sorry about that. It's my fault. I told her she could go on ahead. Is she there with you?"

There was silence.

"Thea?"

"I was talking about Wanda. Who are you talking about?"

"Tammie. She was getting antsy. We haven't seen her since I told her she could go on ahead. What happened to Wanda?"

"She said she forgot something," Thea said, "and she'd be right back. So far she isn't. On the other hand, the installations are looking great, don't you think? And I'm sure Tammie and Wanda will show up for the finale at the footbridge. Which brings me to my second update. I won't be there."

"*What*? Why not?"

"Did you know that the town ducks aren't keeping themselves confined to the mucky banks of the mucky creek in the park anymore? They aren't even keeping themselves confined to the blankity-muck park. And I stepped in what they aren't keeping in the park anymore. It's on my shoes. And now I'm going home."

"You could change shoes and come back."

"These are toeless heels. Picture that. You and Ardis can handle the memorial at the bridge. We've done a good job out here tonight. But I'm going home. I'll see you at Mel's in the morning."

"You're neurotic." I said that after she'd disconnected. It didn't seem right to add to her neurosis by telling her about it. Before I could put the phone away, Joe called.

"Bad news," he said. "Rachel twisted her ankle."

"Oh, heck. Badly? What happened?"

"She said she landed wrong hopping off the low wall

at the post office. She was able to walk on it, but she wanted to go home and ice it."

"Did you get a chance to ask her about the meeting at the bank? Or were you even able to get a word in edgewise?"

"She was kind of quiet tonight, but yeah, I asked her a few questions. Mild, but drifting in the right direction."

"And did you see her twist it? Did she limp?"

"Are we being suspicious?"

"Observant sounds better than suspicious."

"I didn't see it happen. But you can twist an ankle without falling down or making a big fuss. She favored it, but she could walk and didn't want us to bother walking her to her car. Or to go get it for her. Zach offered. She drives a BMW." A gabbling on Joe's end interrupted him, and then he was back. "Zach says not just a BMW— a BMW Z4."

"Tell him I'm impressed and don't tell him I'll Google it later." I told Joe about Tammie and Wanda both going AWOL and about Thea going home for a different kind of foot problem.

"The best-laid plans of ducks and librarians," he said. "See you at the footbridge in a few."

"Wait. Has Ardis checked in with you?"

"No. But we didn't ask her to, did we?"

"No, and they probably have their hands full."

While I'd been talking, Ernestine made herself comfortable on the bench in front of the Extension office. Ardis and Team Needle hadn't hit that bench, but Ernestine had yards of tentacles and a jellyfish bell the size of a golf umbrella to cuddle up to on the bench. She'd nodded off, dozing against the bell, the tentacles spread across her lap and down the front walk.

"Just resting my eyes," she said, opening them and blinking rapidly when I called her name. "That was quite refreshing, and not many people can say they napped with a lion's mane jellyfish. Shall we hang this handsome fellow and be on our way?"

Hanging a monstrous knitted jellyfish on the front of a nondescript 1970s brick office building was good in theory but difficult in practice. We lacked height and the building lacked anything much in the way of protrusions we could turn into attachment points. The boxwood and euonymus struggling to grow in the brick planter running the length of the building made it hard to even get close to the building. But the scrawny bushes finally gave us the answer, and we spread Ernestine's lion's mane out so that it swam along on top of them.

"It's not quite how I pictured it," she said, "but it's very exciting to see it heading for the door and to think of it swimming inside to sign up for the next beekeeping workshop."

As we made our way to the footbridge, Ardis sent a text. "Developments," it said. "Delayed. More later." Ernestine and I laughed about how she treated texts as though she paid for them by the word, like old-fashioned telegrams.

Joe and Zach—what was left of Team Purl—arrived first at the footbridge. Joe's lean silhouette showed against the sky, standing in the middle of the graceful arch. He'd been leaning his elbows on the rail and straightened when he saw Ernestine and me coming. Zach sat on the steps. Ernestine joined him, and after all her worries over the past weeks, about keeping individual projects secret from the rest of the bomb squad so that we could all look forward to being surprised, she excitedly told him every one of her secrets. While she did, the court-house clock struck midnight. By ten minutes past, Ardis and her team still hadn't arrived.

"Do you hear them out there anywhere?" I asked. "You'd think we'd hear Ambrose whacking something with his cane, if nothing else. Shall I call one of them?"

"We can give them a few more minutes," Joe said. "No telling what 'developments' means with those two old coots. Has Ardis told you about the prancing?"

"Wouldn't that be a sight on Main Street? We would've heard more than ducks quacking in their sleep if that was going on, though."

"Why don't we start," Ernestine said, "and anyone else who comes along can join us when they get here?"

"Good idea." I opened the last garbage bag I had—by then I felt as though I'd been dragging it around for hours. "I have some of the crochet. Ardis has the rest. Come on, Zach. Our last hurrah, before us old fogies fall asleep on our feet. Or in the creek."

"That should be we old fogies," Zach said.

"Thank you, Zach. Joe, have you got extra mouth tape—I mean, duct tape?"

We'd made eighteen squares to hang from the bridge rails—nine for each side. Actually we'd cheated—the squares were crocheted, but not by any of us. Wanda had bought a box of old afghans at an estate sale, none of them in a condition worth saving whole. Pieces of them were worth rescuing for our purpose, though. Wanda had washed them, cut them into two-by-two-foot squares, and handed them out to the rest of us. We'd mended where necessary, embellished here and there, and bound off the edges of the squares. They were a mix of patterns and colors and ended up an eclectic riot of creativity and we'd decided they were perfect for bombing the foot-bridge. I took out the nine squares I had in my bag and divided them between Zach, Joe, Ernestine, and me.

"I thought I was going to be too late," a voice said from the other side of the creek. And there was Wanda, her market basket on her arm. She waved and came across the bridge.

"Great job on finding the afghans, Wanda." I held a square out to her. "This final bomb is going to be the bomb. We thought we'd go ahead and start. Here you go."

She ignored the square and put her basket down. "Where's everyone else?"

"They'll be along," Joe said, adding as he turned away, "Most of them."

I held the square out to her again.

"No, no," Wanda said. "I brought my own, a special one. I had to run back home and get this. I can't believe I forgot it. It's what I've been working on—my secret. Ernestine, I've kept it under wraps all this time." She took a folded square from her basket. "I know Ardis wants to dedicate this whole shebang-shebomb to Hugh McPhee, but I'd like to dedicate this one square to my grandmother, Viola Moyes. She taught me everything I know about knitting and crocheting." She held up a granny square in shades of purple.

"What lovely work," Ernestine said. "And a truly lovely idea. Put it right in the middle of the bridge, why don't you, and we'll space ours out on either side of it?"

"*You* should have thought of that lovely idea," a voice said in my ear. I shivered as Geneva laid a chummy arm across my shoulders. "You could have dedicated your yarn spewing to your dear, departed grandmother. Or to me. That would have been a truly lovely idea."

While the others spaced themselves along the bridge and got busy tying their squares to the balustrades, I held up my square as though I was looking it over. "We were getting worried about you guys," I said quietly. "Are the others on their way?"

"I did not wait to find out."

She took her arm from my shoulders and floated around so that she was between me and the square. It was close quarters and her serious face worried me. I lowered the square and took out my phone.

"I rushed here to tell you important news," she said.

"What?"

"I rushed here to tell you important news."

"Don't play around, Geneva." I saw Joe looking at me. I held my phone up for him to see and put it back to my ear. "What is it? What's happened?"

"Ardent could not see or hear me."

"That's—"

"I thought she was being rude and ignoring me whenever I said anything. Then I realized that she did not hear me and did not know I was there."

"That's—"

"And then I got bored because all the yarn they were strewing around just . . . sat. Really. But here is something more interesting than sedentary patches of yarn. Do you remember our discussion about yin and yang?" She repeated her over- and underarm movements of the other day.

"Yes."

"Here is another example. Ardis did not know I was there, and then her old-as-dirt daddy and John's creaky cranky brother were not there."

"What?"

"She did not see me. Then she did not see them. Poof." She illustrated the poof with her hands. "Both of them. Gone."

Chapter 21

"Trouble?" Joe appeared as Geneva poofed her hands again, and I jumped. He was lucky I didn't scream. "Is that Ardis?" he asked.

I nodded and held a finger up to him, then spoke quietly into the phone, looking at Geneva. A calm voice would have been optimal, but I didn't quite get there. "Tell me what happened," I said. "Are Abby and John there? Where's Darla?" Unfortunately for my less-than-stellar acting skills, while I peppered Geneva with those questions, my phone buzzed. I took it from my ear and looked at it. Joe looked at it, too.

"If I am reading your screen correctly," Geneva said, peering at it more closely than either of us, "*that* is Ardis."

I looked at Joe and shrugged. "No wonder she wasn't answering my questions," I said. "We got disconnected." I pushed the TALK button. "Ardis?"

While Ardis was being incoherent on my phone, Joe got a call. It was John. Joe seemed to be getting some sense out of John—sense that had him slipping his backpack off, taking out his flashlight and checking the batteries, putting the pack back on, and saying, "We'll be there in five."

"Kath? Are you there?"

I hadn't been paying attention to Ardis. "I am. What's going on? Hold on a sec, will you? Don't hang up."

Joe had gone and spoken to Zach on the footbridge. Now the two of them were walking back toward me. Wanda had stopped working and followed them. Ernestine didn't seem to have noticed that anything else was going on. She continued working on a square at the other end of the bridge. The misty shadow next to her was Geneva, who'd lost interest in me when I stopped talking to her.

"Hold on, Ardis," I said, again, then muffled the phone against my chest.

"Zach and I are going to give John and Ardis a hand," Joe said. "They've, uh . . ." He rubbed his temples. "They lost Hank and Ambrose. The two of them took off. Or Ambrose took off with Hank. They don't know." He held his hand up. To stop questions? He didn't need to—I didn't know where to begin asking questions. No wonder Ardis hadn't been coherent.

"Darla's not there," Joe said. "She got a call from work before this happened. Abby, Ardis, and John are okay, just confused about how they could lose the old guys so thoroughly. Zach and I'll go see what we can do."

"We can come, too," Wanda said. "More feet on the ground, isn't that what they say? And the sooner we locate them, the better. How long have they been gone?"

Joe held up his hand again. "Thanks, Wanda. What you say makes sense, but give us half an hour."

"And a lost half hour could make all the difference," she said.

"It's what Ardis and John want."

"Call Cole if you don't find them soon," I said.

"Yep."

"And call me when you know what's going on. Let's skip meeting up back at the shop. Unless we hear that you need our help, we'll finish up here and call it a night."

They waved and took off into the dark. Geneva had floated back to my side and she waved after them.

"But let's not just call it a night," she said. "We should call it a strange and eventful night. And here are two more events you might like to know about. Ardis is squawking against your breast and Ernestine has lost her crochet, hook and all, over the side of the bridge."

Sure enough, Ernestine was peering over the bridge railing and Ardis was obviously still on the line. I put the phone back to my ear. "Ardis? Ardis, Joe's on his way." I wasn't sure she heard me.

"—don't think Ambrose will hurt him," she was saying. "The two of them were getting along so well. But neither of them is competent to be out, and I'll never forgive myself if anything happens to Daddy or to Ambrose if Daddy's taken something into his head and dragged Ambrose along. But we don't think Ambrose will hurt him." She was slower and clearer by then, so I could follow her, but I got the feeling she'd been talking nonstop since we'd connected.

"Stay on the line, Ardis. I want to know what's happening. We'll keep talking, okay? Here's what we're doing. We're going to finish up bombing the bridge with the materials we have—" I looked at Wanda.

"I finished my square," she said. "If you don't need me to look for the old me, then I'll see you at Mel's in the morning."

"Wanda's going home," I told Ardis. "We'll plan to use the squares you have another time. Maybe even tomorrow night. Where are you, anyway?"

"The other side of the library. John knitted what looks like several acres of oobleck from the Dr. Seuss book as a surprise for Thea, and we were spreading it around on the grass in front."

While Ardis talked, I went back up onto the footbridge with Ernestine. She stared over the railing, her hands on her hips. Geneva hovered beside her, hands on her hips, too.

"Thea's going to love the oobleck, Ardis," I said. "Ernestine will, too. I need to give her a hand, now."

"Right over the side they went," Ernestine said. "And I don't think I can get down there and make it back up."

"Did you hear that, Ardis? She lost her square and crochet hook over the side of the bridge." "Lost" set Ardis off again.

"How could we lose two grown men? We thought we could *find* them," she streamed into my ear. "John and Abby and I, we all thought we could. I mean, how hard can it *be* to find two gimpy old men who think they're out for a night in a town the size of a bath mat?"

I let Ardis talk and got the flashlight from my backpack. I gave it to Ernestine and asked her to shine it where the hook and scissors fell.

"The square will be easy enough to get," she said, "but the crochet hook and my scissors might be harder to find in the reeds."

I looked at Geneva, raising my eyebrows in invitation. She folded her hands primly at her waist and made no move to come with me.

"Try to avoid stepping on copperheads while you're down there trailing through the mud," she said helpfully, "and try not to worry the dear ducks and ducklings by crashing about."

"And we didn't want to worry anyone," Ardis was saying in my ear. "We didn't want to alarm the rest of you or start a ruckus, especially with Ambrose the way he is—"

I went down the steps at the far end of the bridge and made a wide circuit around the bushes planted along the bridge's rock foundation. The embankment didn't look too steep, but there were plenty of weeds and reeds between me and the area lit by the flashlight. The tall growth petered out farther along to my left and grass ran down to the bank and the gurgling creek. I decided to go that way and then walk along the water's edge to get where I needed to be. And to avoid worrying the copperheads or stepping on ducks in the dark. Although maybe copperheads preferred the water's edge, too. I didn't know.

"You're sure you need the hook and scissors back?" I called to Ernestine.

"I think I see the hook," she said.

"They are her favorites," Geneva said.

"Thank you, Kath," Ernestine called.

I waved back when she waved one of the crocheted squares, and gingerly picked my way to the water.

"Is Joe there yet?" I asked Ardis.

"He, Zach, Abby, and John have spread out to look. I'm staying put in case the old reprobates follow their own trail back this way."

The closer I got to the footbridge, walking along the creek bank, the narrower the bank became. And there were two or three narrow trails leading into the tall reeds and weeds. Not as narrow as snakes.

"Vernon and I used to sit on that creek bank in the moonlight," Ardis said. "Until Daddy caught us one night. But the creek looks real pretty these days, don't you think?"

"Oh yeah."

The town parks department had been working with a University of Tennessee naturalist to rehabilitate the creek, after years of it being straightened and channeled and run through culverts. It certainly looked good and natural, and now that I could smell the mud, I thought that must be very natural, too—but I was beginning to appreciate Thea's feelings toward a natural creek environment.

Ernestine's square was caught on cockleburs—cockleburs that were now caught in my socks and my sleeves. I pulled the square free and tucked it under my arm, no doubt transferring cockleburs there, too. We'd assumed the crochet hook and scissors had fallen nearby, but what Ernestine thought was the hook, and was shining the light on, turned out to be a bicycle spoke.

"John says the hardest part about looking after Ambrose is that he's unpredictable," Ardis said.

"Unpredictable can be scary."

"Boy howdy."

Ardis kept talking. I made listening noises and kept looking. Had the square caught a breeze and fluttered when it fell? Not that there was much of a breeze, and the crochet wasn't like a piece of paper or even lightweight cotton. But the hook and scissors wouldn't have fluttered at all. They would have dropped straight down, and I was a yard or so out from the bridge. I turned around and inched my way back toward it, parting the reeds and weeds, and studying the ground as I went. I was beginning to think I should have given Ernestine the phone and brought the flashlight down with me.

"Shine the light straight down," I called. I'd seen something, but the light wasn't quite strong enough.

"John also says Ambrose has that very strong antagonism that some lawyers develop toward the police," Ardis was saying. "He blamed them for some of the cases he lost."

"Did you lose two squares down here, Ernestine?"

Had I lost my mind, coming down here? It was hard to tell. It was hard to tell what I saw, too. But there was something under the graceful arch of the footbridge, in the dark, not quite hidden by the reeds. I moved closer. Striped or striped by shadows . . . but if it wasn't a crocheted square . . . was it . . . striped . . . socks?

"Ambrose got in trouble for kicking a deputy in the shin after losing one of the cases."

"Ardis—"

"Well, if he reacted like that when he was compos mentis, now that his cogs are slipping you can see why we didn't want to call the police if we didn't have to, can't you?"

"We have to call them now, Ardis. I need to hang up and call the police now."

Chapter 22

But I couldn't hang up from Ardis until I told her it wasn't her daddy dead under the bridge. Or Ambrose.

"Gladys Weems, Ardis," I whispered into the phone. "Oh my God, I think it's Pokey's little old mother in her blue vest."

"And you're sure she's—"

"No, I need to check. And I need to call nine-one-one—"

"Kath, you need to stop, breathe, and listen to me. Are you doing that?"

"I'm standing here breathing, but that's not good enough—"

"Kath, I didn't take Red Cross CPR training for nothing. First thing, tell one of the others to make the call. Tell someone specifically. Assign it so you know it's done."

"There's only Ernestine left."

"Then tell her."

Ernestine had already caught on that something wasn't right, but hadn't heard the muffled details. I gave the two

most important details now—a body, under the bridge.
When she heard them, Ernestine dropped the flashlight
into the reeds at my feet. Geneva swirled down next to me
while Ernestine made the call. Then, with Geneva beside
me, I picked up the dropped flashlight and shone it on
Gladys.

"I'm going to see if there's anything I can do for her,"
I said to Ardis.

"No, stop. The next thing you're supposed to do is
make sure the scene is safe. Or . . . maybe that was supposed to come first. Now I'm confused."

"I'm going now."

I started forward, Geneva still beside me, but stopped
and whispered to her, "You can't, by any chance, tell
from here if she's gone, can you?"

"I am sorry, no."

Gladys hadn't moved in the minutes I dithered. I'd
seen no rise and fall of breath. There were also no broken reeds near her, nothing to indicate that she'd
reached the low space under the end of the bridge from
this side. She must have walked or crawled in from the
other side.

She lay facedown, her feet in their striped socks
toward me, her arms over her head, as though . . . maybe
someone had dragged her. I couldn't see her face, and
was glad of that. Given her position and location, even
with my flashlight I wasn't sure I would see breaths. Especially shallow or dying breaths. I crouched and crab-
walked sideways, awkwardly, farther under the bridge to
get nearer to her head, to get close enough to feel for a
pulse in her neck.

But getting my fingertips on a blood vessel in her

throat wasn't going to be easy, maybe even impossible. A narrow length of crochet, in brighter stripes than her socks, was wrapped around and around her neck, around and around and twisted, twisted, twisted tight at her nape with a large crochet hook.

So instead of laying my fingertips on the side of Gladys' neck to feel for the beat of her heart, I sucked in a breath and made myself touch the crochet. I didn't understand or like the eerie jolt of someone else's emotions running through me—but if I couldn't feel her pulse or her breath, then maybe I could sense her dying emotions. I brushed my fingers against the crochet—didn't want to, but felt I should, felt . . . laughter? Derision. Disdain. Horrified surprise.

I must have whimpered into the phone. Ardis asked several times what I saw, but I didn't answer. Geneva swirled against me, as though to push me away from the body. She couldn't physically push, but her billowing was just as effective. I scooted backward, away from her and to get out of the dark under that bridge, but then Geneva suddenly swirled around behind me, blocking my way out—unless I wanted to move straight through her, and that I did not want to do.

"Her socks," Geneva said in a low voice. "Touch them, too. Go on. See what you feel. Do it before the police get here."

If a siren wailed in the distance, I didn't hear it. I only heard Geneva urging me over and over to touch Gladys' socks. I didn't want to do that any more than I'd wanted to pass through Geneva's misty form.

"The deaths might be connected," Geneva said. "You have a gift. Use it."

I touched the socks . . . but I didn't so much feel anything as . . . heard . . . "quack."

I sat back on my heels. "What the . . ."

"What?" Geneva asked. "What is that silly look on your face?"

"What is it?" Ardis squawked from the phone. "Kath! What's going on?"

"Did you hear that?" I wasn't sure who I was asking— Geneva, Ardis, or myself.

"Hear what?" Geneva asked.

"Quack."

"Shame on you," she said. "This is no time for lame duck impressions. I am affronted on behalf of the deceased."

"No, no, it's what I heard. Didn't you?"

She swirled around me once, making a noise ruder than a quack, and disappeared.

"Who are you talking to?" Ardis asked. "Is Gladys alive?"

"No. No, she's not. It was Geneva."

"She's there?"

"She was. She's gone."

"If she's gone," a voice I didn't know said behind me, "then there's nothing more you can do for her, so come on out of there."

I didn't know that voice behind me, but I recognized its nasal birthplace—Chicago. "Ardis, I think Al Rogalla is here," I whispered into the phone.

"Then watch your back," she said.

"He's *at* my back."

"Okay," she said, "then here's what you do. Turn around, look him in the eye, mention Hugh's name, and see what he does. It's the element of surprise and might be revealing."

Mentioning a murdered guy to someone Ardis didn't trust wasn't the kind of surprise I wanted to spring in the dark, under a bridge, near another newly murdered person. Under the circumstances, just being near the guy Ardis didn't trust would have given me the heebie-jeebies, but before my nerves had a chance to dance that particular jig, the first wave of police arrived in the form of Shorty Munroe.

"Deputy Munroe's here now," I whispered into the phone. "But, Ardis, we need to find your daddy and Ambrose, fast, because—"

"Because there's a maniac on the loose. Tell Shorty, Kath. Tell him and whoever else arrives. Oh my land, and now I'll worry about John, Joe, and the kiddos out there, too."

"You should hang up in case they're trying to call you."

"And so you can concentrate. Call me when you know something," she said, and disconnected.

"What are you doing here, Rogalla?" Shorty said. "You know better than to contaminate a possible crime scene. And who've you got treed under the bridge there? Oh, hey, Ms. Rutledge. You're not with this guy, are you? Did you call this in?"

I acknowledged Shorty's "hey," and then we heard Ernestine hailing him from the bridge.

"Yoo-hoo, Deputy Munroe. I made the call. Kath found the body."

"Hoo boy," Shorty said. "Cole's going to love this. You come on out, too, Ms. Rutledge."

Before making my way out into the glare of his high-powered flashlight, and before my nerves had a chance to run screaming, I quickly brushed my fingertips across Gladys' sock again. The "quack" that time was just as clear—and just as bizarre. I'd never "heard" anything through my fingertips before. But the quack reminded me of the first time I'd seen Gladys. Outside the courthouse, with Clod holding her by the arm, and she'd whomped him in the stomach with her handbag and called him a quack. *Quack?*

"Ms. Rutledge, are you all right?" Shorty was on his hands and knees.

"Kind of rocky, Shorty, but I'm okay."

"Well, you go on out while I see what we've got here."

I crawled past him. I liked Shorty. While Clod's entire persona appeared to be starched, pressed, and at attention, Shorty always looked as though he'd just stifled a massive yawn, and his uniform as though it was still taking a nap. He wore wire-rimmed glasses and made me think of an overworked pencil pusher—more like an accountant than the guy in running shorts who watched me crawl out from under the bridge and get to my feet.

"Are you Al Rogalla?" I asked.

"Yeah." Joe had said Al Rogalla—accountant and volunteer fireman— was a nice guy. But he wasn't so nice that he made any more of an introduction of himself than "yeah," and he didn't ask me who I was in return. Maybe he didn't feel it was the time or place for that kind of polite exchange. He wasn't as tall as Joe or Clod, though easily a head taller than Shorty. Shorty's nickname hadn't taken any imagination. That he had a couple of inches on me wasn't saying much.

Now that I wasn't alone in the dark under a bridge with Al Rogalla, I decided it *was* the time to take Ardis' advice and spring the name Hugh McPhee on him. And while we were there within scream's reach of an armed sheriff's deputy, I decided to up the percentage. "You and Hugh McPhee had a meeting with the Register of Deeds Tuesday afternoon, didn't you? And another meeting with Rachel Meeks at the bank after that?"

"Yeah." Neither his face nor his monosyllable revealed a thing. He did shift slightly from one foot to the other; otherwise nothing.

We heard Shorty speak into the radio at his shoulder. It was possible that Rogalla, from his years as a volunteer fireman, could interpret the answering burst of static. I couldn't. Shorty spoke again, then crawled back out. When he stood he wiped his hand down his face, but he didn't bother to brush the dirt from his knees.

"You look lonely out here by yourself," Rogalla said to Shorty. "Everyone else at the poker game?"

"Backup's on the way. What *are* you doing here, Rogalla?"

"I was out for a run and caught it on the radio." A small box clipped to his waistband buzzed to prove his point.

"And you got here before me? All I had to do was walk out the back door." Shorty hooked a thumb over his shoulder toward the courthouse.

"I run fast. You should try it."

The gibe didn't bother Shorty. I pictured it landing

somewhere on his rumpled khaki and brown and getting lost in the wrinkles. He scratched the back of his neck. "Where'd you run tonight? Were you in the park before you heard the radio?"

"Before? No. I ran the usual loop. Out Depot to Old Stage Road and around to Spring Street. I was crossing the tracks at Fox when I heard the radio."

"Okay. You can clear out, Rogalla. Ms. Rutledge, we're going to have to take a statement. Would you like to wait up there on the bridge with Ms. O'Dell?"

"I'd like to walk Ms. O'Dell home," I said. "But first I need to—"

"I'll walk her home," Rogalla cut in.

"You are being rude and staring at him as though you expect him to sprout horns," Geneva called down from the bridge.

"Ernestine, is that all right with you?" I asked.

"If it doesn't put him to too much trouble," she said. "Deputy, I don't think there's anything I can add to your report except that if you find a crochet hook and a pair of scissors down there, they're probably mine."

"*Crochet* hook," Shorty said as though the piece of a puzzle had fallen into place. "When did you lose it?"

"Shortly before Kath made her discovery. I dropped them and she kindly went to find them for me and found—who did you find, dear? Do we know?"

I looked at Shorty and he shook his head.

"It's unconfirmed, Ernestine."

"We might need to keep Ms. O'Dell here to answer a few questions, too," Shorty said quietly.

I shook *my* head and pointed toward the bridge, toward Gladys, toward the crochet hook twisted in the strip around her neck. I was interested to see that my finger shook slightly. "It's not Ernestine's hook," I said. "She never uses one that big."

"Old woman?" Shorty said, sounding skeptical. "Bad eyesight, right? My grandmother uses one that big. Heck, my wife does."

"Ernestine doesn't," I said firmly. "She was with me all evening. Gladys was dead when I found her."

"All right if I take her home, then?" Rogalla asked. "Your call, Shorty."

"Go on."

Shorty and I watched Al Rogalla climb the bank in a few long-legged steps. On the bridge, he bent his head to hear something Ernestine said. Geneva bent to hear it, too. Then Rogalla took Ernestine's backpack on one shoulder and her on his arm.

"See you in the morning, Ernestine," I called. "Thanks, um, Al." He said nothing in return.

"You could walk *me* home," Geneva said, floating down from the bridge and hovering beside me. "Now that your art project has blown up in your face."

"Excuse me, Shorty, my phone." I pulled it out of my pocket. "Okay if I answer it?"

"No details," he said.

"I'll just go over here." I put a few feet between us. Geneva followed. "What did Ernestine say to Rogalla up there?" I asked her.

"She asked where he bought his running shorts. Will you take me home now?"

While I tried to explain why I couldn't walk her home then and there, Shorty's backup arrived. Shorty shooed me up to the bridge, which was fine with me. I sat on the steps, glad I was at least a little removed from the usual controlled commotion of a crime scene. I didn't want to see them putting Gladys on a stretcher. I didn't want to see Clod, either. It wasn't until I was thinking how strange it was to know what consisted of "usual" at a crime scene that I realized this one was usual, except for a conspicuous absence.

"The sheriff is here," I whispered to Geneva, "but wonder of wonders, Deputy Dunbar isn't."

"Because someone probably walked him home," she shouted back.

There was no point in telling her, *again*, that she could easily find her way back to the Weaver's Cat without me. And there was no point in *re*-repeating that if she stopped moaning about it, she might hear something pertinent to the case. She'd already declared me impertinent and was sulking in a heap on the step below me. Her sulk and Clod's absence—including the absence of his invariably snarky questions and comments—lent my small space in this wretched night a brief sense of calm. False calm, of course, because the word "absence" triggered a barrage of thoughts starting with a guilty one about Tammie. She hadn't shown up at the bridge and we, at least I, hadn't heard anything from her. I tried calling her again. No answer. That could mean nothing, or it could mean I should tell Shorty and—and what a *dolt*. I hadn't told Shorty about Hank and Ambrose. That they were still missing, I was sure. If they'd been found, Ardis, John, Joe—or all three—would have called to let me know.

"Geneva?" I moved down onto the step next to her. "I need to go talk to the sheriff. Do you want to come with me?"

"You were told to wait here."

"I need to tell them about Ardis' daddy and Ambrose."

"What about them?"

"What you told me. They're missing. Remember?"

"I thought it was an escape. From Ardent. I know that is what I felt like doing. That is why I followed them here. Now you are staring at me just as rudely as you did at that nice man who walked off into the moonset with Ernestine."

"If you followed them here, where are they now?"

"To borrow one of your favorite phrases, 'beats me.' Now do you see how defeatist and unhelpful that is?" She heaved a sigh. "No, I am sorry. I do not know where they are. When I saw all of you here at the bridge, I bid the old darlings *adieu.* I have just had a thought, though."

"What?"

"Do you think either of those crotchety geezers speaks French?"

As tempting as it was to say, "Beats me," I opted for grinding my teeth instead.

"Because it's possible that I do," she said. "Or it could just be that I had the good fortune to catch a foreign film or two on television. It is so difficult to know these things, *mais oui*?"

"Come on." I stood up. "We need to go talk to the sheriff. *I* need to talk to him, and please don't interrupt while I do. Then I'll take you home. This night is giving me a headache."

"*Dommage.*"

"Please stop."

*   *   *

Sheriff Leonard Haynes did something I didn't think possible. He made me wish I was talking to Clod. Clod at least listened to me. Clod's condescending attitude came with signs and portents—a snort or a smirk— before he dismissed what I said. He thought I was a meddler, but he did listen. Sheriff Haynes didn't care if I made a statement about finding Gladys Weems or not. My words made no noticeable impact on his ears. What I said seemed to go straight into a void of nonresponse. He didn't make eye contact—not out of some kind of social awkwardness, but out of an obvious feeling that there was no need whatsoever.

I'd been introduced to Sheriff Haynes before. Clod had actually mentioned my name to him as one deserving credit for the help TGIF had given in solving a previous crime. That he didn't acknowledge knowing me didn't bother me. Not much, anyway. And I could understand why he didn't want or need to hear my theory about how Gladys had probably been dragged under the bridge from the opposite side. But he lost my respect when he completely blew off worries over Tammie and then shrugged over the missing old men—didn't think they could have gone far, didn't believe they were in danger, didn't give any credence to the horrible idea that Ambrose might have gone off his mean-as-snakes rocker and attacked Gladys—or Tammie. I didn't want to give credence to that idea, either, but I also knew that stranger things had happened. Ambrose was a decrepit and tottery old geezer, but there was strength in him yet and he swung a wicked cane. And what kind of danger did that put Ardis' daddy in? Sheriff Haynes didn't think any.

Shorty caught up with me as I stomped my muttering

way back to the Cat, Geneva's misty form stomping alongside me.

"How did that man ever get elected sheriff?" I asked him. "I felt like shaking my fist at him, but he wouldn't have cared. He wouldn't have noticed."

Geneva turned around and shook her fist, oddly stomping as easily backward as she'd stomped forward. She turned again and put her arm across my shoulders. *"Les flics,"* she said. "Phooey. Pigs, all of them."

Shorty was more polite and probably more accurate. "He's a good old boy. It's the way he works and what works for him."

"But who's he working for? The community he's sworn to protect, or himself?"

"Right now he's trying to figure out how he's going to tell the mayor that his ninety-three-year-old mother was murdered within spitting distance of the courthouse."

"Which is absolutely horrible." I stopped and Shorty stopped, too. "It really is horrible. I liked her. And now this is going to sound callous, but she's gone, and there are two old men—"

Shorty put his hand up. "A couple of questions and then I need to get back there. "You last saw Tammie on Main sometime before eleven. What's her last name?"

"Fain."

"And this yarn project on the bridge—when did you and Ms. O'Dell start working on it?"

"We started the project about ten. We got to the bridge about midnight."

"Were the old men with you?"

"They were with Ardis and John."

"But they had access to your—materials?"

"*Matériel*," Geneva said.

"Because I saw squares on the bridge," Shorty said, "and one of the guys said he saw long strips tied around streetlights and a stop sign. It's the strips I'm interested in. And who had access to them. And when."

"You mean earlier this evening?"

"Earlier this week. We found the same kind of strip wrapped around Hugh McPhee's neck Tuesday night."

Chapter 23

"I hope you realize that what I just said lets Ambrose Berry off the hook," Shorty said.

I'd closed my eyes when he told me about the strip wrapped around Hugh's neck. I opened them at that remark, and he nodded.

"Pun intended. Sorry. I wanted to make sure you're still with me."

"That doesn't let any of us off the hook, Shorty. We've been knitting and crocheting strips for weeks."

"Like that one?"

"I don't . . . maybe not. I don't know. But that makes it even *more* egregious that Sheriff Haynes didn't take a statement from me. He's got two victims of murder by crochet strip, and there I am, with one of the victims and a bag full of potential murder weapons." I was getting worked up again. I took a breath and tried to lower my voice. And to avoid spitting on Shorty's rumples. "Wouldn't you think Sheriff Haynes would have wanted to see if there was some kind of connection there?"

Shorty gave me a slow, tired blink that did more to

calm me than any amount of deep breathing could have. "Did either you or Ms. O'Dell kill Hugh McPhee or Po- key's mother?"

"No."

"Didn't think so. I'm not at liberty to tell you why, but Sheriff Haynes doesn't think so, either. We know where to find you, though, if we have more questions. And I can pretty much guarantee we will have more questions."

"What about finding Tammie and the old men?"

"I've got you covered. I called Cole."

Shorty headed back to the crime scene. I walked with Geneva the rest of the way to the Weaver's Cat. She floated beside me, humming "Frère Jacques." I said good night on the porch. She stopped humming long enough to say, "*Bonne nuit*," and with a wave floated through the front door. I was about to call Ardis when my phone rang. It was a number I'd thought about blocking. The caller didn't wait for me to say hello.

"We're at your house and—"

There was a muffled scuffling sound, as though two identically irritating people were fighting over the phone.

"And we have something you'll be interested in see- ing."

"Something of interest," the other irritating person said in the background. "I knew you'd get it wrong."

"Shirley and Mercy, so help me, if you're in my house—"

"Hurry," the twin with the phone said, and hung up.

It was the fastest three blocks I'd run in years. I didn't try calling Ardis along the way; her imagination didn't need my out-of-breath voice conjuring up all manner of night-mares for her. Half a block from home, though, I slowed, held the stitch in my side, and got through to Joe. He told me Cole had been in touch, but they hadn't found the old men yet. I told him where I was headed.

"What are they doing out this late at night?" he asked. "Do you want me to meet you there?"

He had a good point. By then it was past one. Surely the twins should have been home, hanging upside down in their bat cave by then. "I'll call if I need you," I said. "Where's Ardis?"

"She and John are waiting back at her place."

"Zach?"

"He and Abby are working a grid beyond the library."

"You think that's safe?"

"It's expedient. Let me know what goes on with the twins."

"Will do." I disconnected and started running again.

My porch light shed a soft glow, welcoming my weary feet and pounding heart home, as I rounded the corner into Lavender Street. Most people in the neighborhood left a front light or lamppost burning overnight. Street-lights were fewer and farther between in the residential blocks away from downtown proper, and our own lights gave a cozy, warm look. They also created the shadows in between that made my feet leery as well as weary, and made my pounding heart skip a beat or two.

Shirley and Mercy were watching for me—one of them at the end of the front walk, scanning the street in both directions, the other at the top of the porch steps, arms crossed. When the one at the end of the walk heard me coming, she held both hands up as though she were a border guard trying to stop a tank. Then she turned her palms to the ground, fingers splayed, making "keep it down" motions. I was gulping like a fish by then, and when she saw my mouth open to suck in another breath, she added another frantic semaphore and topped it with a nicely controlled, barely audible "Keep it down." I was impressed. Not to say I wasn't suspicious.

"What's going on, Shirley?" I was breathing through my nose, again, and this was definitely not Mercy.

"Come up on the porch," she said. "We knew you'd know what to do."

"You did?" I wasn't sure how I felt about having their vote of confidence, and followed Shirley warily up the walk.

Mercy, arms still crossed, stood sentry at the top of the steps. Shirley went on up. When I stopped with my foot on the bottom step, Mercy did a Vanna White, gesturing toward the end of the porch where the swing hung. Granny had known how to grow healthy nandina shrubs, though, and a row of them bordered the porch, screening the swing from the street and sidewalk.

"Am I going to be sorry I did this, Mercy?" I asked.

She answered with a quiet "Shh," and waved me up.

I heard a snort and a snore and saw Shirley put a hand over her mouth—to keep from laughing, judging by her eyes. The snort and snore had come from the end of the porch—from the two old men sound asleep, Hank in his wheelchair and Ambrose in the swing. I looked at the men, and looked at the twins. Shirley and Mercy didn't often surprise me in a good way, but tonight they did. Ambrose and Hank were contemporaries of their own daddy, they said. They'd taken off their matching embroidered sweatshirts and covered Hank and Ambrose against the chill. Their faces, as they watched the men sleep, reflected only tenderness. They'd lost their daddy young.

I called Joe and told him that I had Hank and Ambrose at my place. How they got there could wait for Shirley and Mercy to tell it. Joe said he'd call Ardis and contact Clod. I went into the house and got a couple of blankets for the men and so the twins could put their sweatshirts back on.

"Can I get you something warm to drink?"

"What have you—ow," Shirley said.

"We need to be going," said Mercy.

"But where did you find them? People have been searching for hours."

"Cemetery," Shirley said. "Old people like cemeteries. They were visiting Hank's wife."

"Why didn't you take them to Ardis' house?"

"We did," Mercy said. "She wasn't home. Her line was busy."

"How'd you get them up on the porch?"

"On their own two legs, and they were happy to do it. They both knew Ivy. Mercy and I got the chair up here."

"Someone else can get it down," said Mercy. "Now we've got to go. Don't you realize how late it is?"

Which made me wonder why I hadn't already wondered what *they'd* been doing in the cemetery near midnight. But they were on their way down the steps and I had another question I wanted to ask.

"How did you find out about the meetings with Rachel at the bank and the Register of Deeds?"

Mercy linked her arm with Shirley's and they kept

walking. I glanced at Hank and Ambrose—still snoring—
and I ran down the steps after the twins. At the end of my
front walk, they turned down the sidewalk and marched
toward their ugly beige Buick in the drive. I cut the corner
and got in front of them to make them stop.

"It really would be helpful to know—" I said.

Shirley wagged her finger in my face.

Mercy leaned close. "It might also be helpful for you
to know that Rachel and Hugh were briefly married."

They parted then, moving around me like a wave, a
veritable tide of Spivey inscrutability. I let them go and
went back to wait with the old men dreaming on my
porch.

Chapter 24

Our post-bombing celebratory breakfast and debriefing at Mel's the next morning had the look of a hangover party. Mel put us at a long table toward the back of the room. She made it a private space by pulling her room divider across behind us. She'd made the divider by hinging half a dozen antique doors together and putting the whole thing on casters. It accordion-folded so that when she didn't need it, she could roll it out of the way into a corner. The doors were the kind with frosted windows that private eyes had in old black-and-white movies. They seemed especially appropriate to our mood that morning.

The other breakfast customers clattered flatware against plates and cups. The fresh-baked, -broiled, and -brewed smells coming from Mel's kitchen did their best to call us. But only about half the bomb squad seemed willing or able to answer. John, understandably, hadn't driven back into town after finally getting Ambrose home. They lived in the house they'd grown up in, out in the county. Ardis and I had both offered to put them up for what was left of the night, but John had thought it would be better for everyone if Ambrose woke up in his own bed.

"It's really more of a wake, isn't it?" Ardis said to me as she looked around the table. "Bless Gladys Weems' poor heart. And Hugh's. What the world is coming to, I surely do not know." She absentmindedly took a sip of my unsweetened grapefruit juice. It woke her up enough so that she took another, grouchier, look around the table. "Of course, the percentage of bright-eyed breakfasters would be higher if more of those *who went home early last night* had the decency to look as though they'd enjoyed their good night's sleep." Her emphasis was aimed at Thea sitting across from her, who looked less awake than I felt.

Wanda, down at the other end of the table, had joined Zach and Joe by ordering full platters of eggs, sausage, potatoes, pancakes, and biscuits—what Mel called the Eighteen Wheeler Special. Ernestine and Abby each toyed with fruit cups and I ignored the single slice of rye toast I'd ordered. We hadn't heard from Rachel and we weren't expecting Darla. Tammie wasn't there, either, but I'd had a phone call—and an earful—from her at three. She'd thanked me for sending Clod to knock on her door at two to see if she was home and sound asleep. She'd set her alarm for three so she could return the favor and spread the joy of an interrupted night.

Ardis thumped my grapefruit juice glass on the table and Thea had a delayed reaction to her comment about bright eyes.

"Hmm? What?" Thea fumbled a hand toward the coffeepot and latched onto it. She filled one of Mel's thick white china mugs, added milk and sugar, stirred, drank, then sank her chin on her hand. "Sorry," she said through a yawn. "Late night." She yawned again, missing Ardis inflating in high dudgeon. I moved my juice glass in case it got in the dudgeon's way.

"Yeah," Thea said, somewhat unclearly, because her chin still rested in her hand, "I felt kind of bad about bailing after my footwear mishap." She straightened, drank more coffee, then slumped again, speaking so that only Ardis and I heard. "I spent the rest of the night chasing Hugh McPhee on the Internet."

Ardis immediately relaxed and motioned for Thea to lean forward. "Kath has information, too," she said, "albeit from an iffy source. Not here, though."

"Fast and Furious this afternoon?" Thea asked.

"The posse will be in special session," Ardis said.

"And we can make use of the refreshments that didn't get eaten last night," Thea said. "Excellent use of time and taste buds. I'll spread the word."

Mel stopped by the table with a tray of marmalade muffins and another pot of coffee. "Sorry if I've been ignoring you. Shorthanded this morning. And before I forget, Rachel sends her regrets. She says her ankle is okay, but she's staying off it as much as possible." Mel put the coffee down in front of me and raised a muffin. "To success," she said. "Your work is the talk of the café, if not the town."

"Your work, too," Ernestine said. "Your chicken feet look perfect on the welcome sign."

Mel took a bow. While her head was near my shoulder, I gave her the message about our called meeting that afternoon.

"If I can make it," she said. "I'd like to kill whoever killed Gladys. Don't repeat that." She straightened and addressed the group again. "We all did a great job. I wish our success had not been marred by tragedy—" She stared at her pressed-tin ceiling for a few seconds, hands on her hips. "Gladys deserved better," she said, looking back at us. "But she would have loved the yarn bombing. The marmalade muffins were her favorite, so they're on the house. I have to go chop something."

Joe put an envelope on the muffin tray and started it around the table. "Pictures from this morning," he said. He *had* taken me up on the offer to spend the night, and slept soundly enough after the harried search that Tammie's call hadn't made a dent in his soft snores. But he'd been gone by the time I groggily turned off the alarm.

Thea grabbed the envelope before anyone else could. "Because it was my idea," she said.

"And because you missed most of it," Ardis snapped.

"Never fear," Thea said. "It was for a good and shoe-worthy cause. And you'll see; I *more* than made up for it." She leafed through the pictures, laughing at the squid outside the Extension office and the oobleck spread over the library's lawn. Her laugh brought some of the celebration back to the gathering, and we shared the pictures around the table. The photos of the courthouse columns, lit by the rising sun, were particularly nice.

"Convenient," a starched and sarcastic voice said, coming around the edge of the room divider. Clod Dunbar, in all his officious glory, moved a chair to the end of the table and sat. "If only all my witnesses would gather themselves in a room, life would be great. Pass the muffins, Joe. And pass the photos." He held his hand out to

Abby. She warily gave him the pictures she'd been look-ing at, then scooted her chair farther away.

"Saw you out there capturing the local color this morning," Clod said to Joe. He gestured impatiently for the pictures the rest of us still had.

"These photos have nothing to do with you, Cole-ridge," Ardis said. "Ten documented the art installation as part of Handmade Blue Plum. He's writing an article for the paper in Asheville."

"Good for you, Joe. I'm sure these are prints, though, and you have the images in a file. So you won't mind if I keep this set? They're better than the ones I got with my phone. Oh, and by the by, Ms. Buchanan, it might be of interest to you that the chairwoman of Handmade Blue Plum—that's Olive Weems, in case you didn't know—claims she has no knowledge of your art installation."

"*Well.*" Ardis looked down her nose at him, her dud-geon back in full force.

"I notice you didn't deny that it *is* your art installa-tion," he said. "And for clarification I'm using 'your' in the plural." He smiled around the table. "So, is this ev-eryone? If not, I'd like a list of anyone who's absent."

"Your sarcasm isn't appreciated," Ardis said. "I don't think you're taking this seriously."

"Oh yes," Clod said. He produced a pen and note-book. "I am."

"Are we in trouble?" Abby whispered to Ernestine.

"No, dear," Ernestine said. "He's showing off."

Wanda stood up and said loudly enough to hush the other tables in the café, "I want my lawyer."

Then we heard Mel ask someone to take over for her, heard the creak of floorboards as she left the order counter and came down the room toward us, and saw her spiked hair and blazing eyes. Wanda didn't wait to hear what lay behind Mel's bared teeth. She grabbed her purse, meekly waved good-bye, and crept away. Mel turned to Abby and Zach.

"School," she said. "You're late. Go."

They went without arguing. They weren't late; fall break went for another week. If Clod knew, he didn't argue, either. That left Ardis, Thea, Ernestine, Joe, and me at the table. Plus Mel; she pulled out the chair closest to Clod. Clod was undisturbed, as though this had all been part of his plan. It probably wasn't, but Mel called him on it anyway.

"I haven't got time for games, Dunbar." She hitched her chair around so she faced him. "Tell us what's going on."

"I'd like the names of everyone out there with you last night. Anyone who wasn't with someone else the entire time. Anyone else you saw. If you know, or can make a good guess at the time someone left your group, that will be helpful."

"That's a reasonable request," Ardis said. "You should have asked us that to begin with. There are times I don't know where your manners come from."

I'd told him the same thing once, though in less mannered words. Not that it bothered Clod. Joe said the attitude went with the job. He was probably right. A thick skin was armor.

"I'd also like you to look at a picture." He handed it to Joe. "Pass it around." It went from Joe, to Ernestine, to Thea without comment. Ardis took it from Thea.

"It's pretty. One of us did nice work," she said, and passed it to me.

I looked, put it facedown on the table, and jammed my hands in my armpits, arms crossed tight. Mel picked it up, glanced at it, and handed it back to Clod.

"So?" she said.

"It's the murder weapon," I said. The picture showed a length of striped crochet—more brightly striped than Gladys' socks. And the thought of that piece of crochet knotted around Gladys' neck—I hugged myself tighter.

"How do you know that piece of crochet came from one of our installations?" Joe asked. "That's what you're implying, isn't it?"

"I don't recognize it," Mel cut in. "Narrower stripes in that piece than any of us did, and the whole thing is narrower, too. Except for specialty pieces like squid or Groucho glasses, we kept to a standard five inches wide."

"Easy enough to check," Joe said. "We've got the documentation pictures. I'll send you copies," he said to Clod. "See if anything we made or collected matches."

"What is that strip made with, Coleridge?" Ardis asked. "That might tell us something."

Clod opened his mouth as if to answer, then closed it. Ardis must have recognized the look on his face—equal parts curiosity, suspicion, and mulishness.

"It's not a trick question, Coleridge. The crochet is made of yarn, of course, but I'm wondering what the fiber is. Cotton, wool, acrylic? Something else?"

Before Clod answered, Thea jumped in with her own question. "Could crochet really be pulled tightly enough? That kind of stitch has a lot of give to it. A lot of stretch."

"Twisted it with a crochet hook," Clod said. "Like using a branch or a screwdriver or something to tighten a tourniquet."

"Worst aid instead of first aid," Mel said.

"What crochet hook?" Ernestine cried.

"Not yours," I said quickly.

"Big thing," Clod said. "Big around as my finger."

Ernestine leaned against Thea.

"And she was gone before we got to the bridge, Ernestine. Before you dropped your hook, I'm sure of that." I turned back to Clod. "Do you know when it happened?"

"No. Why would it help to know what the fiber is?"

"It might not help," said Ardis. "But if it turned out to be a type none of us uses, or a brand we don't carry at the Cat, it might tell you something."

"Sounds far-fetched."

"It *is* far-fetched," I said, "because the fiber . . . looked ordinary." It had looked completely ordinary—and horribly out of place around Gladys' neck. And when I'd touched it, when I'd *felt* the derision and horrified surprise—I squeezed my eyes shut, trying to erase that memory. But the thought of squeezing anything made my eyes fly open again. "The fiber's worth checking anyway."

Clod made a note. "What about that list of names?"

"We can't come up with it instantaneously," Ardis said. "We'll have to compare notes."

"Sure. Go ahead."

"We'll have to make phone calls, too," she said. "Umpteen."

"I can wait." He poured himself a cup of coffee, ate one muffin in two bites, and took another.

This was different. Clod with no place else he needed

to be? No one else he needed to annoy? I looked at Joe. He shrugged.

Mel shrugged, too. "Sorry I can't help with the paperwork," she said. She got up and stacked some of the dirty dishes on her arm. "You want any breakfast to go with your coffee and muffins, Cole?"

"Eighteen Wheeler would be great."

Joe took notes as each of us thought back and recalled the who, where, and when of people disappearing and reappearing from our teams. On paper it was a more complicated choreography than we'd thought.

Clod glanced at it. "Don't forget to make your phone calls," he said. "Can I get anyone another coffee?"

He was thanking the waitress who brought his Eighteen Wheeler when Darla, crisp and serious in her khaki and brown, came in through the back door. She had her usual smile and wave for us, but they were subdued.

"Message from Shorty," she said to Clod. She nodded toward the door and he got up. They went as far as the vestibule and stopped there to confer.

"Did you notice his radio's been silent?" I asked.

"Did you notice he isn't wearing it?" Joe asked. "What do you suppose that means?"

"The better to sneak up on us, my dear," said Thea. "All that static and lawman babble spoil a good surprise. I hate to leave this fabulous party, but I need to open the library. I'm doing Little Red Riding Hood at story time this morning, with a wolf puppet guaranteed to scare small children. See you for Fast and Furious." She wrapped two muffins in a napkin, put them in her purse, and left.

Joe was still watching Darla and Clod. "I wonder if she's telling him what I was going to tell you." He took another envelope out of a jacket pocket and handed it to me. "Different pictures," he said. "Put it away; here he comes."

"News?" Ardis asked as Clod sat back down. For the veteran repertory actress she was, I thought she overplayed the bonhomie in her greeting. From the suspicious look he gave her, he thought so, too.

"Where's Thea?"

"Time waits for no librarian," Ardis said. "We need to be going, too. And Handmade opens at noon, doesn't it, Ten?"

"It does. Can I give you a lift home, Ernestine?" He started to get up.

"Hold up," Clod said. "I want to lay some facts out for you. I know you aren't going to stay away from this investigation. It's a given that you're all nosy and stubborn. Please believe me when I say that isn't an entirely bad thing. But I want to try to impress on you—again—that this isn't a game."

"Don't look just at me," I said.

"I'm talking about all of you."

"What facts did you want to lay out?" Joe asked.

"Best they can tell, a piece of the same strip of crochet found with Ms. Weems was used to kill McPhee."

"Do you think it was one of us?" Ardis asked. She circled her finger around the table. "One of *us*?"

"One of your inner cabal?" Clod asked. "Probably not. But someone who knew what you were going to do? We have to consider the possibility."

"Is anyone else in danger?" Ernestine asked.

"With the additional death of Ms. Weems, we have to consider that possibility, too. And with that in mind, Sheriff Haynes suggested that Handmade Blue Plum be canceled."

Joe gave a minimal shake of his head.

"Ten's right," Clod said. "The craft show will go on. One other thing, and then you can leave me to eat my breakfast in peace. Deputy Dye just informed me that they've found McPhee's truck. There's some hope that it will yield information that will further the investigation."

"What year is it?" Ernestine asked. "His truck, I mean. I know what year *this* is."

"Older model. I don't know specifics. Why?"

"No special reason." She smiled at Clod, picked up the pencil Joe had put down, and doodled half a dozen shapes that looked like coat hangers.

"Are we free to go now, Coleridge?" Ardis asked.

"Did you finish the list I asked you for? All your cross-referencing and phone consultations?"

"As far as we were able," Ardis said. "Kath or I will drop it by the department later." She and I got up and pushed in our chairs.

"Or I can stop by the shop and save you a trip," he said. We watched him pour syrup on his pancakes, bacon, and eggs. "Yeah," he said, "why don't I do that? I'll stop by later."

Joe helped Ernestine on with her coat and took her arm. Before walking away, he asked the question that had puzzled him earlier. "Where's your radio, Cole?"

"In my desk, Ten. And there's another fact I should've

laid out." He held up a finger and put a fork loaded with pancake, egg, and syrup in his mouth. We waited while he chewed and swallowed. "I am on what's called administrative — well, we're all friends here, so let's skip the formal designation. The plain fact is, I am suspended."

Chapter 25

Ardis wanted to sit right back down and hear all about Clod's suspension. Joe and I convinced her to let him finish his breakfast in peace, quiet, and whatever dignity someone who pours syrup on eggs is due.

"There is no way on this earth I will ever believe that he did something illegal," she said after we'd opened the shop for the day.

"Hard to imagine," I agreed.

"Impossible."

"You can ask him when he comes by to pick up the list."

"Lord love a duck." She dropped onto the stool behind the counter. "You don't suppose this means he'll have so much time on his hands that he'll spend some of it here, do you? I'm not sure I could bear to teach that man to knit or crochet."

"How about macramé? Say, Ardis, why would Gladys Weems have called Cole a quack?" I told her about seeing Clod and Gladys at the courthouse Tuesday morning.

"Maybe it has something to do with the suspension. I

tell you what—if he parks himself in here, I'll pester him about the suspension until he thinks a swarm of nattering knitters is after him. It'll drive him mad."

That thought put her in a good enough mood that she agreed to call Wanda, Tammie, John, and the teenagers to finish the list and timeline that Clod wanted. I warned her Tammie might be snarky, and went to say good morning to Geneva. She hadn't been in the kitchen when we arrived. Argyle had, and we'd exchanged greetings before he got down to the business of first breakfast. As I passed through the kitchen again, he let me know he was interested in second breakfast. I scooped him up and carried him to the study, reminding him there was more to life than crunchy fishy things. Geneva sat in the window seat, looking out the dormer at the limited view it gave of Blue Plum.

"Drawing," she said when Argyle and I sat down next to her.

Our conversations often began that way. Her sense of time was slippery and not always sequential. I'd gotten used to the ebb and flow of her memories, though, and had developed a theory, after reading up on ghosts in a couple of "authoritative" books. Some ghosts are caught in loops, destined to repeat the same actions for eternity. Geneva seemed to get caught in smaller loops, more like eddies, that took her around again to an earlier conversation.

"I miss drawing more than turning the pages of a book," she said. "I miss holding a book and the feeling of opening a book's covers for the first time or for the dozenth time, but you solved the problem of missing stories for me with recorded books. I don't think even you can solve the problem of no longer being able to hold a pencil in my own hand."

"Have you noticed that you're using more contractions lately?"

"I like to keep abreast of fashion."

"I admire you for that. Do you remember telling me that you saw the bagpiper walking with someone the night he died? Do you remember any more about the other person?"

She swayed in thought for a moment. "I think it must have been a man. Their gaits were well matched. But it wasn't your burglar beau."

"I wish you wouldn't call him that. Why do you say it wasn't Joe?"

"He lopes. His brother marches."

"Are you saying it was Cole Dunbar?"

"I would not want to hang a man for the way he walks down the street. He isn't the only one who marches like a lawman. Or a bagpiper."

With Handmade Blue Plum not opening until noon, folks who'd arrived for the craft and art sale had several hours to wander in and out of downtown shops. I kept busy waiting on customers while Ardis made her phone calls, and enjoyed overhearing delighted comments about giant chicken feet, striped signposts, and Groucho Marx at the courthouse. I was also glad Abby and Debbie were coming in to help for the afternoon. When I'd left the museum world to run the Weaver's Cat, I didn't know how satisfying it could be to exchange skeins of yarn, hanks of floss, and lengths of fabric for money in the till. But retail sales wasn't for sissies or anyone who'd be more comfortable in a desk job.

Aaron Carlin came in midway through the morning.

He showed no interest in browsing while he waited for his "client" to arrive, but he looked more relaxed than he had the day before. He seemed happy making small talk about the weather and between customers, courteously stepping aside whenever someone approached the counter. He'd seen the moray eel when he stopped to pay his electric bill and wondered what it meant.

"Whimsy," said a woman buying a circular needle set. "Something we can all use more of. Keep calm and spread whimsy. I think I'll embroider that on a pillow."

"A pillow shaped like a moray," Aaron suggested.

"You made her day and mine," I said as she went upstairs to pick out moray-colored floss. "How are the, uh . . ." I didn't want to say "Spiveys" and spook him. He caught my drift, though.

"The twin horrors that are my dilemma?"

"Are you safe saying that in public?"

"If I say it real quiet-like, and when I know where they are. They told Angie they're obligated at the craft show for the entire weekend."

I rang up several more customers. Aaron went to look out the front window. Ardis finished her calls and joined me behind the counter. Argyle and Geneva came downstairs—he on his little cat feet, she like a localized fog. Ardis didn't seem to notice her and I wondered if she'd forgotten to put her braided bracelet back on, or if she'd decided not to.

"What time is his 'client' due?" Ardis asked.

By then, Aaron was pacing to and from the window at the front of the room, stopping to scan the sidewalk left and right before coming back toward the counter.

"She's probably even more skittish since last night," I said quietly to Ardis.

"We ought to say something to him," she said. "That pacing is beginning to alarm the customers." She still hadn't warmed up to him enough to approach him outright, though. Instead she circled him, much the way her great-great-aunt sometimes circled *her*.

Geneva, the great-great-aunt in question, floated over and asked what was going on. I took out my phone and filled her in.

"His client was afraid to go to the police?" she asked. "Then don't you see what has happened? The witness won't be coming. She was killed last night."

"His client told him she might or might not have useful information. That doesn't mean she was a witness. It doesn't mean she was—"

"'Might or might not' is a word game for someone with a secret. His client was afraid. She was being careful. She was a witness and she was going to tell *you* what she saw."

"But . . . surely Aaron's heard about Gladys," I whispered. But maybe not. Aaron Carlin didn't live the most on-the-grid life. I motioned Ardis over and told her what we feared.

"I'll cover the counter," she said. "You go break the bad news."

Geneva came with me, and she'd been right. We stood at the front window, the morning sun streaming into a puddle around Argyle, and after I told him about finding Gladys, Aaron put a hand on his heart and bowed his head. I asked if I could do anything for him; did he want a place to sit down, a glass of water ... ? He waved all that away.

"Gladys didn't tell you what she saw in the park that night?" I asked.

She hadn't. And he didn't know if she'd told anyone else that she "might or might not" have seen anything. And of course we didn't know, for a fact, that she'd witnessed the murder. Aaron was certain, though, that she'd been there and seen something.

"She's gone," he said. "Proof enough."

There was a lull in business, and Ardis joined us.

"I'm sorry for your loss," she said. "And I have a couple of questions for you. I attach no judgment to either of them."

He pulled a handkerchief from his back pocket and blew his nose.

"Why wouldn't she go to the police?" she asked.

His eyes shifted left, then returned to center, but he said nothing.

"What kind of 'client' was she?"

"Business." That time his eyes gazed steadily back at Ardis.

"Did that business have anything to do with why she was in the park so late at night?" Geneva asked.

"Good question," I said.

Ardis knew what had happened and covered for me with a quick "Thank you, Kath," and then she looked around the room. Geneva was floating right next to me, though. If she'd had discernible eyebrows, I was sure they'd be raised. I repeated Geneva's question for the ghostless and got Aaron's eye shift to the left and back to center again. Wanting to put him back at ease, I asked a throwaway question.

"Any idea why Gladys would call a deputy a quack, or what the word 'quack' would have to do with her last night?" Ardis and Geneva both gave me looks. Aaron did them one better. He flinched and his eyes went wide. He pulled himself together, but the "no" he mustered was hardly credible, and he looked antsy to be on his way.

"Thanks for coming by, Aaron. I think you were a good friend to Gladys, and I don't mean to worry you, but do you think this puts you in danger? Do you think *you* should go to the police?"

Those questions got him moving toward the door.

"If you hear anything else," I called after him, "will you let us know?"

He turned at the door, touched his finger to his nose, and left.

"Do you think he was mocking me?" Ardis asked.

"Why?"

"Because I do that—put my finger to my nose—and I've never seen anyone else do that in real life. He's a shady character from a shady family and he involved Gladys in some kind of shady business, and you see where that got her. I find his use of my gesture shady and highly objectionable. I'm not sure he was even using it right. And do you see what else he's gone and done?" She was ranting— quietly, because she was, first and foremost, a slave to good customer relations—and she didn't wait for anyone else to answer her question. "He's dropped a piece of the puzzle in our laps. A piece that's so important I now feel obligated to turn it over to Cole. I find that highly objectionable, too."

She noticed a customer waiting at the counter, took one deep breath and a few seconds to ease her blood pressure, and went to see how she could help.

"Aaron always puts her in a bad mood," I murmured to Geneva.

"The murder of her favorite student might have something to do with it, too."

"You're right, Geneva. That's very perceptive of you."

"Also losing the ability to see and hear her favorite great-great-aunt. I believe I was a steadying influence on her. What on earth has happened? Because I'm sure the problem is something here on her end, not on the plane where I dwell."

"That's—"

"Also perceptive. I know. I will go stay close to her so she can at least feel my presence and take comfort."

She floated across the room and over the counter to hover shoulder-to-shoulder with Ardis. Ardis shivered and took a knitted shawl from under the counter. They made quite a picture, aunt and niece, and I hoped I'd be able to convince Ardis to put her bracelet back on. Thinking of pictures reminded me of the envelope Joe had slipped to me at Mel's.

I told Ardis I'd be back, and went to find out what pictures Joe hadn't wanted Clod to see.

Chapter 26

Joe had been busy with his camera. The second set of pictures—the ones he'd slipped to me at the café when Darla arrived with a message for Clod—were of Hugh's truck, inside and out. I told Ardis and Geneva how I got them.

"The burglar beau, at your service," Geneva said. "Very handy."

I ignored her while Ardis looked through the pictures a second time.

"Don't you wonder what the deputies think they'll learn from the truck?" she asked. "Though, you know, it wouldn't have hurt Hugh to run a vacuum cleaner around the interior once in a while. That's something *I* didn't expect to learn about him. But was he truly a slob, or just casual? Don't you wish the posse could sneak over there and go through it from hood to back bumper? The photographs are good—the sleeping bag, the case I assume is for the bagpipes, the selection of CDs. I wonder why he didn't own an iPod."

"*Ardis.*"

"What?"

"How do you think Joe got these pictures? He *was* in the truck. He was in it and he opened and closed the glove compartment and that case and he crawled around under the cap and moved things around to get these pictures."

"I'm sure he put everything back the way he found it," she said. "And we'll hope he wore gloves. Do we know where he found the truck? Never mind. You can ask him that, and if he's drawn any conclusions, when you see him at Handmade."

We'd decided that one of us should go to Handmade Blue Plum—to check out the opening ceremony, stick around for the memorial tribute to Hugh, and find out what his connection to the show might be. As Ardis pointed out, Joe would be busy with his booth and unable to circulate freely. Geneva took the opportunity to point out that she hoped Joe continued to practice careful burgling so he didn't end up in jail and unable to circulate anywhere at all. When Ardis further pointed out that she thought I should be the one to go, I said, "Fine." From the way she and Geneva backed away, I realized that had come out with more bark than I'd meant. The truth was, I wanted to bark at Joe for taking such a chance. But I couldn't bark at him in good conscience; it would be the proverbial pot-and-kettle scenario if I did. At last count, I'd let myself into more places I shouldn't have been than I knew—for an absolute fact—that he had. Telling myself that didn't make me any less testy, but when Debbie arrived, she brought something with her that went a long way toward lightening my spirits.

"I'm calling them 'Yarn Bomb in a Bag,'" she said. "I've made twelve styles, each style with its own tag for leaving at the scene of the yarn crime." She held kits up one by one and read the tags. "'Fibers are fantastic.' 'Crochet is cool.' 'Knitting is nifty.' 'Textiles are terrific.' 'Fabric is fabulous.' 'Needlework is nirvana.' 'Knotting is novel.' 'Purling is pleasing.' 'Embroidery is excellent.' 'Darning is daring.' I've also made one with the Einstein quote Joe used, and then one more—'Hooking's a hoot.'"

By the time she held up "Hooking's a hoot," a customer had picked up "Knitting is nifty" and "Knotting is Novel" and put them in her shopping basket.

"*You're* a hoot," Ardis told Debbie, "and these are going to be a hit."

Abby came in, then, wearing her T-shirt that said THE WEAVER'S CAT IS WHERE IT'S AT. We'd offered her the part-time job when she made the shirt and wore it for the heritage festival during the summer.

Before taking off for the opening of Handmade, I looked around the shop. Abby was laughing over "Needlework is nirvana" and helping Debbie make room for the kits in the window display. Argyle had attracted a sunbeam and tamed it with a nap. Ardis, still wearing the shawl, hummed behind the counter, unaware that Geneva floated by her side, humming the harmony to her melody. It felt good leaving at that point, knowing the shop was in talented and caring hands.

It hadn't occurred to me that "opening ceremony" really meant "opening" and no one would be allowed in the gym until the ribbon tied across the double doors was cut. Looking on the bright side, the wait let me people-watch while we milled in the parking lot. It seemed to be an out-of-town crowd; there weren't many faces I recognized. The two women—Ellen and Janet—who'd been spending time knitting in the front room upstairs at the Weaver's Cat saw me and waved. They'd come prepared with roller bags. Beyond them, toward the edge of the crowd, I saw the back of a head that looked as though it could be Rachel. Probably not, though. The woman disappeared around the edge of the building at a good clip, no limp in sight. I moved to the edge of the crowd and called Joe. He said the artists and crafters inside were standing ready.

"Is that Souza playing in the background?" I asked.

"One of the woodworkers thought it would help gird our loins for the onslaught."

"Everyone happy with their booth space?"

He didn't answer.

"You caught up in the marching in there?"

"Ducking under the table. Everything's fine."

"Those two sentences don't seem to go together, but I'll take your word for it."

"Ceremony's about to start. See you in few."

"Wait. Who's taking the mayor's place?"

"You'll be surprised."

Ardis and I had wondered if Olive Weems would ask someone to stand in for Pokey at the ceremony. It seemed unlikely, under the circumstances, that he would feel like making an appearance. I didn't know how Olive felt about Gladys, but assumed she would ask another member of her committee or someone from the Chamber of Commerce to take over that bit of limelight. Joe wasn't on the committee, but if it came down to asking him to do the honors, I could picture him making a quick snip with his Swiss Army knife and ambling off, and the ceremony going down in Handmade Blue Plum annals as the shortest on record. I moved back into position so I could watch the show.

And imagine my surprise when Shirley and Mercy Spivey appeared, carrying a pair of oversized ceremonial scissors between them. They wore matching maize-yellow blazers and black slacks. I called Joe back.

"How did this happen?"

"Does anyone ever know?"

I pocketed my phone and watched the twins wrestle to get the scissors in position. They succeeded with that, then realized they hadn't welcomed the crowd. One of them let go of the scissors to dig in her pocketbook. The twin left holding the scissors dropped them. The other pulled out what looked like notes for a five-minute speech, and then lost them to a gust of cold wind. Ellen and Janet rolled their bags forward and picked up the scissors. They made the cut, bowed to the crowd, and rolled their bags inside, looking delighted to be first through the doors. Someone inside yelled, "Incoming," and the craft fair was open for business.

I stood to the side and watched people stream in, and only jumped an inch or two when Mercy and her cologne came up behind me.

"Glad to see you're taking this seriously," she said.

I waited for Shirley's contribution, and when I didn't hear it, I looked around and saw why. Shirley was twenty or thirty feet away, talking to a woman standing by a Prius. Shirley put a hand on the woman's shoulder, the woman pulled away, and then I saw who it was—Olive Weems, dressed in black slacks and sweater and wearing sunglasses.

"Tragic," Mercy said.

"Mmm." My murmur was noncommittal. She was probably referring to Gladys' death. Then again, she was a Spivey; she might have been commenting on Olive's rejection of Shirley's shoulder squeeze.

"If we hear anything else, you'll be the first to know," Mercy said.

She was still standing behind me, and it felt as though we were acting in a bad spy film. I decided to go with that. "Any recommendations on how to proceed?"

"Watch your back."

Bad spy film or not, I wasn't about to laugh off her advice. Two people were dead, and Ardis had said the same thing the night before when I was under a dark bridge with Al Rogalla. I thanked Mercy and went inside.

The craftspeople and artists—with their booths, their handmade goods, and even the clothes they wore—had transformed the space before me from a school gym into a market bazaar. Colors, designs, and sounds swirled around the room. People filled the aisles—pressing forward to admire and touch—drawn from booth to booth by textures, scents, and ready smiles. A woman at the door handed me a flyer with a map of the booths and exhibitors on one side and the schedule of Saturday's classes and demonstrations on the other.

"Do you know anything about the memorial tribute to Hugh McPhee?" I asked her.

"Who?"

"McPhee."

"Sorry. I'm only here for the first hour." She reached past me to hand a flyer to the next people through the door.

I checked the map to find Joe's booth—in the far corner. The tide was moving in that direction, so I let myself be carried along. I stopped at a few booths, but passed many more I knew I'd like to get back to if there was time. I saw turned bowls so smooth I wanted to stroke them, woven table linens, knitted socks, mittens, hats, scarves, quilted jackets, carved walking sticks, embroidery on almost every kind of clothing, soap, candles, photographs, pottery, and a line of people waiting for a caricaturist.

A Christmas tree decorated with red, green, and white monkey's fists caught my eye. My grandfather had known how to make the neat, round knots, and I wondered if John did. Granddaddy had told me it was a sailor's knot. A sailor's weapon, too, if it had a long tail for whirling and whacking. That was a nasty thought to have while looking at a Christmas tree. I slipped back into the stream and didn't stop again until I reached Joe's booth. "Booth" was a loose definition for his setup.

"Nice boat," I said.

"You like it? John found it for me."

"Aboard the *Pequod*?"

The "booth" was a large, heavy wooden rowboat, cut in half across the wide midsection and standing, prow up. It must have been seven feet tall, making its original length at least fourteen feet.

"It was orange when John found it," Joe said, scratching his ear. "Took a couple of gallons to cover it." Now it was aquamarine on the outside and white on the inside. He'd built multiple shelves in it to display his watercolors and trout flies. He had a card table beside the boat, with a couple of wooden crates on it, where people were flipping through more watercolors. A coat tree, hung with his kumihimo braids, stood on the other side of the boat.

"The dang thing is heavy as the dickens," he said, patting the boat.

"It's eye-catching."

Other people thought so, too, and I could see he was going to be busy. I asked if he'd heard when or where the memorial tribute would be, or who was doing it. He hadn't. But he had an idea who might know all the details.

"Shirley or Mercy. Fingers on the pulse, those two."

"Are they why you had to duck under the table earlier?"

"No comment."

"Olive might be here, too. I saw her outside. Oh, one other question." I moved closer and dropped my voice. "Where and how did you find Hugh's truck?"

"I was lucky."

"Lucky how?"

"Tell you later." He gave me a kiss. "Customers. Gotta go."

As I turned away, I saw a flash of yellow Spivey blazer. It disappeared down the aisle I'd just come up, and I went to chase after it. But not too fast. It was a Spivey I was tracking, after all, and I knew that Spiveys, like dandelions, always popped back up. With that brilliant piece of philosophy under my belt, I slowed even more to enjoy some of the booths I'd skipped earlier. While I looked over a display of ceramic spindle whorls, I heard someone say my name. But not to me.

As best I could tell, the voice came from the next booth over, but I couldn't hear any more because a couple started chattering behind me. I peered between the displays in the ceramics booth and saw the monkey's fist Christmas tree. And Rachel Meeks sitting in a chair at the back of the booth talking to Al Rogalla.

"Aren't they beautiful? Breakable, too." The ceramicist took the whorl I was paying no attention to from my hand.

I apologized, gave the poor woman my card, and told her if she was interested in selling her whorls locally to give me a call at the Weaver's Cat. When I left her booth, Al was bagging a set of monkey's fist ornaments for a customer and Rachel was gone. I saw her ahead of me at the end of the aisle, though, and was sure she was the unlimping woman I'd seen earlier. I debated going after her, phone in hand—Kath Rutledge, forensic videographer, proving to the world that a banker's twisted ankle was a figment of her prevarication. I didn't do that, but I did move quickly past Al's booth, and was nearly run over by Olive leaving another booth. She grabbed my arm to steady herself, and put a tissue to her eyes.

"Olive, I'm so sorry for your—"

"Next year," she said, slashing a hand through my sorrow, "I won't allow anything with perfume. It is killing me." As soon as the word was out of her mouth, she looked appalled. And then she looked at me, and obviously hadn't realized who she was holding on to. And she held on tighter. "I do not appreciate your sense of humor," she hissed.

"Sorry?"

"You told Lonnie Haynes those ridiculous things at the courthouse—" She made another angry slash with her free hand, but it didn't help her come up with any more useful words.

"It's a form of urban art called yarn bombing, and you're hurting my arm."

"You told him it was part of Handmade Blue Plum. It looks degenerate." She let go of me and stalked away.

"Are you all right?"

I looked at the man who asked—Pokey Weems, sadly watching his wife push her way through the crowd.

"Please forgive her," he said. "She wanted so much for this to be a happy, successful weekend." He hadn't looked at me, hadn't taken his concerned eyes off Olive. I should have offered my condolences, but he sighed and followed in her wake.

My phone rang then. Joe with a lead on the memorial tribute.

"Al Rogalla," he said. "Not verified."

"He has a booth."

"He isn't registered for one."

I told him about seeing Al and Rachel at the booth with the knotted monkey's fist ornaments, and Rachel's fleet and limpless feet.

"I don't remember her name on a booth, either," Joe said. "If you're still looking for the twins, someone saw them down the hall, checking on classrooms for tomorrow."

"I'll take a look."

The pea-green walls made the school hallway timeless—it could be any school, anywhere—and it was a relief to hear nothing but my footsteps after the roar of the crafting crowd in the gym. I didn't find the Spiveys in the first few rooms along the corridor, but according to the map, some of the classes would be held in the art room around the corner and down the next hallway. Mercy's cologne wasn't evident, but it might have met its match in eau de school floor wax.

There were three trophy cases around the corner and I stopped to look at them. Three seemed like a lot, but they held trophies going back decades. I didn't need to read dates on the labels or yellowed newspaper articles—the stratigraphic layers of dust in the cases were clue enough. The progressively more faded team photographs, and the style of uniforms and safety equipment, told the story, too. I looked for a trophy or an article or some kind of ballyhoo over Hugh McPhee's amazing and long-standing record in each of the cases, but didn't find anything. I did find a big trophy with Al Rogalla's name. And was tickled to recognize two young Dunbars in a couple of the pictures—Clod on the football team and Joe on the cross-country team. The difference in sports suited the brothers.

I found the art room. No Spiveys lurked within, but I tested my bloodhound skills and sniffed the air. A trace of Mercy lingered there—not enough to bay about, though. Instead I was nosy and looked at the materials and kits laid out for a needle felting demonstration. While I was examining one of the kits, and thinking Debbie could put some together for us to sell at the Cat, someone ran past the room, going farther down the hall. I went to the door and heard the running feet stop around the next corner.

Another sound came from that direction—a door being rattled? Rattled, but not opened, because then the steps came back toward me, slower. Slower and quietly and . . . carefully? Creeping?

Craven amateur sleuth that I was, I shrank back into the art room, plastered myself to the wall, and closed my eyes. If Geneva were with me, she would have called me pathetic. And she would've been right, too, doggone it. So I steeled myself to open my eyes and act like a—like I didn't know what—like a proud member of the TGIF crime-fighting posse.

And then those furtive steps crept into the room with me.

Chapter 27

"Are you about to hurl?" Zach asked. "Because if you are, I'll move."

I opened my eyes. Nothing but concern showed on his face. For me, or possibly for his shoes. "Was that you running down the hall? If you ran down, why did you come creeping back?"

"Thought I heard someone." He pointed over his shoulder in the direction he'd come from. We listened. He shrugged, then gave one of his quick smiles. "You looked like you'd stepped in what I left on the floor in front of the cafeteria. You want to see?"

We walked down the hall and around the corner to the cafeteria. On the floor, like a doormat, lay a knitted puddle of OMG—old moldy gravy.

"Abby wanted me to put it in the kitchen in front of the sink," Zach said, "but the doors are locked."

"Best yarn bomb ever." I took out my phone to get a picture. And heard footsteps again, farther down the hall. I held myself together this time. And told myself I was being strong because I was there for Zach's sake, and not because he'd moved so that he stood between me and the approaching feet.

Feet that belonged to Al Rogalla. He saw Zach first. "Hey, are you supposed to be back here? Oh, hi. Do you know this kid?"

"We're working on a project."

"Well, you shouldn't be wandering around the school."

"Like you?" I could hear Geneva, in my mind's ear, exclaiming, "You are rude!" Even if only in my mind, she was right. I had no good reason to be rude to the man, especially if I wanted him to answer questions. "Sorry. I saw the monkey's fist ornaments at your booth. Really cute. Where'd you learn to make them?"

"It's not my booth." He looked at the knitting on the floor. "Nice vomit," he said, and walked away.

"You should practice your technique," Zach said.

"Yup."

I didn't stay for the memorial tribute. I finally crossed paths with Shirley and Mercy and they told me it was scheduled for five o'clock.

"I notice your chagrin," Mercy said. "Other plans?"

"Not to worry," said Shirley. "We'll be your eyes and ears."

"Full report later," Mercy said.

I gulped and left.

The posse gathered in the TGIF workroom later that afternoon. I was last to arrive and found them at one of the oak worktables instead of the circle of comfy chairs where we usually sat and knitted. No one was knitting now, and I took that as a measure of how urgent they felt the situation had become with Gladys' death. Everyone but Joe had made it to the meeting. Geneva was there, too, still hovering at Ardis' side. She was somber, too, only raising a hand in greeting, then putting a finger to her lips. They'd rolled the whiteboard in. Ardis nodded her approval when I closed the door and took the seat they'd left for me at the head of the table.

"John suggested the table," Ardis said, "to put us on a more serious footing."

"I like the closed-door policy, too," Mel said. "It'll keep out that law enforcement riffraff that's wandered in a time or two. And I get the feeling our secret plans weren't so secret after all."

"Me, too. How's Ambrose?" I asked John.

"He put a hole in the screen door with his cane when I got him home. Then he slept like a baby and mended the screen when he got up. I think the evening did him some good."

"Daddy, too," Ardis said. "He thinks he and mother were out dancing last night at Pokey's roadhouse."

"Pokey closed that roadhouse twenty years ago," Thea said.

"And Daddy hasn't been there in thirty, but he wants to go at the weekend for the live music."

"Let's get started," I said.

"And let's finish it, too," Ernestine said, "so we can put a stop to this terrible business." She slapped her hand on the table. "Oh." She put both hands in her lap. "We should sit at the table more often. That was very satisfying."

"What's first, then," Ardis asked, "a recap of the questions from the last meeting, or reports?"

"Reports," I said. "They'll answer some of the questions."

"And add more," said John. "It's worked for us before; let's hope it does again."

I went first and told them about the connection between the two murders—that Gladys had seen something in the park that night—and how we knew. "We think she saw the murderer if not the actual murder," I said. "We can't be sure, of course, but it fits, and we know she didn't want to go to the police." I hesitated before using Aaron's name, but decided to go ahead.

"Another person who might not be comfortable going to the police," Ernestine said. "And such a nice young man, too. I hope you warned him not to let anyone else think he knows what Gladys saw."

"I think he's taking the possibility of danger seriously," I said.

"And he's a Carlin," Ardis said, "so he knows how to disappear. But this question of trust in the police brings up an interesting wrinkle. Cole Dunbar's been suspended."

Ernestine and I had heard that at breakfast, but it was news to the others. Reactions ranged from Thea's mouth hanging open to John's fingertips tapping the table as though they were recording the thoughts running through his head.

"Coffee," Mel said. "I need coffee to process that." She'd set the refreshments up on the Welsh dresser, the way we usually did, but brought it all over to the table now. "Help yourselves," she said. "It's nothing but marble pound cake. If I'd known you were going to drop that bomb, I'd have brought rum cake. And possibly left the cake out altogether." She poured a cup of coffee and drank half of it. "Okay. Cole's suspended. Why?"

"He wouldn't say." Ardis crumpled a napkin and

dropped it on the table. "When he came to pick up the list and timetable this afternoon, I gave him every opportunity. I haven't offered that man so much sympathy or so many chances to come clean since he was a boy and put a bar of soap in Dee Dee Williams' sandwich and refused to admit it." She crumpled another napkin. "Dee Dee was a snotty thing and deserved it."

"Are we guessing why?" Mel asked.

"No," said John. "That doesn't sound safe or smart. Or kind. It might be a personal matter."

"Best left under a rock?" Mel said. "Fine with me. He was in uniform this morning. When did it happen?"

"Maybe it had *just* happened," I said. "Nasty surprises like that get sprung on you sometimes." Nasty surprises like a phone call telling you your job's been eliminated, which was what had happened to me. The shared experience of a sucker punch like that should have made me more sympathetic toward Clod. But there was a difference in our situations. My boss had cried when she told me the news and had made it clear it wasn't my fault. Clod's boss seemed to think something *was* his fault.

"He doesn't seem to be paying much attention to being suspended," Ernestine said. "He asked for that timetable and list of names."

"Darla doesn't, either. She was there giving him an update on Hugh's truck this morning. I wonder if she'll tell us anything about the suspension." I made a note to call her. "It's probably hard to step away from a case like this. Cole was pretty psyched about Hugh being in town."

"Speaking of the truck—" Ardis put the envelope with Joe's pictures on the table. "Score one for our team. Joe found the truck first. Did you find out where, Kath?"

"Score zip for my team," I said.

"Oh, poor baby," said Thea. "You're not scoring any these days?" She smiled and moved her chair out of reach of my foot—too close to Mel. "Ow. Okay, let's see the pictures."

They passed the pictures around and I went to the whiteboard. Geneva followed me. Filling up the board's clean expanse with questions, facts, and theories always seemed to help me. Geneva usually left the room when we got it out. Knowing now how much she missed drawing, I could understand. I picked up the marker and drew a tiny ghost in a corner of the board.

"That looks nothing like me. Please erase it."

I rubbed it out and looked at her.

"She isn't wearing her braided bracelet."

I took my phone out and looked at it as though I was checking to see who was calling, then put it to my ear. "I know."

"I didn't notice that until now. Some detective. Some great-great-aunt. Not so great at anything. I will be in my small room. It's like a coffin. That's something I did notice."

"I'll come talk to you later," I said, but I wasn't sure she heard me.

"Are you making notes up there, Kath?" John asked.

"Yeah." I slipped the phone back in my pocket. "Columns, then notes. Columns with all the names we've had floating around. Ardis and I started a list Thursday morning."

"That was yesterday," Mel said.

"Yow. Doesn't seem possible." I wrote *Hugh McPhee* in the upper left corner, and next to that *Gladys Weems*.

"Ardis, will you read the other names from the list? It's in my notebook." I wrote them across the top of the board as she read—"Olive Weems, Sheriff Haynes, Cole Dunbar, Al Rogalla, Rachel Meeks." For good measure, I added Tammie Fain and Wanda Vance.

"Does anyone know who the Register of Deeds is?" Ardis asked.

"Lois Poteet," Ernestine said. "Why?"

"I'll let Kath tell you," Ardis said. "It's her report. I'm still skeptical, but . . ." She let the thought hang while I started to write *Lois Poteet* on the board. I got as far as *Lois Pot*, stopped, and turned around.

"Oh boy—with everything else going on last night, I forgot that I heard something else, and this one's a doozy."

"We haven't heard the first part of your report yet," Mel said, "but go ahead and lay the doozy news on us."

"Hugh and Rachel were briefly married."

That was an even more impressive bomb than the news of Clod's suspension. No finger tapped, no hand reached for the coffee.

"None of you knew that?" I asked.

"Did you hear this from the same source?" Ardis asked. "The *Spivey* vine?"

"Is *that* where you heard about the meetings at the bank and the courthouse?" Thea asked. "And you wanted to rearrange the teams to follow up on *Spivey* information?"

"The meetings have been confirmed," I said. "What Ardis and Thea are talking about is something the twins told me Thursday afternoon—that Hugh and Al Rogalla, on *Tuesday afternoon*, met with Lois Poteet at the courthouse and then with Rachel at the bank. At the bridge last night, I asked Al, and he confirmed it."

"And I can now confirm the marriage, through the wonders of online public access records," Mel said, holding up her smartphone.

"Did Al tell you why they met with Lois and Rachel?" Ardis asked.

"No."

"Any more reports from Spivey Central?" Thea asked. "Because I'd like to go next. I clearly need to redeem myself, both for doubting the Spivey Fount of All Knowledge and for last night's duck disaster. I have more background information on Hugh. Although the fact that I totally missed the marriage blows my mind."

"Forget your mind," Mel said. "Will the shoes recover?"

"That jury is still out. Okay, here are my notes, raw and in order of discovery, not in timeline form." She settled a pair of reading glasses on the end of her nose. "Age, fifty-three; graduated from UT Knoxville 1983; English major, history minor; junior year abroad, Edinburgh University, Scotland; graduate studies at Edinburgh, attaining a doctorate in Scottish studies and fluency in Gaelic; learned to play the bagpipes, too, in case you didn't notice. An interesting aside—he was one of the injured in the Sheffield Soccer Riots of 1989. Suffered a head injury but made a full recovery. He returned stateside, bounced from job to job, ended up back at UT Knoxville working in the math library, there not being much of a job market at American universities for someone with his expertise. He's been at the library for fifteen years."

"In Knoxville," Ardis said, "and never came back here."

"At least not with the kind of splash he did this time,"

Thea said. "And maybe not ever. He wasn't hiding over there. He just quietly faded into the background. Except when he's playing the bagpipes. Hard to fade into anything when you're blowing them and dressed to the teeth. The guy whose funeral he played for—Walter Jeffries—was a colleague at UT. Hugh was somewhat active in an online Gaelic society. Not into other social media, though."

"Anything else?" I asked.

"I think that's darn good for one night." Thea folded her glasses and set them on the table. "I will now sit back with a keen ear for further points of online inquiry, and fortify myself for tonight's foray." She refilled her coffee and took a slice of pound cake.

"Good job, Thea."

"Of course."

"How does it change things, if we know Rachel and Hugh were married?" Ardis asked.

"That's one of our new questions," John said, "with a whole cascade of questions below it. Are there any other reports before we jump to those?"

"A few observations from Handmade," I said. "They might give some direction to the new questions, but I'll try to keep them objective. Rachel was there. She wasn't limping—and as an aside, Joe was beginning to ask her questions last night, working his way toward the bank meeting, when she twisted her ankle and went home. He didn't see it happen. She said it wasn't bad."

"But she called me this morning and said she was staying off it," Mel said.

"And I really didn't see anything wrong this afternoon."

"Did you talk to her?" Ernestine asked

"No, but I saw her talking with Al Rogalla in one of the booths. They were sitting behind the display table. Al seemed to be manning the booth, but Joe said that neither Al nor Rachel is registered for one."

"He should be able to tell you who *is* registered for the booth, though," Ardis said.

"I'll ask him. The booths have been a major headache, partly because of the way people were allowed to register for them. More than one person might be involved with a booth, but the registration only asked for one name."

"Isn't there a master list of registrants?" John asked.

"Supposedly. But Olive has it and Joe says she's enough of a technophobe that she only has a hard copy and only the one copy."

"Good Lord," John said.

"Hey, don't knock it," Thea said. "If her system works for her, it works. You won't catch me with files of personal information available for any hacker or voyeur to find."

"Or librarian," said Mel.

"That's hardly the same thing as keeping accurate records in an accessible format," Ernestine said. "I'm a firm believer in working smarter, not harder. I love spreadsheets." She reached over and patted Thea's hand. "I'm sorry, dear; sometimes I revert to my secretarial days. Pokey is Mayor Weems, and Olive is Mrs. Mayor Weems, but they still live over on Third Street in the brick ranch they started in. I don't believe Olive ever had the good fortune to stretch her wings beyond joining her various social clubs. And I hope you know that I mean that only in the nicest possible way."

"Olive was there today," I said. "And Pokey." I told them about the Spiveys standing in for Pokey at the ribbon cutting, and about being run into by Olive. "Olive and Pokey both looked pretty ragged, and she wasn't happy that we let the sheriff think the yarn bombing was part of Handmade."

"It is part of it," Thea said.

"Not officially, and she doesn't seem to have much of a sense of humor. Oh, but you know who does?" I took out my phone and showed them Abby's OMG puddle. While John and Ernestine were chuckling over it, a text alert came in.

"Shall I see who it is, Kath?" Ernestine asked.

"Sure."

"Look at this, Thea." Ernestine turned to her, flashing my phone. "Do you think Olive knows how to retrieve a text? *I* do. Oh my goodness." She dropped the phone. "It's *them*."

John looked at the display. "Spiveys," he said, and pushed the phone across the table to me with the tip of a gingerly finger.

"Hoo boy." I took a swig of cold coffee and read the text aloud. "Fistfight at O.K. Gymnasium. Al from Chicago versus Cole Dunbar. Yippee-i-o-ki-ay."

Chapter 28

"Right." Ardis stood up. "We need to get over there. This could be the break in the case we're looking for." Hands on her hips, chin up, she looked like a seventy-something Valkyrie in a popcorn stitch shawl. "Who has their car here?"

John raised his hand. "Unfortunately it's Ambrose's old MG. I take it out a couple of times a month to keep it running."

"Damn. Never mind. You take Kath, John, and the rest of us will walk."

"The rest of us might walk down the stairs and see them off," Thea said, "and read about the bloody noses in the *Bugle* on Thursday. But the fight will be over by the time we can get there on foot. And before we do go, tell me why Olive and Sheriff Haynes are on the whiteboard. What am I looking for if I troll for them tonight?"

"Anything," Ardis said. "If reports are accurate, they were both shocked to see Hugh."

"Gladys was tickled," I said.

A car horn blared in the alley and another text alert burbled on my phone.

"Spiveys again. All it says is 'WAITING.' All caps. Shall we go, John?"

John and I headed down the stairs, a stream of advice rolling after us as the others followed. The car horn blared again, drowning the back door as it baaed. And there, idling in the alley at the bottom of the steps, stood the Spivey mobile, with Spivey One and Spivey Two gesturing madly for me to hop in.

I sat between Ardis and Mel in the backseat of the Spiveys' Buick. They cinched their seat belts tight, and I hoped they'd keep me from flying forward in case of a sudden stop. Not that Shirley made any stops between the shop and the school.

"I'm rarely terrified," Mel said on one side of me. "But I wish I had a Saint Christopher medal."

"This thing is as safe as a tank," Ardis said on my other side. "Step on it, Shirley."

Shirley did, and we arrived before John and Ernestine in the MG. Thea had opted to stay behind, saying she'd do more good with her fingers on her keyboard. She was right, of course, that the fight was over before we got there.

"We did our best," Mercy said. "You might chip in for gas money sometime." They dropped us at the door to the gym and went to park.

We got the bare facts of the fight from Joe. He'd gotten them from Shorty, because he'd missed it, too. The fight had erupted on the other side of the gym from Joe's boat booth. Al Rogalla, standing under the basketball goal, had been delivering his memorial tribute to Hugh Mc-Phee. Clod showed up, listened, and waited until Al finished; then the two came together. No one was quite sure what triggered the fight—Al said or did something, or Clod did, or it was a mutual conflagration. No one was sure who swung first. And although the fight was over before most people were aware of it, there were plenty of people in the gym who might have seen something.

"A veritable who's who of our whiteboard," Ardis said, scanning the crowd.

Olive and Pokey stood under the basketball goal talking with Darla. Sheriff Haynes walked past us and out the door. Tammie Fain, encumbered by one grandchild, chased down an aisle after another. To our right, Wanda Vance was trying on a quilted jacket.

"Everybody but Rachel," Ardis said.

Ellen and Janet, who'd spent so much time knitting in the front room upstairs at the Weaver's Cat, saw us, and rolled their bags over. They were beginning to seem like old friends.

"This is certainly the most interesting Handmade Blue Plum we've been to," Ellen said.

"Not very small-town friendly, though," Ernestine said. "I am so sorry we haven't shown you our better side." Her eyes didn't look sorry; they looked ready to catch round two of the Rogalla-Dunbar match.

"I wouldn't worry too much about it," Janet said. "You know what they say about bad publicity. The crafts this year are top-notch. We'll be coming back."

"You didn't happen to see how the fight started, did you?" Mel asked.

They hadn't. But they'd been struck by how much the scuffle reminded them of middle school boys.

"Posturing," Ellen said. "A lot of blowing and not so many blows. I teach eighth-grade science and I see it too often. Circling each other like dogs with their hackles raised."

"These two 'boys' each got in a couple of good pops, though," Janet said. "Are you ready, Ellen?" They waved again and rolled their bags out the door.

"Where's Cole now?" I asked Joe. "And who's watching your booth?"

"Cole's in a classroom cooling off. Al's in another. Zach's got the booth, and I'd better get back there."

"Here comes Darla," said John.

Darla, bless the heart she wore on her sleeve, said we could go in and talk to Clod; he wasn't under arrest. John and Mel thought it would be good if they talked to Al, but Darla said he'd already left. Neither of them was hurt beyond bruised ribs and knuckles—not having aimed at noses, which I knew to be a very satisfying target—and neither intended to press charges. Al apparently hadn't minded running a potential gauntlet of stares to leave the building.

"Go stuff—a mushroom," Clod said to Mel when she asked him why he was hiding in the classroom.

"Keep a civil tongue in your head, Coleridge," Ardis snapped. But she'd snapped automatically and concern showed in her eyes. "Aren't you even one bit remorseful?"

He didn't look it. He didn't look as though he was hiding, either. He leaned back in the teacher's chair with his feet, crossed at the ankles, on the desk. Except for his regulation boots, he was out of uniform. His jeans and T-shirt hadn't gotten the memo, though. They probably weren't starched, but they couldn't quite carry off casual.

"Perhaps it would help if you told us what the fuss was all about." Ernestine's hands, clasped at her waist, gave her the look of a mole as Mother Confessor.

"There was no *fuss*," Clod said. "It was merely a disagreement between two people who've never liked each other."

"And yet you and I never break out in fisticuffs," Mel said. She and Ardis sat down at desks directly in front of Clod.

John had stepped out of the room with Darla. I stayed by the door, keeping an ear on them, but watching Clod. Posturing, Ellen had said. He was still doing it, still putting up a front. But what lay behind it? Ernestine joined me at the door, and when John saw her, he motioned us into the hall.

"You might learn more without the whole crew in there," he said. "Why don't Ernestine and I walk around Handmade? Which booth was Al working?"

"One with a Christmas tree covered in balls that are really monkey's fists."

"A coincidence?" John asked.

"Sorry?"

"There was a monkey's fist in one of the pictures—" He stopped and coughed. "A picture Ambrose showed me the other day. Shall we go?" He took Ernestine's arm, raised his eyebrows at me behind Darla's back, and headed for the gym.

The pictures of Hugh's truck were still on the table at

the Cat. If there was a monkey's fist in one of them, I'd missed it. But John wouldn't have.

"Monkey's fists and Rogalla," Darla said, watching my face. "Interesting. We found a monkey's fist in that pouch Hugh McPhee had with him. One in his truck, too." She looked at me and nodded. "Interesting. What pictures was John talking about—that Ambrose probably didn't show him?"

"If I tell you that, will you tell me what's going on with Cole?"

Her eyebrows thought that over, maybe weighing risks and benefits.

"Or, if you can't tell me that, is there any way you can let me see Hugh's pouch? See what was in it? I know that's irregular—"

"And I know you've got notes. That you're all working on this."

There wasn't any point in denying it.

"So," she said, "you show me your notes and I'll try to do both. But first, I want to hear what kind of bull he's tossing to Ardis and Mel."

We slipped back into the room, staying near the door so we didn't interrupt the show. Mel, Ardis, and Clod hadn't changed seats, but the dynamics between them had shifted. Clod was still posturing and still sat with his clodhoppers on the desk, but now Ardis was in charge. Sitting in the front row, she wasn't the former teacher; she was the director of a piece of reality theater. Clod might be throwing out bull, but not with impunity; Ardis was digging for the motivation behind the bull. Mel, rapt, slid down in her seat and turned slightly so she could see both their faces and miss none of the nuances.

"But your attitude toward Hugh is different," Ardis said. "I want to understand why."

"Why not?"

"Too glib," she said. "That answer isn't good enough. There's more."

"Then it was the bagpipes."

"And that's not funny."

"You can always find something funny about bagpipes," Clod said. "Just not always ha-ha funny. Here's a bagpipe riddle that's been bugging me for the last few days. How easy is it for someone to sneak up on a bagpiper playing in the dark and strangle him? You want to know the answer? The sneaking-up part isn't too hard."

"Tasteless," Ardis said.

"Speaking of which, it's time for supper. I'm going home. Any reason I need to stick around, Deputy Dye?"

"None at all, Deputy Dunbar, dear."

"Then you-all have a dandy evening." He slammed his feet to the floor. More posturing—it made him wince, and he put a hand to his ribs on the way out.

Ardis and Mel got up, too, and the four of us watched him walk down the hall.

"Any idea what started the fight?" I asked Darla.

"He wouldn't say. Had to be Rogalla."

"That isn't loyalty talking?" Mel asked.

"Nothing wrong with loyalty." Darla stood up straighter and suddenly seemed . . . crisper. She had more of an edge, anyway. "Rogalla knows how to needle. Not just about Hugh. He's the kind of guy who gets the jab in with a smile. Hugh's death probably brought it to a head. Rogalla loves rubbing the house in Cole's face."

"What house?"

"He lives in the old McPhee house."

"I'm not sure I knew that," Ardis said.

"And what of it?" Darla swirled a finger in the air. "The big hero's big house with the big columns in front. Big whoop."

"Big mortgage, too, I expect," Ardis said, "for a house that looks too formal to be comfortable. I've never been impressed by it. But you say Coleridge was?"

"That's part of Rogalla's needling," Darla said. "He let Cole and everyone else believe he bought that pile right after McPhee inherited it. Now it turns out he was renting all these years until McPhee finally decided to sell."

"Do you know why Cole's attitude toward Hugh changed?" Ardis asked.

"My guess? Something to do with taking Hugh out to dinner that night." She shrugged. "Heroes don't always live up, you know?"

"Why was Cole suspended?" Mel asked. "That's something I cannot get my mind wrapped around."

Darla didn't answer.

"He's a public employee," I said. "It'll be reported in the *Bugle*."

"True enough. It's a crock, though. Sheriff Haynes accused him of mishandling a case."

"What case?"

"That's a crock, too. It isn't even a case; it was an anonymous complaint. About someone stealing ducks from the park."

Chapter 29

Darla's radio did a Donald Duck imitation on her shoulder and she had to leave. (Or "fly," as Mel said.) I asked her to give me a call when she had a chance. Then Ardis, Mel, and I went to find Ernestine and John, Mel wondering if she'd be able to keep herself from quacking the next time Clod came in the café.

"You could throw a roll at him and yell, 'Duck,'" Ardis said.

"Add duck à l'orange to the menu," said Mel.

"Or ask him if he wants quackers with his soup." It felt good to laugh—at Clod's expense in particular—but now we had another piece and no obvious place to put it. It felt as though we were collecting odd and unrelated bits for another yarn bomb installation, with no idea what we were creating. "There're connections we're not making," I said, "and right now quacks and ducks are at the top of the list."

"Including the Case of the Condescending Clue," Ardis said. "Dabbling in detective work, indeed." She told Mel about Clod tossing us the clue and telling us to knock ourselves out.

"Prophetic?" Mel asked. "I hope he hasn't knocked himself out of a career."

Ernestine and John were watching Joe demonstrate the kumihimo, and I could see John's fingers itching to try it. Ernestine told us what they'd found out about the monkey's fist booth.

"I only wish it had taken more ingenuity or skill," she said. "But there's something to be said for simply asking questions."

"Asking the right questions takes insight and perception," Ardis said.

"Or, as in our case, walking up to the young woman behind the table and saying, 'Who's in charge of your booth and did you know Hugh McPhee?'" Ernestine said the young woman standing behind the table at the booth had promptly burst into tears. "But I gave her a clean hankie and held her hand, and John got her a bottle of water."

The booth was being run by volunteers from several area pet rescue groups. Enough of their members were crafters as well as pet lovers that they thought they'd give the show a try as a way to raise awareness and money. Hugh had been a supporter of the group from Knoxville. He'd donated the monkey's fist Christmas ornaments to the effort and offered to sit at the booth for an hour. When I saw Al Rogalla there, he'd been filling in for Hugh.

"The sweet girl doesn't know who Rachel is," Ernestine said. "She thought Rachel was probably just visiting with Al. And here, dear, I thought I should contribute to their cause, so I bought one of Hugh's ornaments for you."

John said he'd drop Ernestine at home. Mel, Ardis, and I looked at each other and agreed without discussion to walk. Ardis used her six feet to scan the immediate area for the twins. She declared the coast clear and we snuck out—Ardis walking with her knees bent to give her a shorter profile. Mel peeled off when we reached the café, and left us with a quack and a guffaw. I told Ardis I was going to stop at the Cat and stare at the whiteboard for a while.

"And check on Geneva?" she asked. "How's she doing?"

"Wondering why you took the bracelet off and left it off."

Ardis rubbed her wrist.

"Will you put it back on?"

"I'll think about it. Having her in my life puts a new twist on the notion of the sandwich generation." She tried to laugh, but it sounded worn-out. "I'm not sure I'm capable of learning how to be niece to an aunt who is both one hundred and fifty years old and twenty-two. My seventy-year-old brain can take only so much boggling, and Daddy's prancing might be more than enough to keep up with for the time being. Now, I'd best go rescue the sitter. I'll see you in the morning."

Argyle and I were squinting at the whiteboard I'd scribbled all over when Geneva floated down from the study.

"Squinted eyes are cozy and inviting in a cat," she said. "You merely look dyspeptic."

"Thanks."

"I believe honesty is necessary in relationships."

"You're probably right."

"Have you made any progress on the case? On either case?"

"Not a lot. They're connected—connected in ways that are probably right in front of our eyes, but I'm not seeing them."

"Did you draw those ducks up there?"

"Yeah."

"You are not much of an artist."

"I have no illusions."

"That's good. Why are you obsessed with ducks these days?"

I told her about the stolen-duck complaint and Clod's suspension, and ended up telling her about the fight at Handmade Blue Plum. To say she was sorry she'd missed it would not capture the scope of her disappointment.

"Careening around corners with the darling twins?" she said. "Two strapping fellows defending their honor? And I missed it? I am dragged down into the depths of despond. And all you can say is 'we missed it, too.' That is hardly the point."

"What *is* the point?"

"That if Ardis had not been so ardent, if she hadn't pestered me mercilessly—"

"If you hadn't given as good as you got?"

"And then she had the gall to rebuff me by taking off her bracelet and I thought it was *my* fault." She billowed back and forth in front of the whiteboard. Argyle slunk off my lap and crouched under the table.

"Stop it."

"And of course," she said, "of course, once again, I am wrong and you're asking me to stop."

"I am. I want you to stop this. Ardis doesn't deserve your rudeness. Think about it and be honest with yourself. You're taking advantage of a situation, of being a ghost. I know you have no control over that, but you do have control over how you act and how you treat other people."

"You don't know what it's like to be me."

"I know what it's like to be a person. I know what it's like to be angry and resentful. I know what it's like to regret things that I've done or said. And to be depressed, disappointed, and jealous. And vindictive."

"Lost?"

"Not to the extent you have, no." I waited a few seconds, then asked, "Are you still interested in being honest?"

She billowed some more, but listened.

"You say you're lost, and I think I get that. But you've been dead for how long? More than a hundred years, right? So get over it."

She whirled straight at me and I sat there. It wasn't easy, but I pretended nonchalance, crossed my legs, studied my nails, tried not to run screaming from the room. Eventually she seemed to whirl herself out, and she drifted, like the ash from a leaf fire, onto the table.

"If I don't let you, Geneva, you can't hurt me."

"Hmph."

"Don't let what Ardis does hurt you."

"There are all kinds of hurt," she said. "Hurts that scar."

"There are. You're right. Oh, hey, do you want to know how Hugh got that scar on top of his head?" I told her about the soccer riot when he was a graduate student.

"How terrifying! And fascinating. And I'm the only one who noticed the scar. But it sounds like a red herring."

"Cases are full of them."

"Ducks are, too, depending on where they live," she said.

"You quack me up."

Before going home, I snapped a picture of the whiteboard, with the notes I'd added to it, and sent the picture to the posse and to Darla. The board needed more pairs of eyes trying to decipher it. I didn't erase it; it had taken too long to get the notes and questions up there, and we would probably end up adding more. I locked the workroom door, though, and thought that was good enough, that the information was safe. And that was my mistake.

Chapter 30

The notes and questions on the whiteboard prompted a string of events and conversations the next day. Darla started it, calling way too early, even for a day I needed to be up and opening the shop at nine. We met at seven, and she let me in the door at the back of the courthouse. It was the same door Shorty had rushed out of when he'd answered our 911 call. Visiting public usually reached the sheriff's department by climbing the courthouse steps, passing the row of columns, and entering the overlarge front doors.

"Come on in, quick," Darla said. "This is definitely irregular."

"Let's not do it if you're going to get in trouble."

"I'll be all right. It tends to be quiet this early on a Saturday. Come on down here."

"Down here" was a dim basement corridor. The present courthouse dated to 1912, built on the foundations of previous structures. It kept in touch with its history with whiffs of old drain and flooding problems. Darla unlocked a door halfway down the corridor that opened into a room the size of a small bedroom. Two narrow windows high on the outside wall let in dingy light. She flipped on an overhead fluorescent that did nothing to improve the looks of the place. Metal cupboards and steel shelves lined the walls. A chipped and scratched six-foot folding table took up most of the floor space. It reminded me of the storage rooms I'd so often seen in underfunded museums.

Hugh McPhee's clothes, and the belongings he'd had with him when he died, were laid out on the table. I stopped in the doorway and seriously considered backing out of this.

"It gets me like that, too," Darla said. "Come on in. Come on over. If there's any chance you can help, I'll be grateful and so will he, wherever he is."

"You're a good person, Darla." I crossed to the table and looked without touching until she told me it was all right. I still didn't touch the wool of his tartan kilt, or any of his other clothes, and the sporran only gingerly until I knew it was safe. It was a handsome piece. About nine inches wide by seven high, the face of the pouch was black fur—probably rabbit—with three tassels. The back of the pouch and the front flap were leather. The flap was embossed with a graceful Celtic knot pattern.

"Here's the book that was in it." She showed me a slim dark green paperback that would have barely fit in the sporran. *"The Naughty Little Book of Gaelic: All the Scottish Gaelic You Need to Curse, Swear, Drink, Smoke, and Fool Around,"* she read. "The guys got a kick out of the title. Why do you suppose he was he so fascinated by a dead language?"

"It isn't dead," I said. "It's endangered, like a lot of

living things." I took the book from her and thumbed
through it. "It's a signed copy. Maybe he knew the author. What about the paper with Ardis' name on it?"

She showed me. Just a slip, a scrap with Ardis' name
and address.

"It seems to be nothing more than a note so he could
look up a favorite teacher," she said.

"Were there other names? Ardis couldn't remember
if you said there were."

"I didn't tell her, but there was another name and a
phone number—Al Rogalla."

"That must've thrilled Cole. Darla, can I ask you
about his suspension?" She tipped her head and I took
that as a guarded yes. "Last night you said it's a crock.
Do you really believe it's a trumped-up charge?"

She tipped her head to the other side, eyes steady but
slightly narrowed. Then she looked back at the table and
picked up Hugh's camera. "Nothing helpful here. Tourist
stuff. A few pictures of the house. Speaking of pictures,
though, what about those pictures John wished he hadn't
mentioned?"

I'd been working out a way to answer that without
landing Joe in a pile of something. I'd decided to go with
a less-is-more approach. "He managed to get a peek at
pictures of Hugh's truck."

"How?"

"You came into Mel's and told Cole you'd found it,
right? He told us. It wasn't exactly a secret." I held my
breath, but we skated smoothly forward on that thin
edge of truth.

"Speaking of pictures," she said, "we didn't find any
matches between the ones you took to document the

yarn bomb materials and the pieces used to strangle Hugh and Gladys. And those two strips are definitely from a single piece."

"There were a lot of people making strips."

"And you know how people are," she said. "Excited about a project one day, toss it aside the next."

"Some of the strips people made probably didn't end up at the Weaver's Cat."

"No, they didn't," Darla said. "They very definitely didn't."

I looked at the dingy windows, wishing they let more sunlight in, or that I could leave through one of them. But I was there for a reason. Better get on with it. "So, what about the monkey's fist that was in the sporran?"

"Cole and Shorty thought it was a weapon, and you could sure do some damage with one if whatever you made the knot around—whatever you put in the middle—is heavy enough and you give it a good swing." She held up a knot the size of a Ping-Pong ball, made of smooth brown cord, with a foot-long tail.

"But you don't think this one's a weapon?"

"See what you think. It feels too light, and the material isn't really something you'd use for a weapon." She held it out and I took it in my hand.

I was cold. On a cold floor—I hoped it was a floor, not a slab. Surrounded by knots. And a circle of monkeys. "Not my monkeys," I muttered. "Not my monkeys, not my circus." Thank goodness there were no ducks. No way. No ray. No . . . Rachel.

"This is not good, not good, not good."

That was someone else muttering. Not me. Not I. I

was all tangled up. Tangled in knots. But I did not care. Neither here nor there. It made no difference. Indifferent. In knots.

"Come on, Kath. Make sense."

That was that other person. That made sense, because I was here and she was there. Where? Oh yeah. Right here. "Hi, Darla."

"You scared the *spit* out of me," she said.

"Sorry."

"Should I get you to a doctor?" She was kneeling beside me.

"No. No, I'm . . . fine." I sat up and looked around warily. "Is the monkey's fist—"

"I had to pry it out of your hand."

I put my hand to my head. Didn't feel a lump.

"You didn't fall. I thought you might. As soon as I laid you down, you came out of it."

As soon as she'd pried the monkey's fist out of my hand. "Good. Thanks." I got to my feet. The monkey's fist was on the table. I didn't go near it. I looked at Darla. She was watching me and there was something going on with her eyebrows.

"Did I ever tell you that I grew up in a holler away out there in the county?"

I shook my head. I was glad it didn't make me dizzy.

"My folks still live out there, and my grandmother, too. My grandmother used to tell me stories about the old days and the old mountain ways. Stories about granny women."

"Healers and midwives, sure."

"Sure. But sometimes, she said, they were more . . . unusual than that. Were and are, because she says there are still some granny women around. Not many, but she told me she had occasion to call on one once, down in Blue Plum. A weaver woman."

I couldn't think of anything to say.

"She was real sorry to hear about your granny passing this spring, Kath, and she told me something to tell you—though not until the right time—but that I would know when it *was* the right time. She says it's a gift that passes down the female line. She also says this isn't something folks are meant to talk about, so I won't mention it again."

"And your grandmother's always right?"

"Smartest woman I know. Grannies tend to be, don't you think? Are you really feeling okay now?"

"Yeah, I am. Kind of weirded out, but otherwise okay. And I, uh, I think you're right about the monkey's fist. It's too light to be a weapon. Sometimes they're tied around a weight—a rounded rock or a big ball bearing— but not this one. If I were you, I'd take it apart and see if Hugh used something else."

"Like what?"

"A ring? I don't know. But take a look."

When I left the courthouse, there was plenty of time to go back home for breakfast before heading to the Weaver's Cat. Instead I took a detour through the park and walked along the brick path that followed the creek. The trees were beginning to change color—some of the maples looking lit from within. Patches of ironweed bloomed deep purple on the other side of the creek. The range of vibrant colors in yarn bomb squares we'd attached to the railing on the footbridge tied the whole scene together—

grass, reeds, ironweed, trees, all of them rising toward the blue of an October sky. I stood in the middle of the bridge, looking from the clouds sailing high over me to the water flowing under me, and thought about ducks.

Ardis called as I combed through the weeds below the bridge. She was drawing on her theater skills again. "Motive is to a murderer as motivation is to an actor," she said.

"Okay." I'd stood on the bridge where Ernestine had when she dropped her crochet hook and scissors and determined my search area.

"Motive is missing from your picture of the whiteboard. *Why* did someone kill Hugh?"

"That's what we're working on, isn't it?"

"We have names. We have possible suspects. We're aware of relationships between these players. But we're short on motives. So here are some questions that might help us get where we need to be. Are you ready?"

"Do you want me to write this down? I'm in the park and I don't have paper—"

"No, I've written it all out," Ardis said. "I'll bring the script when I come in. Are you ready?"

"Sure."

"One, what did the murderer want? Two, did Hugh put an obstacle in the way that would have prevented the murderer from reaching that goal?"

"Or *did* prevent."

"I'll add that later," she said. "Good point. Three, was Hugh himself the obstacle? And four—this is a multipart question, with a preamble—we have to believe that Hugh's sudden appearance in town changed something. What, how, and why? Was his presence alone enough to prompt that change? Or did he say something to someone? Did he, or did his presence, deliver a message that motivated someone to murder?"

"Wow, Ardis."

"Exactly."

"That's really good. Wow for you, but also wow for me—I just found Ernestine's favorite crochet hook and scissors."

"That's wonderful. You should stop by Mel's to celebrate, and as long as you're there, bring me a large coffee and a couple of doughnuts. I think I'll need them."

Mel's Saturday breakfast special was buttermilk banana pancakes with banana cream. I didn't try very hard to resist them. I sat at one of the tables in the front window. Mel brought the pancakes herself, and joined me for a cup of coffee.

"I got your picture. I studied it. Here's the question I keep coming back to." She took a gulp of coffee. "What kind of old lady witnesses a murder in the park late at night, and then goes back out to the park two nights later?"

"That is a good question."

"It's got a good answer, too, and it's the only one I can come up with. First of all, she was a *great* old lady." She stopped and leaned across the table, teeth as fierce as her spiked hair. "And I stand by what I said yesterday morning about wanting to kill the person who did this. But again, don't repeat it." She sat back and took another gulp of coffee. "So here's the answer. She was the kind of old lady who wasn't worried, because she knew the murderer had a specific reason to kill Hugh, but had no reason whatsoever to kill her."

"Until the murderer found out she was a witness."

"And how did *that* happen?" Mel asked.

"That's another good question. According to Aaron, she either didn't want to or couldn't go to the police, and she told him very little and no details. But she planned to tell *us*, hoping we could help. If we can trust Aaron, it sounds as though she was being careful."

"I think we *can* trust him," Mel said, "and here's why. She was careful enough that she felt perfectly safe going back to the park alone at night two nights after the murder. She wasn't afraid of the murderer."

"Huh."

"We have to wonder why she was afraid to go to the police. We have to wonder why Sheriff Haynes blanched when he saw Hugh."

"Blanched, according to Olive, who calls Haynes 'Lonnie,'" I said, "and who also blanched."

"And why Cole Dunbar is suddenly 'mishandling' cases."

"A charge we both heard Darla call a crock, which could be loyalty to Cole, despite evidence of his doofusness, *but* . . ."

"*But.*" Mel nodded. "And here's one more thing. Gladys still did the Sunday crossword puzzle in ink. She was the old lady I want to be if I live that long. And *she* should've lived longer. Food for thought, Red. Now I have to go serve food to customers."

It was enough food for thought that I got to the back door of the Cat and realized I'd forgotten the coffee and doughnuts for Ardis. Rather than go back down the alley, I went around the corner into Main Street to see how the yarn bombs there were doing. The signposts and streetlight had never looked so good, and I laughed out loud when I saw a new bomb—a tasseled hat on a fire hydrant with the "Knitting is nifty" tag from one of Debbie's kits. But I turned thoughtful again when I saw Rachel pulling away from the curb in front of Mel's in her BMW Z4—a nifty piece of automotive engineering that made my thoughts switch gears back to motives. If Rachel and Hugh were married way back when, what sort of secrets did they know about each other? Secrets that could stall a successful financial career? And what happened in a brief marriage to make it fall apart so thoroughly that it seemed completely forgotten?

I went into Mel's for Ardis' coffee and doughnuts, and absentmindedly bought two for me as well.

Clod arrived so soon after Ardis unlocked the front door that he must have been waiting and watching. That was an unpleasant image, so I was surprised when the first thought springing into my mind wasn't "creepy Clod," but "poor dope." It was probably good that I kept it to myself, though, just as I kept most of my knee-jerk reactions to him. He marched up to the counter, his posture and gait not having received the suspension memo any sooner than his jeans or shirt.

"I would like to clear up a misapprehension," he said. Sententious clod.

"Very good, Coleridge," Ardis said. "Confession is good for the soul. If you'll remember, Ernestine gave you the chance yesterday."

"Clearing up, not confessing. Apparently it has been suggested that I hold a grudge against Al Rogalla over the fact that he grabbed the McPhee house out from under me."

"That didn't happen?" I asked. I shifted my dough-nuts to the left, out from under his interested eye.

"That did happen."

"Then where does the misapprehension come in?" Ardis asked.

"That I care a rat's—"

"*Language*, Coleridge."

"Yes, ma'am."

"How did he grab it out from under you?" I asked.

"Pfft. He got it through EMT Realty," he said, giving the name of the realty company in air quotes. Then he looked at our faces, mine probably a mirror of Ardis' total blank. "It's not a real company; it's a shi—a *shifty* kind of insider trading in properties. Happens all the time. EMTs, firefighters, cops—they go out on a call for, say, a heart attack. But the attack is massive and the per-son dies before they can transport. If one of the guys is in the market, and likes the look of the place, he takes the opportunity to do a walk-through. And he's first in line if it comes up for rent or for sale."

Now our faces were probably mirrors of dumbfound-edness.

"Yeah," Clod said. "Now you get it. So, McPhee's grandfather owned the house. Had a stroke one night. Left the house to Hugh. *Great* house."

"How long ago?" I asked.

"Twelve, fifteen years. Rogalla got to Hugh first. Hugh had no interest in coming back here."

"But it turned out he held on to the house all that time," Ardis said, "and only this week sold it to Al."

"Everyone thought he bought it back then. With his accountant's salary."

"But you didn't then, and still don't, give a duck's diddly-squat," I said.

Apparently not; he didn't comment. He did, however, take my two doughnuts and leave.

"Nice segue into the ducks," Ardis said. "But I wonder if you aren't obsessing."

"I'm not. Darla thinks Cole's suspension is a crock, but what if Gladys wouldn't go to the police because she saw a policeman kill Hugh?"

"Not Cole!"

"No. But what if he's being railroaded with this suspension? Olive said Sheriff Haynes looked as though he'd seen a ghost when Hugh played his pipes Tuesday afternoon. I didn't tell you, but Geneva saw Hugh with someone Tuesday night."

"No, you did not. *Why* didn't you?"

I looked around but didn't see Geneva. Even so, I spoke quietly. "At first she didn't know if the person with Hugh was a man or a woman. Now she says it was someone about Hugh's height who marched like a lawman or a piper."

"Not the most reliable witness."

"No. But what do we know about any history between Hugh and Sheriff Haynes?"

Ardis thought for a minute. "Leonard Haynes was coach at the high school. Unreliable witness or not, it bears looking into. This might get nastier than it already is."

Thea called shortly before noon. She spoke so softly it was hard to hear her.

"Modeling good library behavior?" I asked. "I thought you didn't care so much about it being like a mausoleum."

"It's my day off. I'm in my office with the door closed. If they don't hear me, they hardly know I'm here, and I can troll without interruption. Stealth librarian at your service."

"Cool. Anything new?"

Her first two offerings we'd already learned—Rogalla living in the McPhee house, and Sheriff Haynes coaching at the high school while Hugh attended.

"Any hint of problems when he was coach?"

"Not so far. That's the era of sweeping things under the rug, but I'll keep looking."

"Can you do another search for me?" I told her what we knew of Clod's suspension—including our duck gibes—then asked her to look for the original complaint about stolen ducks.

"How do you mishandle a complaint about ducks?" she asked.

"By making dumb jokes, like we're doing?"

"A complaint might be in the public record," Thea said. "But if it's anonymous, what's it going to tell you?"

"I don't know. See what you can find."

"Hey, I'm a miracle worker, not a magician, but I'll see what I can do."

"Thanks. Anything on Tammie or Wanda connecting them to Hugh?"

"No, but that reminds me. There's something I've been thinking about that's getting me more and more steamed. Something that's creeping over me like a red haze ever since Gladys died." The red haze was creeping into her voice, too.

"Are you going to blow your stealth there by getting upset and shouting?"

"It'll be worth it," she said. "Okay, so two people are dead. That's the worst part of this, I know that. But the murderer also took advantage of the yarn bombing. *Our* yarn bombing. The murderer *knew* we were knitting and crocheting strips, and used one to kill Hugh and Gladys. That was not a spur-of-the-moment decision. Or maybe killing Hugh while he was blowing his pipes at midnight *was* a spur-of-the-moment decision, but we hadn't bombed anything at that point. So using a crocheted strip, and part of the same strip to kill Gladys, means the murderer knew beforehand about the bombing and took advantage of us. Took advantage of all our planning. Of our *art*."

"Of TGIF."

"And that's what really gets me," Thea said, "the betrayal. Because it had to be a member of TGIF."

I didn't want to think the murderer was a member of TGIF, but knew I had to face that possibility and told Thea so.

"Or not," she said.

"Wait. You just told me—"

"My brain won't turn off, so hear me out. It could've been loose lips. Bomb squad members were knitting and crocheting. Other members of TGIF were knitting and crocheting to help the cause. And we don't know who or how many others were supplying us with strips, even though we asked everyone to keep quiet."

"True."

"Lots of strips, too many lips."

I sighed, thanked Thea for continuing her Internet search, and hung up. She was right; there were too many lips involved to lay blame anywhere in particular. And there could easily have been several loose pairs. But that didn't stop me from sifting through my favorite candidates for the role of Loose Lip Louse. I tried to be objective, weighing Tammie's excitement and calling attention to herself in the middle of Main Street against Wanda, who took notes during meetings, disappeared during the bombing, and then reappeared, and weighing both of them against Rachel, who'd been married to Hugh and "twisted" her ankle. Objectivity wasn't actually all that hard; any one of them could have told someone else about the yarn bomb project.

Then Geneva shrieked into the room. "A spy!" she shouted. "Upstairs! She's reading the whiteboard to someone over the phone, and spilling all our supersleuth secrets!"

Chapter 31

Geneva swirled up the stairs ahead of me, and I arrived, heart thumping, and clutched the doorframe of the TGIF workroom. Tammie, her back to me, stood in front of the whiteboard, phone to her ear, spilling our sleuth scribblings. She turned when she heard me gulping air at the door. Geneva went into the room and threw herself in front of the whiteboard, arms spread wide — protecting our data about as effectively as I had done. Tammie disconnected after a quick "see you later."

"The door was locked," she said, "and you-all were busy. I didn't like to be a bother, so I thought I'd try the key for the supply closet in the kitchen. You know — old doors, old keys, and there you go. Here's the key back."

"You can put it on the table." I stayed in the doorway. Call me overly cautious, but I didn't like the idea of being in an enclosed space with Tammie Fain.

"You don't usually keep the door locked, do you? But I can see why you would now, with all that going on—" She waved at the whiteboard.

"Did you need something in here?" I asked.

"My snips. I couldn't think where I'd left them, and then I realized it must have been here the last time I brought the grandbabies. Found them, though, and now I'd like you to move away from the door and let me out."

I stepped aside, and she moved past me. Not too close.

At the top of the stairs she stopped and said, "You scare me."

"Who were you talking to?" I asked.

But her phone rang and, rather than answer me, she answered it as she ran down the stairs.

"It might not be so bad," Ardis said when I told her about Tammie breaching our limited security. "She could've been on the phone with someone in Alaska for all we know."

"Only if she's going there. She said, 'See you later,' when she hung up."

"And Geneva didn't hear a name?"

"No."

"I hope she doesn't feel too badly about that. She did us a great service by giving the alarm." Ardis darted glances around the room. "Is she here?" she whispered.

"She vowed to stay in the workroom and guard the whiteboard with her life."

"How worried do you think we need to be? Should we warn the posse to be vigilant?"

"I think we should. But Tammie doesn't know who all has been working on the board, and it only has my handwriting. So you're right; it isn't so bad."

"Except for you," Ardis said. "I don't like the sound of that. No walking home alone at night until this is over. In fact, I'll worry about you being alone in the house."

"Well, you know, there is that guy named Joe who hangs around sometimes."

"And I've a mind to call him up and tell him to hang around more permanently."

"That's kind of you, Ardis, but we can probably make our own arrangements."

"*Permanent* ones, hon? Am I the first to hear the news?"

"What news?"

"Never mind. Joe's tied up with Handmade this evening, though, isn't he?"

"Until the last booth is taken down and taken away."

"Then I want you to come eat supper with Daddy and me tonight. And if we can get him in his chair, we can take him for a tour of the yarn bombing."

"Not the footbridge."

"No, I suppose not. We'll skip that part, and we'll let Joe know he can pick you up at my place when he's finished."

So much for letting us make our own arrangements, but it sounded like a nice way to spend the evening. So after a day of normal yarn shop activity, tinged with abnormal worries about a murderer loose in our fair town, Ardis and I walked up the hill to her house. At the last minute, before leaving the shop, I'd run up to the workroom and invited Geneva to come with us. She declined, saying her new catchphrase was "vigilance is vital." It wasn't easy to read subtle expressions on her face, but at a guess, her vigilance was slightly wistful.

In Ardis' big, homey kitchen, she whisked eggs for an omelet. I tossed a salad and made toast. And in the den, her daddy caught the tail end of *Top Hat*, and got the itch to go dancing.

*   *   *

"Come on, Fred," Ardis said to her daddy after supper. "If you'll hop in your carriage, we'll go downtown and cut a rug."

"I've got a better idea," her daddy said. "Let's go to Pokey's."

"Does Pokey's sound okay to you, Kath?" Ardis asked.

"I can hardly wait."

"Me, neither," her daddy said. "Oh my, oh my."

Ardis got Hank in his wheelchair and we strolled and rolled down to Main Street. Hank sang snatches of songs and we showed him the striped signposts, the giant trout flies, and the new beanie on the fire hydrant. It had only been a few days, but we were happy to see that most of the yarn bombs were still intact, including the Groucho glasses and pouting lips on the courthouse columns, despite Olive's assertion that they were ridiculous.

It was another evening that smelled of woodsmoke and early frost. Not many people were out. Ardis asked her daddy if he was warm enough. He said he felt fine and dandy, oh my, oh my.

The moray eel had disappeared from the electric company, and that was disappointing, but we hoped someone had loved it so much that it now swam in a bedroom somewhere. Ardis hadn't seen the lion's mane, so we headed down the street to the Extension office. My phone rang. It was Thea.

"I saw you three out walking as I was on my way home," she said, "and I thought you'd get a kick out of this. I looked up Pokey's roadhouse of thirty years ago — for grins, but the trivia might help Ardis and John with those old boys. You never know. Anyway, the live music Hank remembers? None other than Ms. *Oh My*. And I think you have to say it like that to get the flavor of it— *Oh My*. Ever heard of her?"

"No." I slowed as I listened to Thea, and Ardis and Hank got to the Extension office ahead of me. Ardis lifted part of the lion's mane and waved it at Hank.

"'My' is short for Myers," Thea said. "'Oh' is a cute way of designating the first initial. Ms. O. Myers. O for Olive. Olive Myers, who became Mrs. Pokey Weems. She was a roadhouse singer, Kath, and pretty hot."

"Interesting." Interesting, too, that Mrs. Pokey Weems, taking her Boston terrier for a walk, was up ahead there and talking to Ardis' daddy. As I closed the distance between us, I heard Hank swearing on his life that he'd seen her in the park Thursday night.

"Oh my, yes," he said. "I'd know you anywhere."

"You still there, Kath?" Thea asked.

"Oh my," I said faintly.

"That sounded completely lifeless," said Thea. "Try it like this: *Oh My*."

"It *is* Oh My, Thea. Olive's here." But I wasn't sure Thea heard me, because Olive had grabbed my phone and smashed it.

Chapter 32

"Oh *my*! She still has the moves," Hank said. He clapped as Olive did the two-stomp on the remains of my phone.

"What good did that do?" I asked her. "This is downtown Blue Plum. There are three us. And your dog just jumped into Hank's lap." I was surprised to hear how calm my voice sounded. "If you're trying to get away with murder, you're doing it wrong."

Ardis' daddy was delighted by the happy dog licking his face. "A lap dancer!" he cried, and started the wheelchair moving in a slow spin. "Oh my, oh my, she makes me sigh!"

"Stop that, you old fool," Olive said. She kicked pieces of the phone into the gutter and tried to grab the handles of the wheelchair without letting go of the dog's leash.

"I'm either dazed or confused," Ardis said. "Tell me if I've got this right. Daddy, in a moment of clarity, aided by a somewhat risqué long-term memory, just ID'd Olive and placed her in the park Thursday at the crucial time. And Olive, through her panicked reaction and lack of denial, as much as confessed to Gladys' murder."

"And your daddy is wrapping up the case, but could use some help."

Her daddy had gotten the hang of spinning the wheelchair, tangling the leash around Olive's legs in the process. Before Olive could free herself, Ardis and I grabbed Ernestine's giant lion's-mane jellyfish from the bushes. In a pincer move so smooth we might have been practicing it for months, and accompanied by her daddy's cackling and the dog's yips, we wrapped the piece of knitting around Olive like a straitjacket, pinning her arms. Ardis tied the package tightly with the tentacles.

"Olive-stuffed jellyfish," she said with satisfaction, and added another knot for safekeeping. "A Blue Plum yarn bomb specialty. Oh my."

Between Ardis' daddy singing a rousing rendition of something about a girl from Ypsilanti whose dress was red and scanty, and Olive's dog encouraging him with more licks and yips, our strange party attracted the attention of several other folks abroad in Blue Plum that evening. Clod and Darla had just left Mel's and they advanced on us in a synchronized quickstep. Darla had the pleasure of reading Olive her rights and making the arrest. Clod seemed happy to stand back and watch. More than happy, as Ardis noticed.

"There is a look of extreme satisfaction on your face, Coleridge," she said. "Why?"

Her "Why?" was more of a demand than a request,

and Clod didn't always react well to demands. But Ardis was right; his extreme satisfaction led him to give us an answer that satisfied us, too.

"Because Ms. Weems made anonymous complaints about stolen ducks," he said, "and then claimed that I mishandled the complaints. To my mind, murdering two people trumps mishandled duck complaints, and Olive Weems doesn't have a duck leg to stand on."

"And *that* is why I reported you," Olive sputtered. "Your jokes at my expense are inappropriate and unprofessional."

"She has a point," Ardis said, "but I will gladly be a character witness on your behalf if it's necessary. She didn't inherit her granddaddy's house, but she sure did inherit his sense of humor."

"He had no sense of humor," Olive snapped.

"Exactly what I meant," said Ardis.

"No sense of humor," Olive repeated, "and he was a fossil. I had as much right to that house, but that idiotic, patriarchal old man favored his son's son over his daughter's daughter. *I'm* the one who loved the house. It should have been mine."

Darla repeated her warning about speaking without an attorney present.

"Oh, do let her sing," Ardis' daddy said.

And Olive did. "*I'm* the one who would've taken care of the house properly. I would've made it a showplace. It would've been the perfect home for a rising political career. An *estate*. But would he give it to the granddaughter who loved it and loves this town? No, the *grandson* got it. Cousin Hugh, who never cared. Never cared and never came back."

"So why didn't you offer to buy it from Hugh?" Clod asked.

"Because I thought he'd already sold it," Olive said. "How was I supposed to know he'd been renting it out all these years? No one knew that but Al Rogalla, and he acted as if he owned the place. And when I offered to buy it from *him*, he laughed."

"You would've known all that if you'd talked to Hugh," Ardis said.

"I hadn't heard from him since he left, and I had no idea where he was. I thought he was lost or gone for good."

"You never thought to look for him?" Clod asked.

"It wouldn't have been that hard to find him on the Internet," I said.

"Why should I?" she asked.

"Joe says she's a technophobe," I told the others.

"If he didn't have the house, then he didn't have anything I wanted," Olive snapped. "And I had more important things to do than look for him. But when I heard he'd only just sold the house Tuesday afternoon—when I knew that it could have been *mine* all these years—" Her voice rose higher with each word. "I want you to know that Hugh took something away from me. His *existence* took something away from me." At that point she howled unintelligibly.

Ardis' daddy rolled himself backward several feet. "I believe I'd like to go home now, Ardie," he said.

Shorty and another deputy had arrived by then. So had Al Rogalla. He stood several yards away, a brindled Scottie at his heel. We all watched as Shorty, the other deputy, and Darla extricated Olive from the lion's mane.

Shorty put Olive in the car, and Darla handed the giant jellyfish to Clod. Then she took Olive's dog from Hank and climbed into the backseat beside Olive.

"Nice use of knitting," Al said as the car pulled away. "You make that . . . thing yourself, Dunbar?"

"Since when do you have a dog, Rogalla?" Clod asked.

"Bruce belonged to Hugh, Dunbar. Sheriff Haynes gave me permission and his blessing to take him. Bruce seems to be a serious dog, though, with a law-and-order take on life, so I thought I'd improve his name. I toyed with the idea of calling him Deputy Bruce, but then I realized he's better than that. Classier, too. So I'd like you to meet Inspector Bruce of Scotland Yard."

Clod shoved the wadded-up lion's mane at me and stalked off into the night.

Ardis and I relaid the jellyfish on the bushes in front of the Extension office, and then we took her daddy home.

In the days after Olive's arrest, pictures of her and Hugh as children and young adults emerged, taking shape from the snippets and pieces of gossip popping up around town. Hugh never had cared for glory. Olive craved it. His status as a sports hero never meant anything much to him. He accepted the talents and gifts he was given as though they were nothing or simply expected. Olive worked for everything her whole life, and everything was hard. Darla told us that when they asked Olive why she killed Gladys, she confirmed that Gladys had seen her.

"She told us that Gladys was out there catching ducks again," Darla said, "and she blamed Cole. She said if he'd followed up on her complaint and stopped Gladys, then she wouldn't have had to—but then she started howling and we didn't get much more sense out of her."

Thea told us more of the duck story. In her search for the anonymous complaint about stolen ducks, she came across half a dozen complaints made by Gladys Weems against the ducks.

"She hated them," Thea said. "And I don't blame her. Look what they did to my shoes. She complained they were too messy, too noisy, and there were too many of them. She was fed up and wanted the town to get rid of them or at least thin the flocks."

Joe filled in the final pieces of the duck story. Aaron Carlin gave them to him in exchange for Joe's first attempt at making a sporran with a piece of deer hide.

"Gladys really was a pistol," Joe said. "She started her own duck abatement program. She caught them at night, because they don't see well in the dark, sold them to Aaron, and then he turned around and sold them at the flea market. He says he didn't ask where she got them."

"Do you believe that?" I asked.

Joe rubbed his nose. "That he didn't ask? Sure. But he knew what nights to park his truck on Fox Street for a few hours, leave it unlocked, and go for a stroll. He said it backfired Tuesday night when he drove back to the campground. He and Angie are living in an RV out there. Hugh was staying there for the few nights he was in town, too. I saw his truck Friday morning when I went out to see Aaron. Hugh must've walked to town with his pipes that night. It isn't much of a hike."

Rachel came into the Weaver's Cat a few days later to thank me. Darla had asked permission to open the monkey's fist from Hugh's sporran. Inside was Rachel's wedding ring. She said that when she'd left him, she threw the ring at him. Later she'd regretted that, because she'd liked the ring, if not him, but he'd never returned it.

"There was never really enough between us," she said. "That's the way I saw it, anyway. I loved this town more than I loved him. So I stayed and he went, and I've never been sorry. But I think he was. That tune he played on the courthouse lawn that afternoon was "Mairi's Wedding." He played it at our wedding. And the tune he played at midnight is played at funerals. I think it was his farewell to Blue Plum. He'd sold the house and had nothing else to tie him here."

She said she had a couple of confessions to make, too.

"My feelings for Hugh weren't so completely indifferent after all. Being out there that night, and being so near where he died, was too much for me. I pretended I'd twisted my ankle. I should have been honest."

And because she was friendly—and had always been friendly—with Olive, she'd spilled the yarn bomb beans to her several weeks earlier, and recruited her to crochet a few strips for the cause. When she saw Olive on Tuesday afternoon, she'd told her about Hugh selling the house.

"She acted as though the yarn bombing was an affront to Handmade Blue Plum," I said.

"Distancing herself from it," Rachel guessed, "so people wouldn't know she'd made strips, too."

Shirley and Mercy Spivey also came into the shop one morning. They rarely bought anything when they came in, but this time they piled the counter high with skeins of pink baby yarn.

"You'll never guess," Shirley said. "We're going to be grandmothers!"

"I'm going to be a grandmother," said Mercy with a glare. But then a remarkable thing happened—she threw her arms around Shirley and said, "*We*. You're right. *We're* going to be grandmothers. Angie's having a baby."

And they both burst into tears.

But they pulled themselves back together, and after they paid for the yarn, I asked them, again, where they'd gotten the information they'd passed on to me about Hugh's movements on that Tuesday.

"Olive," Mercy said. "We were duped."

"Duped by a disgraceful excuse for a cousin," said Shirley.

"*Why* did she give you that information?" Ardis asked.

"We aren't sure," said Shirley. "But we think she wanted our help to frame Al Rogalla."

"And we want you to know, Kath," Mercy said, "that we will never act toward a cousin the way Olive did."

"I believe you."

Ardis started wearing her braided bracelet again a few days after Olive's arrest. She didn't announce it, but I noticed and then Geneva did. They were wary of each other, but each was obviously on her best behavior.

They were both absorbed in the pieces of stories people brought to us. Geneva usually lay curled around the ceiling fan, chin propped in her hands. When the twins came in, she floated down to the counter and nestled in their pile of pink wool. Ardis had to pretend a sneeze to cover her urge to laugh. When the twins left, Geneva wafted over to the mannequin and perched on its shoulder.

"This talk of disgraceful cousins made me think of a question," she said. "Is it easier to be friends than relatives?"

Ardis looked at me.

"Be my guest," I said.

"Okay," she said. "Here's what I think. I'd say being relatives is unavoidable. Those are knots that are tied the moment you're born. Being relatives is an accident, and not always a happy one. Liking your relatives and actually being friends with them is hard."

"Olive and Hugh were relatives," Geneva said, "but not friends."

"And she felt she had no choice. But here we are, only aware that we're relatives by the strangest of circumstances." Ardis touched her braided bracelet. "But also by choice."

"What do you choose?" Geneva asked.

"Relatives," Ardis said, "*and* friends."

Tunnel of Fudge Cake with Ginger

Ingredients

CAKE
1 cup white sugar
¾ cup brown sugar
1¾ cups butter, softened
6 eggs
2 cups powdered sugar
2¼ cups unbleached white flour
¾ cup unsweetened cocoa
2 teaspoons vanilla
1½ cups chopped, crystallized ginger

GLAZE
¾ cup powdered sugar
¼ cup unsweetened cocoa
4–6 tablespoons milk

Directions

1. Preheat oven to 350ºF. Grease and flour a 10-inch Bundt or tube pan.

2. In a large bowl, cream sugar and butter until light and fluffy. Beat in eggs 1 at a time. Gradually add the 2 cups of powdered sugar, blending well. Stir in flour and remaining cake ingredients. Pour batter into prepared pan. Spread evenly.

3. Bake at 350ºF. for 45 to 50 minutes or until top is set

and edges are beginning to pull away from the sides of the pan. Cool in pan on a wire rack for 1½ hours. Turn out onto serving plate and cool completely.

4. Combine glaze ingredients in small bowl, adding enough milk for desired drizzling consistency. Spoon over top of cake, allowing some to run down sides. Store tightly covered.

Roasted Beet and Radish Salad
à l'Orange

Ingredients for roasted vegetables

1 bunch red radishes cut into wedges ½ inch at wide end
4 beets (tangerine to orange in size), peeled and cut into
*   ½-inch dice*
2 carrots, peeled and cut into ¼- to ½-inch slices
½ red onion, sliced into ¼- to ½-inch rings, then rings
*   into quarters*
2 Tbs. olive oil
1 Tbs. fresh thyme
½ tsp. salt
¼ tsp. black pepper
2 Tbs. balsamic vinegar

Ingredients for curried pecans

1 tsp. olive oil
⅓ cup pecan halves
½ to 1 tsp. curry powder
¼ tsp. salt

Fresh ingredients to finish the salad

3 to 4 cups mixed greens (spinach, romaine, etc.)
1 seedless orange, segments cut into bite-size pieces

Directions

1. Preheat oven to 450°F.

2. Toss prepared radishes, beets, carrots, and onion with olive oil. Spread on a rimmed baking sheet in a single layer. Sprinkle with thyme, salt, and pepper. Roast for about 20 minutes, turning once or twice, cooking until the vegetables are tender and the edges are beginning to caramelize. Roasted vegetables are good—caramelized vegetables are superb.

3. When you think the vegetables are 3–5 minutes away from being perfect, stir in the balsamic vinegar and finish roasting.

4. Let cool while you prepare the pecans, the greens, and the orange.

5. Heat olive oil in small skillet over medium heat. Add pecans, curry powder, and salt. Stir until pecans begin to brown. Remove from heat.

6. Put greens in a large salad bowl. Add the roasted vegetables. Top with the orange and the pecans.

The salad doesn't really need a dressing, but an oil-and-vinegar Italian is nice, and Asiago peppercorn is great.

Yarn Bomb Bunting

Designed by Kate Winkler, Designs from Dove Cottage 2015

Designed for Molly MacRae's *Knot the Usual Suspects*

Almost any knitting or crocheting can become a yarn bomb. Swatches (I am sure you always work a gauge swatch) can be joined together in strips to wrap poles, trees, etc., or attached to i-cord or crocheted chain to make bunting.

The easiest knitted yarn bomb is a simple length of garter stitch. You can use any yarn available, but using up odd bits of yarn in various colors and textures makes the result even more fun. Use a needle one or two sizes larger than you would normally use for a garment made with the yarn; in the case of mixed weights of yarn, go with the size you'd use for the heaviest yarn in the mix. Variegated yarns add extra interest. You can join as you go, or make up a "magic ball" by knotting yarns together with a simple overhand knot. Don't trim the tails—they'll add to the impact of your yarn bomb.

Bunting Pattern

This pattern uses short rows to shape the pennants. There are many ways to avoid a hole at the short row "turn"; consult a knitting reference work or search for "short row tutorial" on the Internet. I prefer German short rows, which do not require a wrap.

Materials

Worsted-weight yarn in a variety of colors
Size 9 (5.5mm) needles
Crochet hook, size G or H
Tapestry needle
Abbreviations: (crochet terms are US usage) K=knit,
    SR=short row, ch=chain, sc=single crochet, sl st=slip
    stitch, rep=repeat

Knitted Pennant

Cast on 31 stitches.
Row 1: K28, turn
Row 2 and all even-numbered rows: K to end
Row 3: K24, turn
Row 5: K20, turn
Row 7: K16, turn
Row 9: K12, turn
Row 11: K8, turn
Row 13: K4, turn
Row 15: K7, incorporating SR stitch or wrap when you come to it; turn
Row 17: K11, incorporating SR stitches or wraps when you come to them; turn
Row 19: K15, incorporating SR stitches or wraps when you come to them; turn
Row 21: K19, incorporating SR stitches or wraps when you come to them; turn
Row 23: K23, incorporating SR stitches or wraps when you come to them; turn

Row 25: K27, incorporating SR stitches or wraps when you come to them; turn

Row 27: K31, incorporating SR stitches or wraps when you come to them

Bind off all stitches. Knit as many pennants as desired.

Crocheted Cord

Ch 50, *sc in every ridge across top of pennant, ch 25; rep from * until all pennants are attached to chain, ch 25.

Turn, skip first ch and sl st in every ch and sc across. Fasten off.

Weave in ends.

FROM NATIONAL BESTSELLING AUTHOR

Molly MacRae

The Haunted Yarn Shop Mystery Series

When Kath Rutledge moves to the small town of Blue Plum, Tennessee, she inherits her grandmother Ivy's fabric and fiber shop, The Weaver's Cat. She also winds up joining T.G.I.F.—Thank Goodness It's Fiber—the name of the spunky group founded by Kath's grandmother, who are determined to help Ivy run the shop and carry on her grandmother's legacy. But soon Kath is tasked with more than needlework as she adds sleuthing to her very busy schedule...

LAST WOOL AND TESTAMENT
DYEING WISHES
SPINNING IN HER GRAVE
PLAGUED BY QUILT

"Full of loving crafting details and quirky, sassy characters."
—*Library Journal*

Available wherever books are sold or at penguin.com

facebook.com/TheCrimeSceneBooks

OM0167